For Jen, who has been there every step of the way
as these stories have come to life.

PRAISE FOR
DEATH GRIP

"An unsettling thriller that dives deep into the twisted mind of a predator and the relentless pursuit of justice by those determined to stop him."
–Niamh McAnally, author of *Following Sunshine*

"Tougaw spins detective agency associate Brad Cummings off his *Marcotte and Collins* series like John Sandford's pivot from Lucas Davenport to Virgil Flowers! Double the mystery and triple the thrills!"
–Cam Torrens, award-winning author of the *Tyler Zahn* mystery suspense series

"Tougaw's latest thriller has action that leaves you on the edge of your seat from the first page to the last."
–Lena Gibson, award-winning author of *The Edge of Life, Aftermath,* and the *Train Hoppers Trilogy*

"Tougaw captures the majesty of the Montana wilderness as his characters work to solve the mystery. The pace of action is relentless and builds to a satisfying conclusion that will leave the reader looking forward to the next book."
–Gary Gerlacher, author of the *AJ Docker series*

"On one hand, you have methodical investigation in small-town America. On the other, white-knuckle survival in the woods. Both will have you frantically turning the pages."
–Luke Swanson, author of *Epicenter* and *Spectators of War*

"Tougaw is a gifted writer and does a fine job setting the scene. He is particularly good at getting into the twisted mind of the killer. If you enjoy thrillers, especially those with vivid bad guys, *Death Grip* will provide a few hours of absorbing reading."
–Nancy Stancill, author of the *Annie Price series*

MARCOTTE AND COLLINS INVESTIGATIVE THRILLERS - 4

DEATH GRIP

TRAVIS TOUGAW

Black Rose Writing | Texas

ISBN: 978-1-68513-648-2

LIBRARY OF CONGRESS CONTROL NUMBER: 2025933751
PUBLISHED BY BLACK ROSE WRITING
www.blackrosewriting.com

Printed in the United States of America
Suggested Retail Price (SRP) $22.95

Death Grip is printed in Georgia Pro

*As a planet-friendly publisher, Black Rose Writing does its best to eliminate unnecessary waste to reduce paper usage and energy costs, while never compromising the reading experience. As a result, the final word count vs. page count may not meet common expectations.

DEATH GRIP

CHAPTER 1

As soon as he saw her, he knew he would kill her. He knew how he would do it, that it would be close and personal. Thoughts of her invaded every waking moment. He could feel her skin under his fingers as he squeezed out her final breaths and she clawed, kicked, and screamed.

Her routine was simple: depart for work at 7:25 each morning and arrive back home just after 6:00 in the evenings. On Mondays and Wednesdays, she ran before dinner, on Tuesdays and Thursdays, attended yoga in a neighborhood studio, and on Fridays, met friends for drinks. Saturday nights brought the occasional date, but she came home well before midnight and always got out of the guy's car at the curb and went into the house alone. No pets, no roommates, and no security system.

He drove his white panel van to her house on a Wednesday afternoon. Wearing coveralls and work gloves, he pulled a billed cap low to shade his eyes. A quick glance up and down the street confirmed no one was watching. Carefully making his way to the back of her house, he used a crowbar to force the back door open. The jamb splintered with a shriek, but an oak tree crowded the property line with the only neighbor who could have seen the back door, giving him plenty of cover.

He walked through the house and found the door leading from the kitchen to the garage. He opened the garage door and went back to his van. Peering in all directions, he checked the street again. His heart thrummed as he threw the van into reverse and backed up her driveway and into her garage.

Once the garage door closed, he climbed on top of the van and unplugged the opener. He left the sliding side door of the van open and curled up in the back where the seats used to be. He set an alarm on his watch and drifted off to sleep.

His alarm woke him at 5:30 p.m. He stretched, drank from his aluminum water bottle, and entered the house, where he waited by the front door. Every car driving down the street made his heart race. The seconds ticked by. At 6:05, he heard the familiar sound of her red Dodge Charger. No all-electric vehicle for that granola-eating, yoga-posing woman. He pictured her reaching up to press the button for the garage door before pressing it again. She probably cursed under breath as she pushed it a third and fourth time before finally resigning herself to entering through the front door.

The engine shut off. A half wall next to the front door in the small entryway provided cover for him. The lock turned. The door swung open. He held his breath.

The door closed. Footsteps stomped out of the entry.

He exploded from his hiding place and clamped a hand over her mouth. She fought hard, first trying to pry his fingers away, then stomping toward his instep. He anticipated the move and dodged her foot.

As he predicted, she next swung an elbow toward his solar plexus. He absorbed the blow, though she struck with more ferocity than he imagined. He dug the syringe out of his pocket with his left hand and jabbed her neck. As he pushed the plunger down, she continued thrashing against him. He kept his right hand over her mouth until she fell limp.

He swept her up and carried her into the garage, where he bound her hands and feet with duct tape, put a strip over her mouth for good measure, and secured the side door. He plugged the garage door opener back in and opened it. She had parked in the middle of the driveway.

Not willing to risk being seen moving her car or leaving DNA inside it, he backed out at an angle, running over the mulch bed along the left side of her driveway. He made it into the street, threw the van into gear, and drove away, keeping to the speed limit and stopping at every red light.

They had a long way to go before reaching their destination. With a little luck, traffic leaving town would be sparse, and she'd still be asleep when they arrived.

CHAPTER 2

July 18, 2025. Burgess County, Montana.
Brad shouldered his overnight bag and locked his truck. He surveyed the area and let out a slow whistle. Eddie had hit the retirement jackpot. The fishing resort consisted of a series of cabins nestled into trees at the base of a mountain. A river rippled by just a hundred yards from Eddie's front door. A rack outside the cabin held Eddie's waders and fly rod.

The door burst open, and Eddie rushed out. "I thought that was you," he said, offering a warm handshake.

"You haven't lost your detective skills," Brad said, and Eddie rolled his eyes at the tired joke.

"Come on in." Eddie pulled Brad toward the cabin. "I made dinner. You can tell me all about the race while we eat, and I'll give you the grand tour afterward."

Brad followed him into the cabin, which consisted of a cramped living room and kitchen. Two open doors revealed a bathroom and a bedroom.

"It's not quite a palace, but you'll sleep great in the mountain air," Eddie said. "The couch folds out, and it's plenty comfortable."

"It'll be perfect. I really appreciate you letting me stay."

Eddie motioned for him to sit at a card table in the corner. The table leaned to one side, and its cracked vinyl top showed years of wear. Eddie went to the stovetop and came back with a platter of pancakes so high Brad couldn't see over the top of it. Another trip to the kitchen yielded bananas, a bottle of maple syrup, and a six-pack of Budweiser.

"Eddie, what's all this?" Brad asked, trying not to sound ungrateful.

"Dinner," Eddie replied with a grin. "Carb loading, right? Need your energy for the race."

Brad helped himself to a pancake and a banana. He had a healthier idea of fueling up, but he didn't want to offend his host. "Thanks," he said. He nodded toward the beer. "I really can't have alcohol the night before a race, though. Mind if I get some water?"

"Suit yourself," Eddie said. "These won't go to waste."

As they ate, Eddie grilled Brad on the next day's adventure race, the Broadwood Blitz. Brad explained that it was a sprint course, meaning it would last somewhere between six and ten hours. He and his partner wouldn't know the route until the next day, but they expected the race to include cycling, rock climbing, rappelling or zip lining, and kayaking.

"And a lot of navigation," Brad added. "We can't bring our phones or any smart devices on the race. They'll give us a map with coordinates to the first challenge, and we'll have to find our way there. Each time you complete a challenge, they give you coordinates to the next one until you reach the finish line."

"Sounds awful."

"You'd probably like it," Brad said. "Big outdoorsman like yourself."

Brad shook his head when Eddie offered him a refill on pancakes. Eddie shrugged and loaded his plate. "Who's this partner you're racing with?"

"Shelly Cantwell. We've known each other for years. Done several races together."

Eddie nodded. "You two more than friends?"

Brad laughed. "No. Actually, we met because I was dating a friend of hers. That didn't work out, but Shelly and I got along great. We're more like brother and sister. We'd booked a hotel near the racecourse, but her boyfriend decided to come at the last minute. So, here I am. Thanks again, by the way."

"The boyfriend racing, too?"

"No, he's never gotten into adventure racing. Not sure why he came at all." Brad rolled his eyes.

"You're not a fan?"

"We fought at the same MMA gym in Chicago. Never really got along, and he accused me of taking a cheap shot on him last time I beat him."

They finished the meal, and Eddie led Brad back outside. "The resort is technically in unincorporated Burgess County. You'll be going a little north of us to Broadwood, which is also along the Missouri." Eddie gestured toward the river that ran through the resort. "If you follow the river south, you get to the Missouri River Headwaters. You probably passed it on the way in if you came through Bozeman on I-90."

Eddie continued the tour of the resort. There were a dozen cabins, ten of them for guests and two for fishing guides, including Eddie. Further up the gravel road, a two-story lodge loomed at the edge of the forest.

"That's where my cousin and his wife live," Eddie said. "They run the place. The cook stays there, too, and the bottom floor of the lodge is where the dining hall is for people who aren't privileged enough to eat my pancakes for dinner. Trent, that's my cousin, takes groups on the river, too, when we're full. It's been a slow summer, though. Not sure we'll get full this year."

They walked along the river, watching the trout jump. A man in his early twenties with a tie-dyed bandana around his head and a three-day stubble on his cheeks exited the lodge. A man and a woman, who both looked to be in their forties, followed him, carrying fishing gear.

"I'd go downstream a ways, Wyatt," Eddie called out. "They were feeding good near the bridge earlier."

The young man gave him a thumbs up and motioned for the couple to follow him. Eddie turned and started back toward the cabin. The sun dipped behind the mountains and cast long shadows throughout the resort.

As they walked, Brad caught Eddie up on the happenings at the Fleck, Collins, and Marcotte Detective Agency. Eddie was the Fleck in the group and the founding partner before he retired.

"Lot of background checks," Brad said. "Not super interesting, but it's steady business."

"You must have worked at least one good case by now," Eddie said.

Brad grinned. "Hadley and I cracked a case a couple months ago." Hadley was the Collins at the agency, leaving Vince Marcotte as the final partner and employee. Brad was the lone associate. "You ever hear of the MacDougal corporation in Fort Collins? Big real estate developer up there. Randy MacDougal had a daughter with another woman. Big secret, apparently. When his wife died, he wanted to find the daughter since she's now the heiress to his fortune. Vince and Hadley searched for months. Vince went on vacation, and I took another look at the case while he was gone and found her. She was in Loveland, practically in her father's backyard."

"I bet Vince was thrilled you cracked it without him," Eddie said.

"You know Vince," Brad said. "He doesn't care who gets the credit as long as the cases get cleared."

Once they reached the cabin, Brad refilled his water and folded the sofa out into a bed. The coils poked his back through the sparse padding, and he tried not to think about what might have stained it. The hotel at Broadwood had been completely booked up, though, and he couldn't think of anything less appealing than sharing a room with Shelly and Aaron. That left staying with Eddie or camping. He didn't mind roughing it, but having a decent meal and a roof over his head would make him that much more competitive the next day.

He tossed and turned for a while before cracking a window open. Eddie was right; the mountain air did the trick. Before long, he drifted off, dreaming of the race that lay before him.

CHAPTER 3

Ten Years Earlier.
August 7, 2015. Chicago, Illinois.
The bell rang to start the third round, and Brad knew he had to make up points. Aaron had gained an advantage in the first round and extended his lead in the second. He had to take some risks to win.

The two fighters circled. Physically, they were an even match. Aaron stood an inch taller than Brad, but Brad had more muscle. They matched each other in speed, reaction times, and techniques.

Brad had dark hair that he wore in a buzz cut. Aaron let his blond hair flop to his shoulders. Sweat glistened off both men. The crowd, somewhere between seventy and 100 people, murmured for more action. Blood from a previous fight stained the ring.

Brad took his shot early. He lunged forward, bending in a fluid motion and grabbing for Aaron's leg. Aaron dodged, but Brad got a hand on Aaron's foot, knocking him off balance.

Brad jumped back into a fighting stance and propelled himself forward as Aaron stumbled. He threw a series of rights and lefts. Aaron instinctively protected his face, and Brad landed blows against his body, driving both men to the ropes.

The crowd cheered the onslaught. Aaron wrapped his arms around Brad, cupping his hands around Brad's head and pulling him close. Brad resisted Aaron's efforts to slow down the fight, but his opponent was powerful, and he couldn't pull away.

Brad kicked Aaron's calf, but Aaron stood strong. The referee's footsteps neared, and Brad knew he would pull them apart, giving Aaron a chance to regroup. In a last-ditch effort to prevent that, Brad grabbed at Aaron's arms. His hands slipped from Aaron's sweaty limbs, and his right hand raked across Aaron's face.

Aaron let go, howling, and turned away from Brad, his hand covering his eyes. Brad advanced, grabbing Aaron from behind and throwing him to the ground. As Aaron regained his feet, Brad moved in again, delivering a roundhouse kick to Aaron's side and landing a combination of punches to the head.

The referee stepped in front of Brad before he could strike again and signaled to the judges' table. The bell rang, and the crowd continued cheering and jeering the two fighters. With Aaron on the judge's right and Brad on his left, the judge grabbed Brad's hand and lifted it. Brad turned to shake Aaron's hand, but Aaron shoved him away and went back to his corner. Brad ignored him and soaked in the crowd's applause, his heart still racing from exertion and adrenaline.

Back in the locker room, Brad showered, examining the welts from where Aaron had landed kicks and punches. He'd have a few good bruises the next day. He luxuriated under the hot water a moment longer before changing at his locker.

With his backpack over his shoulder, Brad headed for the exit. Aaron waited just outside, still in his fighting clothes and his face filled with rage. He glared at Brad through a swollen and red left eye.

"Good match, Reynolds," Brad said.

"Shut up, Cummings." Aaron shoved Brad's chest, knocking him back a step. Brad dropped his backpack and put his hands up in a fighting stance. "You cheated. You gouged my eye. I should have won."

"Wait…I did that?" Brad asked.

Aaron's hands shot forward again, but Brad blocked him and knocked his arms away.

"Yeah, you did this," Aaron said, gesturing toward his eye. "You knew I had you beat, and the only way you could win was to cheat."

"I had no idea," Brad started.

"Yeah, right."

"Seriously. The ref should've stepped in."

"Well, he didn't, and now I have a loss on my record that shouldn't be there."

Another wave of anger passed over Aaron's face. He lowered his head and charged. The speed of his advance caught Brad off guard, and Aaron plowed through Brad's attempted block and slammed him against the wall.

Aaron stepped back and delivered an uppercut that caught Brad under the chin. Brad's head snapped back and struck the concrete wall. A right hook to his temple sent him reeling to the ground.

Aaron would not relent. He drove forward, kicking like a wild man. Brad rolled into the kicks, wincing with each blow, but he came close enough to wrap his arms around Aaron's thighs and pull him to the ground. Brad rolled on top of him, pinning Aaron's arms to the ground with his knees.

Aaron thrashed and kicked. Brad leaned forward to avoid his legs.

"Calm down, Reynolds," Brad said. "I'll explain what happened and see if they'll change it to a draw."

Aaron wheezed something incomprehensible before spitting at Brad. Brad drew back a right hand, but before he could launch the blow, a voice behind him said, "Cummings, knock it off."

Brad dropped his hand and stood, stepping away from Aaron. Doyle Burton, the gym's owner and unofficial bouncer, pushed his way between the two men. "Reynolds, get up," he said in his raspy baritone. At six foot four, Doyle towered over the two fighters, and though he was in his sixties, neither man wanted to tangle with him. A pair of golden gloves hung in Doyle's office, proclaiming the success of his youth as a boxer in the Chicago area. Lean with ropy muscles, he looked like he could step into the ring and go a few rounds at a moment's notice.

Aaron tried to explain what happened, but Doyle cut him off with a wave of his hand. "This is my gym, so my rules," he said. "Rule one is whatever the ref says goes. Did he miss a call? Don't know. Don't care. He made the call, and we're living with it. Understood?"

Aaron nodded and looked at the ground. Doyle stepped back and turned so he could see both men.

"Rule two is you do your fighting in the ring. None of this extracurricular garbage. I see this again, and you won't be allowed back through my doors. Got it?"

"Yeah," Brad muttered.

"Yeah," Aaron said.

"Good. Get out of here."

Doyle remained rooted to his spot. Aaron gave Brad a final glare before skulking inside to the locker room. Brad shouldered his pack and headed home. He glanced over his shoulder once and saw Doyle still standing at the gym door like a sentinel, arms crossed over his chest.

CHAPTER 4

July 19, 2025. Burgess County, Montana.
Brad stood in the bed of his F-150, scanning the crowd for Shelly among the sea of racers. He guessed at least 100 competitors were there, maybe more. He wore medium weight hiking boots, gray tactical pants, and a long-sleeved, moisture-wicking T-shirt in a lighter shade of gray. He also wore his lucky hat, a faded Chicago Cubs ball cap, and a pair of wraparound sunglasses.

"There you are," said a familiar voice behind him. He swiveled, and the grin vanished from his face when he saw Aaron with Shelly.

Brad hopped out of the truck and offered Shelly a warm hug. "Glad you found me," he said. "I was starting to worry you changed your mind."

"No way," Shelly said. "I've been looking forward to this for months. You remember Aaron, don't you?" She took Brad's elbow and led him forward a step closer to Aaron.

"Couldn't forget him," Brad said, trying to keep the sarcasm out of his voice.

Aaron buried his hands in his pockets and gave Brad a reverse nod. "Hey, Cummings."

Shelly rolled her eyes at the two men. "We'll go pick up our race bibs at check in. Aaron, you might as well head back to the hotel. You have at least six hours before we'll show up at the finish line."

Aaron nodded, leaned in, and gave Shelly a long kiss. As they pulled away, he caught Brad's eye and smirked. Aaron swung the backpack off his shoulders and handed it to Shelly.

"Be careful out there," he said.

"We'll be fine," Shelly assured him. Brad watched as Aaron strutted away, following a gravel path back to the main road.

"Where'd you park?" Brad asked as he fetched his own pack.

"At the hotel. There are so many racers, and the hotel is just down the road, it didn't make sense to fight for parking. How was your stay with your friend?"

"Good. Not really a friend as much as an acquaintance, but Eddie's a good guy. I'll have to tell you all about him."

Because it was a sprint race, Brad packed light. His backpack contained a basic first aid kit, a spare shirt, leather gloves, trail running shoes, protein bars, and two large bottles of water. Longer races could stretch over multiple days, and he was glad he didn't have to schlepp a tent, sleeping bag, and more food.

They found the check-in station. A young man, maybe twenty-two years old, wearing a bright red polo and thick glasses, greeted them. "Names please?" he said.

"Brad Cummings and Shelly Cantwell," Brad said.

The man gave Brad a dirty look and said, "Ladies first. I like her better." His voice had an edge to it. Brad took a deep breath but blew it out and stepped behind Shelly. It wasn't worth getting into a scuffle with a volunteer before the race began.

The man riffled through a bin and handed Shelly a race bib encased in plastic to protect the GPS tracker from dirt and water and an envelope with their first destination.

"Don't open the envelope until the starting gun, my dear," the man said. The words sounded strange coming from someone so young, and Brad didn't like the way he leered at Shelly and made sure their hands touched as he handed over the materials. He stepped forward.

"Brad Cummings," he said.

The man clicked his tongue. "Patience, my man," he said. He grinned at Shelly, and Brad's skin crawled. "Enjoy the race."

He found Brad's race bib and reminded him that they'd share the info packet he gave Shelly. Glad to be rid of the strange volunteer, Brad guided Shelly away from check in.

"That was weird," Brad said.

"He's probably just nervous," Shelly said. "He might not get to talk to strangers very often." Just like Shelly to always see people in the best possible light, Brad thought.

They followed the crowd to the starting point. Brad checked his watch; they had ten minutes until the gun. He led Shelly through the crowd, making their way as close to the front as they could and drawing plenty of dirty looks from other competitors.

"How are things with Reynolds?" Brad asked.

"He has a first name," Shelly chided. "It's been fine. I know you don't like him, but he's been good to me."

"It's not so much not liking him as it's our history," Brad said.

"And that history colors your perception of him."

"Fair point. But it's not just my history with him. I know other things about him, too."

Shelly waved him off. "Let's not do this, Brad. I've told you before, I can take care of myself, and I don't want to hear whatever deep, dark secrets you think you know about Aaron. Let's just enjoy the race."

Brad backed off. He adjusted his backpack and stretched. One minute before the starting gun, a loudspeaker came to life with a crackle of static.

"Racers, welcome to the Broadwood Blitz," the master of ceremonies said in a nasal voice. "This race is the largest adventure race in Montana." The racers whooped and cheered. "Over the next several hours, we'll test you in a number of skill sets. We'll have volunteers posted throughout the course, and aid stations are clearly marked on your course map. Have fun, race well, and we'll see you at the finish line."

A gunshot sounded, and the air filled with envelopes ripping open. Shelly tore open their first clue, and Brad peered over her shoulder to read their instructions.

The envelope included a course map and a neon pink half-sheet of paper. The half-sheet instructed them to navigate to the first checkpoint found at B2 on their map. Brad studied the grid and found where the B, along the horizontal axis, intersected with 2 on the vertical axis.

His strategy in adventure races was to make quick decisions and separate from the pack while other racers weighed their options. Shelly took the same approach, so they made a good team.

"This way," Shelly said, tracing a route with her finger. "We have to go through the woods at some point, but going this way keeps us in the open the longest."

Brad followed the path she designated and nodded. They would have to cover more ground, but it decreased the chances of mistaking a game trail for the race route and losing time in the trees.

They took off, leaving most of their competitors at the starting line staring at their maps. Shelly led the way with Brad at her heels. After a half hour, they found an entry into the forest. They had to fight through branches of some of the larger pines to find the main trail, and Brad consulted the map frequently, making sure they continued to make progress toward their goal.

After another half hour, the trail spit them out into the open. A checkpoint stood 100 yards away, a card table in front of a corral of mountain bikes.

"There it is," someone shouted from behind them.

Brad looked over his shoulder where two men emerged from the woods. They looked like a father and son, both tall and thin. The older one took off his cap to wipe his brow and revealed a bald head. The younger did the same thing, his movements a replica of the older man, and revealed a receding hairline. Both sported short goatees and wore matching yellow shirts. They were the first racers Brad had seen since they entered the woods.

"Come on," Shelly said, pulling Brad's arm. They sprinted to the checkpoint where a round woman in denim shorts and a T-shirt with "Bozeman, MT" emblazoned on the front stamped a spot on their map. She handed them another neon pink half-sheet with the coordinates to their next location.

"The fun part is next," she said. "The twins will get you set up with a bike."

Two pre-teen girls in matching outfits waited among the bicycles. Each bike had a helmet hanging from its handlebars. Brad selected a black bike, and Shelly grabbed a green one. The girls checked the fit of their helmets and gave them a thumbs up to ride.

"I think we're ahead of the pack," Shelly said. "Let's see if we can lose the yellow shirts."

Brad agreed. They compared the coordinates to the map and saw that they'd be riding up a ridge, then down the back side of it before they reached the next checkpoint.

They took off at a fast clip. The first mile remained flat, and their pedals flew with ease. Brad glanced over his shoulder and saw the father and son, a pair of yellow specks behind them.

"They're still back there," he said. Shelly pointed at an arrow marking the turn to begin the ascent up the ridge. Rocks littered the path, which gradually became steeper. Shelly stood on her pedals to create more leverage. It didn't take long before Brad did the same. He looked back and saw the yellow specks had taken on human form and were only fifteen yards behind them.

Just before Shelly reached the ridge, the father called, "Make way. On your left."

Grudgingly, Brad pulled to the side to let them pass. Shelly did the same. Brad watched as the other pair reached the top of the ridge and disappeared over the other side.

A minute later, Shelly and Brad summited. Shelly motioned for Brad to stop. She took off her pack and found a water bottle. Brad did the same, glugging liquid as fast as he could.

"That was brutal," Shelly said.

"Downhill's gonna go a lot faster," Brad said, motioning at the steep decline in front of them. Ruts and rocks filled the downhill expanse. Brad watched the yellow shirts increase the gap between them.

"Better get going if we're going to catch those guys," Shelly said. "I wish I'd trained at altitude like you."

They pushed off from the ridge, pedaling into the decline at a reckless speed. Brad stayed a bike length behind Shelly. Though curious if anyone had appeared behind them, he didn't dare take his eyes off the treacherous path.

Shelly hit a rut, and both her tires left the ground. Brad steered around the rut but hit a patch of loose gravel. His bike spun sideways as Shelly landed and wobbled back into balance. Gritting his teeth and leaning to his left, he somehow kept the bike upright. Then he hit a chunk of granite, and the impact shuddered through the bike all the way up to his teeth.

They braked at the bottom of the hill and coasted into the checkpoint. One set of bikes was there already but no others. They were racing the yellow shirts for first place.

A sullen teenage boy wearing earbuds took their equipment, while a sixty-something man marked their map and gave them the next half-sheet of pink paper. Shelly compared it to their map.

"Looks like we're running," she said. "And it looks like it's going uphill for a while." Brad checked his watch. They'd been on the course for two hours. Based on where their next checkpoint was, he guessed they'd be doing some rock climbing and then doubling back to the finish line, possibly via a kayak in the Missouri River.

They each took a protein bar and water bottle from their backpacks and began their run, eating on the go. The terrain was rocky, with plenty of hills, but it didn't pose a navigation challenge. They had a straight shot to the next checkpoint, and as they crested hills, they could see the yellow shirts in front of them.

"We're gaining on them," Brad said.

"Let's go," Shelly said. They increased the pace, and within fifteen minutes had passed the father and son. The checkpoint was only another fifteen minutes ahead of them.

"I don't see anyone else behind us," Brad said as they reached the top of the final hill. "You're crushing it."

"You, too," Shelly said. "We should do this more often."

"You should come to Denver."

"Can't. Aaron's job is in Chicago."

Even better, Brad thought, but he kept it to himself. They sprinted the final fifty yards to the checkpoint where they received climbing helmets.

"Follow the path to the rock outcropping," the man who marked their map said. "A volunteer will meet you there to get you secured in your safety harness and give you the location of your next destination."

The father and son arrived at the checkpoint behind them, so Brad and Shelly sprinted to the rock climb. A college-aged woman waited for them, smiling as they arrived.

"First customers of the day," she said then blushed. "Sorry...I'm not supposed to tell you what place you're in."

"We didn't hear anything," Brad said.

"Good. You can only go up the rock one at a time. When you reach the top, you'll rappel down the other side. Here's your next destination." She handed over another half-sheet and helped Shelly into the harness.

Once secured, Shelly began her ascent. At five-foot-five, she had to strain to reach some of the handholds, but her petite frame also had advantages as she was able to glide over the rock face.

"She's killing it," someone said. Brad turned to see the yellow shirts. "I'm Glen," the older one said, sticking out his hand. "This is my son, Gus."

"We've been calling you the yellow shirts," Brad said with a grin. "Now, I'm going to call you G&G."

"We've been calling you the super freaks," Gus said. "You guys don't let up."

"We're in it to win it," Brad said. A clang sounded from the top of the rock, and Brad looked up to see Shelly ringing a bell.

"We'll give her a minute to start down," the volunteer said. "Then, you're up."

Brad harnessed while they waited. When the woman gave him the go ahead, he turned to G&G. "See you at the finish line," he said. "Good luck."

He started up the rock face, unaware of what waited on the other side.

CHAPTER 5

He waited in the trees near the bottom of the climbing rock. The woman appeared first, and he smiled. He had hoped she would be the one, but he needed some luck for his mission to succeed. Fortune had indeed smiled on him. Not only was he getting her alone, she was the first one, which simplified his task immeasurably.

She rang the bell and let out a whoop that echoed across the wilderness. Her strength and athleticism would pose a challenge, but he would overcome her, he had no doubt. He had a canoe beached nearby at the river, which he could follow around a bend where an ATV waited. He would move quickly and be gone before anyone knew he had been there.

His heart pounded, and his fingers tingled. He glanced further into the trees where a volunteer lay, his throat slit. He'd never had to kill to take a victim before. He didn't get the same excitement out of it as he did killing one of the women. It was too impromptu. He enjoyed planning and thinking through his options. He'd been planning the next kill since he first heard about the race, sketching out every detail, except the most important one, who his victim would be. He left that up to chance, and it gave him a rush none of his other victims had before.

She gripped the rope and descended the rock. He gripped the syringe in his pocket, breathed deeply, and prepared to put his plan in motion.

•　•　•

Shelly stretched for the top of the rock, the muscles in her shoulders and core straining as she pulled herself up. She saw the bell and rang it as hard as she could, howling into the clear blue sky. She looked below and gave Brad a quick thumbs up, but he didn't notice. He was talking to the yellow shirts and the volunteer. No time to wait; she walked to the edge of the rope and began the rappel.

The ground rushed toward her as the rock loomed larger above her. The race came at the perfect time; things had been tense with Aaron lately, and work had been no better. She could never tell Aaron, but she was disappointed when he insisted on coming to Montana with her. Not that she minded having a weekend away with him; she just wanted to catch up with Brad properly and unburden some her stresses on her friend.

She reached the bottom of the rope and put her feet back on solid ground. Back to the race; she'd have time to wallow in her thoughts later. Once unhooked from the rope, she took off her helmet. She looked around but didn't see a volunteer. She assumed someone would show up to send the equipment back up for another climber.

Footsteps pounded on the rock behind her. She turned, but before she could get a look at who approached, the person knocked her to her knees with a vicious punch. The person grabbed her around her neck from behind. Dazed, she was slow to reach for the arm that restrained her. Something sharp pricked her neck. Then she was floating, watching the ground move by underneath her, as her eyelids grew heavy and the world around her went dark.

•   •   •

He didn't bother taking her backpack off. He slung her over his shoulder and started toward the river. As he dumped her in the canoe, he noticed the race bib pinned to the front of her shirt. He snatched it, the pins ripping through fabric. He grabbed a rock from the riverbank and shoved it inside the plastic cover that held the bib and its GPS tracker. He threw it into the river, climbed into the canoe, and paddled away.

He put his back into it, gouging into the water with the oar, switching sides on each row. Seconds after he rounded the corner, the bell rang. He had a minute or two until her partner was on the ground. Probably less than five minutes before he figured out what was happening.

The man rowed harder, whipping up a frenzied wake as he navigated the next portion of an S curve. He beached the boat and hauled the woman out of it. He shoved her into the waiting ATV and fastened a seatbelt around her. He grabbed a roll of duct tape from the floor between the seats and slapped a length over her mouth. At the front seat, he picked up a circular magnet, about eighteen inches in diameter, reading "MEDIC." He affixed it to the front of the ATV. That would explain the vehicle's presence if anyone happened to catch a glimpse.

In the distance, he heard someone bellow, "Shelly!" He started the engine, floored the accelerator, and took off down the gravel path that ran alongside the Missouri. After 100 yards, he took a sharp left without slowing down and ventured as far as he could before tree growth choked out the path.

He jerked the woman from the vehicle and put her down inside the trees. She hadn't woken yet. He pushed the ATV as far into the trees as he could and covered it with branches he had cut down for that purpose. With the woman back on his shoulder, he continued on foot until he came out the other side of the trees.

He buckled her into the passenger seat of a waiting pickup truck. He pulled the tape from her lips to avoid suspicion of other motorists.

Once in the driver's seat, he followed a dirt road that led to a state highway that led to the interstate. Once he hit the paved roads, they'd never know which way he went. By the time they organized a search party, he could be on his way to anywhere in the country.

CHAPTER 6

Brad had to hand it to Shelly; she made the ascent up the rock face look easy. He knew G&G were watching, and he didn't want to look bad in front of the other racers, but the climb was strenuous.

He gritted his teeth and found the next handhold. The rock dug into his fingers, but he pressed himself into it and lifted his body. The next reach pulled him on top of the rock. He found his footing and looked down. Glen was getting into his safety harness.

Brad turned and looked for Shelly. He didn't see her at the bottom, though her helmet and safety harness were piled below. He thought that odd but assumed the volunteer working that side of the climb had stepped away for a bathroom break. Maybe Shelly had done the same. He clanged the bell a few times to let her know he had made it.

After latching onto the rappelling rope, he unclipped from the climbing one. With a foot on each side of the rope, he began his backward hike down the rock. Happy to let gravity do its job, he kept his feet moving as quickly as he could and finally hit the ground. He caught his breath, disconnected from the rope, then removed his harness and helmet. He dropped them next to Shelly's.

"Shelly," he said in a normal speaking voice. "Where'd you go? G&G, the yellow shirts, are right behind us."

No answer. Shelly wouldn't have gone so far to not be able to hear him, and she'd answer when he called. His stomach churned, but he dismissed the possibility of anything happening to her. They were on a controlled racecourse, and she was between challenges; nothing could have happened to her.

The bell at the top of the rock rang, and Brad glanced up to see Glen flexing. They needed to start running to the next checkpoint. Brad rushed to the edge of the trees, but he didn't see any signs of her. He sprinted to the river. He couldn't see down it too far before it drifted around a bend.

"Shelly!" Brad called.

"What's going on?"

Brad turned and found Glen looking at him from the base of the rock.

"My partner, Shelly, isn't here. There should be a volunteer here, too, but it's just you and me."

"Weird," Glen said. "Maybe she needed a bathroom." He gestured toward the trees.

"Shelly, if you're in the trees, say something," Brad called. Still, no answer.

The bell rang yet again, and seconds later, Gus started his descent.

Brad stood in the triangle between the base of the rock, the edge of the trees, and the riverbank. With hands on his hips, he took a deep breath and yelled for Shelly once more. The back of his throat burned.

"Want us to help you look for her?" Gus asked.

Brad sighed. "No, just go on. If you see her ahead of us, send her back this way."

Glen held up his map. "There's an aid station not far. We'll see if they can radio to get more help in here."

"Thanks," Brad said. "I'm sure it's nothing."

"I hope so," Glen patted Gus on the back, and the two of them galloped off toward the next checkpoint.

Brad went back to the tree line and stared among the branches. "Shelly, are you there?"

He wondered if he could climb back up the rock and tell the volunteer on the other side to get help, but G&G would reach the aid station first. Instead, he plunged into the darkness of the woods, peering into the shadows for any sign of Shelly and calling her name every few seconds.

He crept through the trees until the branches grew thicker and overlapped. As he turned around, something caught his eye. He squinted and leaned forward. He stepped backward in shock as he realized what it was. Then, he crashed through the branches to get to the body.

His heart pounded. He had a momentary relief when he realized the clothes and hair weren't Shelly's. He tensed again and turned the body over to reveal the gray face of a young man, his throat cut from ear to ear. His EMT training kicked in, and he checked for pulses, but based on the body temperature and pallor of the skin, he was wasting his time.

He laid the body back on the ground and stepped away gingerly, trying not to contaminate the scene anymore than he had. With his stomach roiling, he pushed his way out of the trees and bent over with his hands on his knees, gulping in fresh air. The smell of death hung in his nostrils and left him lightheaded.

The crackle of a radio got his attention. A slim woman with dark skin and ebony hair in braids rushed toward him. "One of the other racers said you need help?"

Brad gathered himself and pointed at the trees. "There's a body in there. A dead man." The woman gasped and dropped the radio. "My race partner is missing. Shelly Cantwell. Did you see a single female racer?"

The woman shook her head. She trembled, and Brad worried she might faint.

He grabbed the radio. "My name is Brad. Who are you?"

"I'm Angel," she said, her voice a strangled whisper.

"Angel, I'm going to make a call on the radio and get more help. Is this radio on the right channel?" She nodded. He slung his backpack to the ground. "There's a bottle of water in there. Why don't you have a sip while I call this in?"

As Angel rummaged through his bag, Brad took a deep breath, pushed the talk button, and said, "This is Brad Cummings. I'm with Angel at the end of the rappelling station. We've come across a deceased person in the woods, and my partner, Shelly Cantwell, is missing. We need help immediately."

He released the button and waited. A rush of static sounded, and several voices talked at once in a stream of gibberish. Finally, an authoritative voice cut through the chaos and said, "This is Graham. All station monitors, stop activity and hold racers at your checkpoint until further notice. We're calling the sheriff now. Angel, switch to Channel 3. Everyone else, remain on this channel and await further instructions."

Angel reached forward and took the radio from Brad. She tuned it to the new channel. "Graham, are you there?"

"Right here. We're calling the sheriff. It's going to take him a little while to get to your exact location. Are you sure there's a body in the woods?"

"I haven't seen it personally," Angel offered.

Brad leaned in to talk. "This is Brad. I'm a racer. I found the body. Definitely deceased. Male, likely in his twenties. Bled out from lacerations, likely from a knife."

Angel started trembling again. Graham answered, "Is there anyone else there?"

"Just us," Brad said.

"Are you safe?"

"Yeah, I think so," Brad said. "No sign of anyone around. Including Shelly. Has anyone seen her?"

Angel shook her head. Graham said, "I'm putting a call out on the other channel to see if she's shown up at any of the checkpoints. We're checking the GPS tracker on her bib to see if we can get a location. You two hold on, and help will be there soon."

Angel kneeled in the gravel and drank more water. Brad stared at the river. He ran to the edge and peered into the water. There was a gentle current, nothing Shelly couldn't handle. He didn't see her falling in and drowning.

"There was a canoe on the other side of the river," Angel said.

Brad whipped around, his eyes widening. "Where?"

"On the other side of the S-curve. I saw it on my way over."

"I'm checking it out."

"Graham said to wait."

Brad didn't answer. He ran along the river, adrenaline and the lack of backpack boosting his speed. He skidded to a stop when he saw the canoe on the opposite riverbank. Brad bounded into the water.

The cold took his breath away, but he pushed forward. The water reached his chin at its deepest place. He emerged on the other side, soaked and shivering.

The canoe was empty. He didn't see any signs that Shelly had been there. He looked beyond the boat and saw tire tracks in the dirt leading away from the river. He took a step around the canoe when the sound of a motor cut through the silence.

Two motorboats came upstream. A stubble-faced man with long, gray hair drove the first boat. He wore a khaki police uniform and sunglasses. A younger man with a buzz cut and a matching uniform sat next to him.

"Son, what are you doing?" the driver asked. When Brad took a step toward the river, the man raised a shotgun and said, "Stop moving and answer my question."

Brad froze and held up his hands to show they were empty. "I'm Brad Cummings. I called in the body. I'm looking for my friend, Shelly."

"She's the missing racer?"

"Yes."

"Get in. We need to see where you found the body, and then we'll look for Shelly."

"Sir, no offense, but there's nothing you can do for the dead guy. There are tire tracks over here. We need to follow this lead before it goes cold."

The driver turned around and pointed at the boat behind him. Two guys who couldn't have been much more than twenty rode in it, each wearing shorts and a T-shirt. "You two, check out the tire tracks. I need to go to the scene." He rotated his body so he was pointing at Brad. "Get in the boat. I need you to show me what you found and fill in all the details."

Brad grudgingly made his way to the boat as the two young guys pulled up to the riverbank. "I'm Sheriff Yellington," he said. "Most of the folks around here call me Old Yeller, but if I catch you doing it, you're a dead man." The man beside him snorted.

Brad thought it was a bad time to make jokes, but he'd come across this kind of guy before. The two other guys climbed out of their boat. As Brad stepped into the sheriff's boat, he said, "No offense, but I think we're making a mistake. We need to stay on the tire tracks and find Shelly."

The sheriff ran a hand though his long hair and said, "Son, have a seat next to Deputy Cooper." He started the boat again and continued upstream toward the rappelling station. "Our priority is the dead body. After I see that, I'll know what kind of investigation we're running, and we'll figure out if your friend is even missing. More times than not, an adult goes missing, they just want to be alone. Turn up again in their own time."

Brad wanted to argue, but they'd already arrived. He checked his watch and climbed out of the boat behind the sheriff and his deputy. Angel stood near the water, clutching the radio to her chest.

"Where'd you find the body?" the deputy asked.

"Over here," Brad said.

As he led them to the trees, he explained that he and Shelly were the first two over the rock. He expected to find both Shelly and a volunteer at the bottom, and when he didn't see them, he went looking in the trees. He pointed them into the woods.

"About twenty feet in," he said. He had no desire to see the body again.

The sheriff led the way. A few seconds after they'd entered the woods, the deputy came out looking like he might retch. The sheriff followed a minute later. He looked fine, but the bravado had left his voice.

"Tell me again what happened."

Suppressing an eye roll, Brad went back through the story of Shelly going over the rock first.

"How far back were you?" Deputy Cooper asked.

"It took five minutes to get to the top of the rock," Brad said. He continued the story, explaining how he didn't see anyone on the other side. When Gus and Glen came down, they offered to send help from the aid station. Brad went into the woods, found the body, and came out as Angel arrived.

"She told me about the canoe, and I went to check it out. That's when you arrived."

The sheriff nodded. He clenched and unclenched his jaw several times before digging a cell phone from his pocket. "Graham," he said. "We've got a real mess here. Looks like a murder scene with a possible missing person. I need you to clear all the racers from the course. Have them go back to the starting point and wait for us. Can you do that?" He listened for a moment, nodding though Graham couldn't see. "Get the check-in sheets, and we'll make sure no one is unaccounted for. Hold all the volunteers. Coop and I will want to talk to each of them. It's going to be a long afternoon."

The Sheriff told Angel she could go back to the aid station and return to the starting line with the other volunteers.

"Coop, you got a camera?"

"In the boat."

"Get it. Take as many pictures of the body and the whole area as you can. I'm going to look at those tire tracks." He tilted his head toward Brad. "You, come with me."

As they rode, the sheriff fired more questions at Brad. "How long were you on the ground before the next racer came over the rock?"

"I don't know. Five minutes."

"How did you know where to look for the body?"

"I didn't. I stumbled upon it while I was looking for Shelly."

"Was Shelly carrying a knife?"

Heat rose in Brad's face. "No," he answered. His voice came out in a growl.

Sheriff Yellington parked the boat behind the other one. The two young guys rushed forward to meet him. "Cody, Noah, this is Brad." The two guys nodded at him, and Brad had no idea which one was which. "What'd you find?"

The taller of the two guys pointed at the tire tracks. "Looks like a four-wheeler," he said. "Tracks go all the way back to the trees, then they stop."

"Show me."

The foursome followed the tracks until they stopped. The sheriff unclipped a flashlight and shined it into the trees. "Over here," he said. He led them to a pile of branches. He shifted one and revealed an ATV. He shined the light on the ground and motioned for the other men to follow. They walked along a game trail that exited the trees. They continued to the edge of a two-lane highway.

"Look at the grass here," the sheriff said. "It's been pressed down. My guess is that there was a vehicle here. Your friend could have driven off."

"Been driven off," Brad said. "Trust me, she didn't leave on her own."

Yellington made a noise that sounded like a combination of a snort and a burp. He motioned for Brad to follow and retraced their steps back to the river.

"Let's go get Cooper," Yellington said.

As they motored off, Brad said, "Can you show me where that highway is on a map? As soon as we get back, I'm taking my truck and looking for Shelly."

"Son, you're not going anywhere," Yellington said. "We still need to take your statement."

Brad slapped his Cubs hat against his knee. "I already told you everything I know. Someone needs to find Shelly."

"Maybe she doesn't want to be found," Yellington said, as he pulled up to the bank near Deputy Cooper. "Wouldn't be out of the question considering the body left behind at her last known location."

Brad's jaw tightened. "What's that supposed to mean? You think Shelly's a suspect?"

"I think it's best to leave no stone unturned," Yellington answered. "Coop, we're going to leave the body here. Paramedics are at the starting point; you can show them how to get back here, and they can figure out how to haul the body back once the ME clears the scene."

Cooper joined them in the boat and drove, and Yellington barked out orders over his radio. They arrived near the race's starting line, and an ambulance waited for them. While the deputy coordinated with the paramedics, the sheriff led Brad into the chaos, where the other racers milled about. Yellington commandeered a microphone and told everyone to form a line.

They would check out with him, so he could ensure everyone was accounted for.

"You might as well take a seat over there," he told Brad, pointing to a folding chair near the check-in station. "I'll get to you at the end."

Brad fumed as he watched each racer give their name to Yellington. He marked them off the check-in sheet and asked each a couple of questions that Brad couldn't hear. G&G approached. The sheriff marked them off. After he asked his questions, he pointed for them to wait on the other side of the line, away from Brad.

Finally, the last of the racers departed, leaving Brad, Gus, and Glen. About twenty yards away, Graham Detweiler, the race master, stood amid a gaggle of volunteers. He saw the sheriff walking toward Brad and beelined in their direction.

"Sheriff, all the volunteers are accounted for, except three. We're trying to track them down."

The sheriff creased his brow and crossed his arms. "Why aren't they here?"

"It's not unusual for folks who had early morning duties to leave for a while and come back at the end. Maybe catch a nap, do their grocery shopping, that kind of thing."

"Keep me posted, Graham," Yellington said. As Graham departed, the sheriff turned his attention to Brad. "Go through your story again. Tell me everything."

Brad closed his eyes and counted to five. He opened them and walked Yellington through the events again.

"Your girlfriend ever been up in this area before?"

"Friend," Brad corrected. Yellington made the snort/burp sound again. "No, this is her first time in Montana."

"She know anyone up here? Old friend from school, maybe? Someone else who was racing?"

"No," Brad said. "We picked this one because she wanted to see someplace new, and we were looking for a quick race. Since we don't train together, we didn't think a multi-day challenge was a good idea."

Without a word, the sheriff went back to G&G. Gus answered his questions, speaking animatedly and waving his hands. Brad checked his watch. It was 4:00; four hours since he'd seen Shelly.

Gus and Glen walked away, and Yellington came back to Brad.

"I'm going to let you go," the sheriff said. "They backed up your story. I need to get a cell phone number from you and an address if you plan on staying in the area."

Brad gave him his phone number and provided the address to Eddie's fishing resort. "The guy I'm staying with is an ex-cop," Brad said. "Homicide detective. If you need an extra set of eyes on anything, I'm sure he'd be happy to help."

Yellington crossed his arms and narrowed his eyes. "Son, if I need help, there are plenty of active officers in the area I can call on. If you don't have any other info to share, you can hit the road."

Brad swallowed hard. "There is one thing," he said. "Shelly didn't come to town with me. She came with her boyfriend. Aaron Reynolds. He has a history."

CHAPTER 7

Ten Years Earlier.
September 2, 2015. Chicago, Illinois.
Brad finished his routine on the heavy bag and peeled the practice wraps from his hands. Sweat coated his torso, and his arms felt like Jell-O. He took a long drink from his water bottle before moving to the jump rope station.

He grabbed a rope and went through his routine, whipping the handles to move the rope as quickly as possible. He counted fifty jumps on both feet, before switching to complete fifty on each foot. He did fifty more on both feet and 100 alternating legs. Dropping the handles, he threw his head back and howled at the exposed duct work in the ceiling.

A strong hand clapped his shoulder. "Good workout, I take it?" Doyle asked.

"The best," Brad said. "I feel like crap." Both men laughed.

"When do you fight again?" Doyle asked.

"Two weeks. Joe Olivero."

"He's good," Doyle said. "Quick. You should do another round on the jump rope." Brad laughed, but Doyle remained stone-faced.

Brad put his water bottle down, retrieved the rope, and repeated his routine under Doyle's watchful eye.

"Faster," Doyle said.

Brad turned the rope and kept jumping. His heart felt like it would leap through his chest.

"Faster," Doyle said in a near-shout.

Brad found a gear he didn't know he had. The rope was nothing more than a blur skimming the gym floor as he hopped first on his left foot, then on his right. When he reached 100, he dropped the rope again.

"You're trying to kill me," he gasped as he grabbed his water.

"Better me than Olivero," Doyle said. He watched Brad drink before continuing. "Seriously, Brad, if you beat Olivero, I think you're ready for the next step."

Brad raised his eyebrows. "City championships?"

"To start with," Doyle said. "I could see you in the Midwest Region MMA. Do well there, and who knows?" He clapped Brad on the shoulder again. "First things first. Take care of Olivero."

While Brad showered and changed, he couldn't stop thinking about what Doyle said. Doyle knew fighting; he wouldn't push Brad in a direction he couldn't handle. Brad had seen Joe Olivero fight before. Olivero was faster than him, but Brad was much stronger. He had no doubt he would win that fight.

He combed his hair, slung his backpack over a shoulder, and started for the back door with a skip in his step. He exited the building, turned the corner, and found Aaron Reynolds and his girlfriend, Monica Robson, in the midst of a heated exchange.

"I forgot," Monica said, throwing her hands in the air. "It was a simple mistake."

"Whenever I make plans, you conveniently forget," Aaron said, mimicking Monica's voice on the last word. "I'm sick of it."

Brad stopped walking. Monica stared at him, causing Aaron to turn around.

"This is a private conversation, Cummings," Aaron growled.

Brad held up his hands. "I'm just walking here."

"Walk somewhere else," Aaron said, his voice menacing.

Brad was not letting Aaron Reynolds ruin his evening. He walked around the couple, giving them a wide berth. When he was about ten feet past them, he heard Monica yelp. He turned and saw Aaron with his forehead against her, whispering in her face. He clamped his left hand around her wrist. His right hand was on the back of her head.

Aaron jerked his right hand down. Monica's head dipped, and she let out another yelp. Aaron shoved her away and turned toward the gym. Monica followed him. Brad dashed around her and gave Aaron a shove of his own.

"I saw you, Reynolds," Brad said.

Aaron wheeled on him and raised his hands, ready to fight. "This doesn't concern you, Cummings."

"I'll decide what concerns me," Brad said, dropping his backpack. "Right now, I'm concerned about a weak man who thinks it's okay to beat up a woman."

Aaron chuckled. "I didn't beat up anyone. We had a misunderstanding, that's all. She's fine. Aren't you, Monica?"

"I'm fine," Monica said, avoiding eye contact with Brad. "Really, it was nothing."

"Get out of here, Cummings," Aaron said, his hands still raised.

Brad looked from Monica to Aaron before retrieving his backpack. He leaned close to Aaron and said, "If I ever hear about you laying your hands on a woman again, that last beating I gave you in the ring will seem like a paper cut."

•   •   •

Three days later, Brad hobbled out of the gym after another strenuous workout. He passed Aaron on the sidewalk outside. Aaron kept his head down and didn't offer so much as a grunt to acknowledge Brad. Brad ignored Aaron and continued to the deli down the block.

He'd barely taken a bite from his hot beef sandwich when Monica came in. Dark circles lined her eyes. Her hair looked dull, and Brad swore she'd lost weight since he'd last seen her. She looked out the window before scurrying to Brad's table and flopping into the chair across from him.

"I watched you come in," she said. "I was hoping to catch you after you left the gym. Aaron doesn't know I'm here." Tears filled her eyes. Brad didn't know what to do.

"Do you want some water or something?"

She shook her head. "I need help. I'm leaving Aaron, but I need to go to his apartment. He has my cell phone and my credit card."

"Wait, what?" Brad asked. He looked out the window toward the gym and half-rose from his seat.

"Don't," Monica said. "It's over between us. He won't accept that. He'll never accept it. I'm getting out of town. I need someone to come to his apartment with me in case he gets back before I leave. I'm parked down the block. Please."

Brad fished some bills from his wallet and left them on the table. "Let's go," he said. "I hope he does come back."

The tears flowed freely down Monica's face, and she shook her head. "You don't understand what he's like," she said. Her sobs increased, shaking her shoulders. She handed the car keys to Brad and pointed him toward an ancient Honda Civic.

She cried the entire way to Aaron's place, giving Brad directions between bursts of tears. Once at the apartment, she had Brad park at the office. "The super works late," she said. She dried her eyes with tissues from the glove box. "He likes me. He'll give me a key."

Brad waited outside the office, eyes peeled for any sign of Aaron. A couple minutes later, Monica and a stoop-shouldered, gray-haired man appeared. "Just bring the key back when you're done," he said with a wheeze.

Aaron's apartment consisted of a bedroom, bathroom, living room, and kitchen. A pair of TV trays sat in front of a sagging couch. The place smelled of sweat and mildew. Brad stayed in the living room, eyes on the front door, while Monica searched the bedroom for her things.

"I don't mean to pry," Brad said, though that's exactly what he meant to do, and he thought serving as a bodyguard for someone he barely knew gave him that right. "What happened with you and Aaron?"

"Nothing in particular," Monica said from the other room, but there was a catch in her voice. "It's been over for a while, and I finally had enough."

She didn't offer anything else, so Brad remained in his spot by the door, arms at his sides, ready to pounce if the doorknob turned. After five minutes, Monica came out with her phone and a wallet.

"Found it," she said. Relief filled her voice, though tears filled her eyes again. She stood in front of Brad before turning her back on him. She lifted her shirt. A line of bruises covered her spine. She dropped the shirt and started for the door.

Brad stepped in front of her and went into the hallway first. He led her back to her car.

"I can drop you somewhere," she said. "Then, I'm going to my aunt's place out of state. Don't ever tell him you helped me."

"Don't worry about it," Brad said. As they drove toward his apartment, he asked, "Aaron did that to you?"

Monica nodded.

"Has it happened before?"

She shook her head. "He's been escalating."

They rode in silence the rest of the way. As they pulled onto Brad's block, he asked his final question. "Why me? Why didn't one of your friends help you?"

"All my male friends are Aaron's friends," Monica said. "When you're with Aaron, you don't really get to have relationships that he's not the center of. I needed someone not connected to us, and I remembered how you stood up for me the other day. Thank you again. You saved my life."

He got out of the car and watched her disappear. He committed to honor his promise not to say anything to Aaron, though he wanted to go back to Aaron's apartment and give him a fair fight. He cracked his knuckles and hoped they'd get one more turn in the ring together before he moved on to bigger and better fights.

CHAPTER 8

July 19, 2025. Burgess County, Montana.
Brad shifted his weight on the metal folding chair. After he told Yellington about Reynolds's past, the lawman brought him to the sheriff's department in Broadwood while Deputy Cooper fetched Aaron. He checked his phone again. No messages from Shelly. He texted her, "U OK?" and watched it join the half dozen other messages he'd sent without a reply. Not that he expected one; her phone was back in the hotel room. He held out a sliver of hope that she'd show up at the hotel, see the messages, and call him.

He scrolled through his social media apps without paying attention to the content. He checked his texts again and shifted in the chair once more. Across the room, the young guy who checked them in at the race sighed and looked at his watch. A middle-aged woman who had helped direct parking that morning sat next to him. On her other side, a woman about the same age talked on her cell phone. From what Brad could gather, she was giving instructions to someone on what to make for dinner.

"I have no idea when I'll be back," she said for the third time, a slight edge creeping into her voice. She listened and replied, "Because they're interviewing all the volunteers. If I had stayed at the course, I would have been done by now."

The check-in guy looked at her and gave a sad nod. They were apparently the three volunteers who hadn't been accounted for at the race. True to his word, Sheriff Yellington planned to take their statements.

The waiting room door opened, and Deputy Cooper walked in. He looked tired. He motioned for the check-in guy and said, "Come with me."

The woman on the end put her phone to her chest and said, "Coop, when's Old Yeller gonna call me back? I have kids to feed, you know."

The deputy shrugged and disappeared into the depths of the police station with the young man behind him. The door had barely closed before it reopened and Aaron Reynolds stormed in. He headed straight for Brad.

"What'd you find out?" Brad asked. "Is he sending someone to look for her?"

"We mostly talked about whether or not I'm abusing her," Aaron said. Though he kept his voice low, fury filled his words. He cocked a fist back and let it fall at his side. Both women leaned forward to watch the scene unfold.

"Can't run from your past forever," Brad said.

"That's it," Aaron growled. He jumped forward and grabbed Brad's shirt. Brad knocked his hands away and leaped from his chair, standing toe to toe with Aaron.

The door opened behind them, and the sheriff appeared. "What's going on?" he asked. He moved straight to the two men and put a hand on each of them, shoving them backward. Brad fell back into his chair. Yellington pointed Aaron into another one. "That's enough of that." He turned to the woman on the cell phone, "Wanda, come on back with me. Naomi, you're next."

The sheriff and the cell phone woman departed. Aaron kept his arms folded across his chest and glared at the floor. "Is he looking for Shelly?" Brad asked.

"He didn't share his plans with me," Aaron said.

A few minutes later, the door opened, and the deputy took Naomi for her interview. Brad scrolled through his phone again. He looked up when the door opened, and he spied Eddie Fleck.

"You made it," Brad said, relieved to see a friendly face.

"Left as soon as I got the message," Eddie said. "Now, tell me what's going on."

Brad recounted the story of Shelly's disappearance once again. Eddie nodded and took quick glances in Aaron's direction. "I don't think the sheriff believes she's really missing," Brad said as he concluded. "We're wasting time, and Shelly could be getting taken further and further away."

Eddie shrugged. "Not sure you want to hear this, but he's doing what he's supposed to do." Brad opened his mouth, but Eddie waved him off. "The Sheriff's Department is small and covers a large county. They have an apparent murder and a missing woman. He doesn't know if those events are related, but she's an adult, and you don't send your limited resources looking for an adult when you need to focus on solving a murder. If she left on her own, that would be a major mistake on his part."

"She didn't leave on her own," Aaron said.

"Who's he?" Eddie asked, jerking a thumb toward Aaron without turning around.

"Reynolds," Brad said. "Aaron Reynolds. He's Shelly's boyfriend. He's right; Shelly didn't leave voluntarily. Something happened to her, and we need to find her."

Eddie leaned back in his chair and tented his fingers. "What are you basing that on? Signs of a struggle? Witnesses?"

"No," Brad said. "I just know Shelly, and she wouldn't run off like that."

"Maybe not," Eddie said, "but the sheriff doesn't know her, and he has to make decisions based on evidence."

Sheriff Yellington came back into the room, carrying a styrofoam cup filled with steaming coffee. He slurped from it as he appraised the newcomer.

"Who are you?"

Eddie stood and offered a hand. "Eddie Fleck. I'm a friend of Brad's."

"Great," Yellington said. He made no move to accept Eddie's handshake. He looked from Aaron to Brad. "I know you're both concerned about your friend. If it looked like she'd gotten lost in the woods or fallen off a cliff or gotten stuck somewhere, I'd have every available man in the county looking for her, but that's not how it looks."

"But—" Brad started. Yellington cut him off.

"That's not how it looks," he repeated, his voice raised a notch. "No one reported seeing or hearing a struggle. It's a reasonable assumption that she took the boat we found, got on the ATV, and took it to the highway. That's an independent adult acting on her own volition. She disabled the GPS on her race bib. That sounds like someone who doesn't want to be followed. I can't say I agree with her methods, but it's not the place of the law to go after her in these circumstances. Now, I have a ton of work to do related to this afternoon's other case, so please see yourselves out. If you haven't heard from your friend by this time tomorrow, check in with me, and I'll reevaluate the situation."

"Don't you think the proximity of the sites of Shelly's disappearance and the murder victim is worth investigating?" Eddie asked.

The sheriff slurped the coffee again then stroked his ponytail. "Who are you, again?"

"Name's Eddie Fleck. I'm a retired homicide detective and private eye."

"Well, Detective Fleck," Yellington said, contempt dripping from every word, "I'm not inclined to release what details I think are important to my investigation to civilians. Not even retired policemen. Good evening."

He left the three men alone in the waiting room. "Now what?" Brad asked.

"Let's go find your friend," Eddie said. "Just because the police aren't looking for her, doesn't mean we can't. Can you show me where the ATV led you?"

He held out his phone with the map open. Brad enlarged it and scrolled before dropping a pin at the nearest road. Eddie studied the phone, his brow furrowed.

"That's not good news," he said.

"What?" Aaron asked, peering over his shoulder.

"That's County Road 15. See how it runs into 287 less than a mile away? Take that highway north, you could get on Interstate 15. Take it south, you hit I-90."

"You're saying Shelly could be anywhere," Brad said. He flopped into a chair and held his head in his hands.

"Basically, yeah," Eddie said. "Not good news."

"What do we do?" Aaron asked.

"We don't have enough daylight left to get in much of a search in the woods," Eddie said. "So, we go to the point where you think she left the woods. We drive the county road to 287 and then go in each direction to see if there are any nearby businesses with cameras, any traffic cams, anything that might tell us which direction to look in. If we don't get any leads, we come back tomorrow, round up a search party and walk the woods looking for any clues."

Brad sprang from his seat, eager to do anything after helplessly sitting all afternoon. "Let's go," he said.

"I'm going, too," Aaron said.

"I think it's best you sit this one out," Brad said. Eddie cocked an eyebrow at him. "I'll explain some other time," he muttered.

"I'm going," Aaron repeated.

"You got wheels?" Eddie asked. Aaron nodded. "You can follow us out. I need to talk to Brad about some personal business, anyway."

They left the police station and drove back past the race's starting point. A row of police cruisers lined up in the parking lot.

The finish line remained intact, a table filled with finisher medals set up nearby. Eddie checked his rearview mirror.

"So, what's up with lover boy?"

Brad looked over his shoulder and saw Aaron tailgating. "I met him back in Chicago," he said. "We used to train and fight out of the same gym. Had a bit of a rivalry for a while. The big thing is I know some things about him. He's a bad dude."

Brad recounted the story of meeting Monica and helping her escape. "She said he was controlling, and I see signs of it with Shelly. He wouldn't let her come on this trip on her own. I just don't trust him."

"Fair enough," Eddie said. He slowed down for a sharp turn. He pointed through the windshield. "We're getting close."

Brad looked back at Aaron again. "I think we should consider Aaron a suspect in Shelly's disappearance."

"Whoa," Eddie said as he coasted to a stop. He steered onto the shoulder and put his flashers on. "You think Aaron tagged along on this trip, so he could hide out on a racecourse—that only the race staff knew about—so he could do something to Shelly? How does the volunteer's murder fit into all this?"

"I know it sounds crazy," Brad said, "but let's not rule him out."

"It doesn't sound crazy," Eddie said. "It sounds like someone who's letting his past cloud his judgment." He held eye contact with Brad for a moment. Aaron approached from the passenger side. "Fine, we won't rule him out," Eddie said. "But you need to stay objective. Shelly needs you to."

They stepped out of Eddie's Jeep. A hint of cool replaced the heat of the day as a breeze wafted off the mountains. The smell of pine trees filled the air, and flecks of fuzz from cottonwoods speckled the sky.

"How far to the ATV?" Eddie asked.

"Just a few minutes," Brad said.

"Let's check it out while it's still light out," Eddie said, motioning them toward the trees.

Brad led the way with Eddie behind him and Aaron bringing up the rear. They crept at a snail's pace, paying attention to every branch and looking for any sign of a disturbance.

The ATV came into view. As they approached it, Eddie cautioned them not to touch it. "If Shelly's really missing, someone is going to take fingerprints from it eventually," he said.

"What are we looking for?" Aaron asked.

"Anything that will connect Shelly to the ATV," Brad said. "We want confirmation that she came this way. A hair, a bit of torn fabric, anything."

"I was asking the detective," Aaron said.

"Brad is a detective," Eddie said. Brad couldn't help feeling smug as the surprise registered across Aaron's face. "And he's completely correct."

Footprints marked the ground where the sheriff and his men had tramped around the vehicle that afternoon, so Brad stepped closer, looking at it from all angles. He leaned in the open side, careful not to touch the frame. He peered at the passenger headrest.

"Nothing," he said.

"I concur," Eddie said. "How tall is Shelly?"

"Five-five," Aaron said.

Eddie gestured at the driver's seat. "We'd need to open it up and take some measurements to be sure, but the seat position looks like it's set for a taller driver."

Brad took photos with his phone and led the way back through the trees to the Jeep. "Let's check out 287," Eddie said. "We can all ride together." Brad started to protest, but a sharp look from Eddie cut him off.

Eddie eased on the gas and crept along the county road. "Keep an eye out for anything unusual," Brad told Aaron.

"Broken branches on the side of the road, any sign of a struggle, or anything that belongs to Shelly. And any cameras."

They reached the highway without finding anything. Eddie turned north. He had to speed up to stay in the flow of traffic. The first building was a mile after the turn, a gas station with four pumps and a convenience store not much bigger than a toll booth. Eddie pulled off. Brad looked the exterior up and down.

"No cameras," he said. "I'm going in."

He approached the counter, flanked by a drink machine and a rack of candy bars. Shelves behind the counter held cigarette cartons. The register displayed a neon pink sign advertising lottery tickets.

"Were you here earlier this afternoon?" Brad asked the attendant, a skinny blond guy with a tattoo of a Viking on his neck. "Between noon and 1:00?"

"Yeah." The guy kept his eyes on a magazine featuring trucks and guns.

"Did you happen to see this woman?" Brad held up his phone, a picture of Shelly on the screen.

The guy looked up from the magazine, squinted at the photo, and shook his head. "Nope."

Brad thanked him and returned to the Jeep. Over the next two miles, they passed another gas station and a burger and taco fast food place. The restaurant did not have any cameras, and the manager did not recall seeing anyone who resembled Shelly.

The gas station attendant did not remember Shelly, either, but the building had a security camera on the highway side.

"How far does the camera reach?" Eddie asked. "Can you see all the way to the highway?" The worker, an attentive man in his 30s, looked nervously at the three visitors.

"I'm not sure I should answer questions about our security," he said.

"We need to see if anyone drove by this afternoon," Eddie said. "We're searching for a missing person, and it's really important that we explore any possible lead."

The guy swallowed and adjusted his collar. "You a cop?"

"Used to be," Eddie said. He pulled his Colorado Retired Police Officers Association card from his wallet and slid it across the counter. "This case isn't officially a police matter yet, but we could still use your help."

The guy swallowed again. He looked past them, then leaned close and lowered his voice. "The camera doesn't work," he said. "The owner put it up as a deterrent a couple years ago. Got knocked out by a power surge during a thunderstorm, and he's never bothered to repair it. Don't tell anyone."

Eddie put his index fingers to his lips in a shush motion. "Your secret is safe," he said. "We'll take it to our graves." Brad struggled to suppress a smile.

They piled back into the Jeep and turned south. That side of the highway did not yield any better results. They found no security cameras and no one who saw Shelly within two miles of the turn from the county road.

"That was a bust," Eddie said as he pulled even with Aaron's car.

"What now?" Aaron asked. "Search again tomorrow?"

Eddie nodded. "Give Brad your number. He can send you the details."

Brad and Aaron exchanged information. Brad watched behind him as Aaron pulled away. "He was quiet," Brad said. "Not much to say. That's not like him."

"His girlfriend's missing, and he doesn't know if she ran off or got kidnapped," Eddie said. "Cut the guy some slack."

Brad crossed his arms. Eddie did a U-turn and headed back toward Broadwood. He pulled into a diner. "Hungry?"

"Not really," Brad said. "But I should probably eat something."

"You need your strength," Eddie said.

Inside, they found a booth in a back corner. Gus and Glen occupied the next table. No longer in matching outfits, Gus wore a faded polo, and Glen sported a Boise State Broncos T-shirt.

"Find your partner?" Gus asked.

Brad shook his head. "Nothing yet." Gus flexed out the veins in the side of his neck; Glen made a similar gesture.

"Must be worried," Gus said.

Brad nodded. "We're planning on looking again tomorrow morning. Eight o'clock." He looked at Eddie who nodded.

"We'd love to stay and help, but we have to get back to Boise," Glen said.

Gus jumped from his seat and strode across the diner. He came back a moment later with Graham, the race coordinator. Bespectacled and balding, Graham looked more like an accountant than an adventure race enthusiast.

"Graham can help spread the word about the search," Gus said, his voice bubbling with enthusiasm. "He knows everyone around here."

Graham looked like someone had just punched him in the gut. "I've never had anything happen like today's race," he said. "Not even close."

Eddie motioned for him to sit down at the booth. Graham sat, looking over his shoulder and signaling to someone across the restaurant that he'd be a few minutes. Eddie peppered him with questions about who knew the racecourse, how the GPS trackers worked, and if any volunteers were unaccounted for.

"I answered all this for the police earlier," he said.

Eddie waved a hand dismissively. "They're trying to solve a murder. We're interested in finding Shelly. You got the names of all the volunteers to the sheriff? Any chance we can get that list from you?"

Graham shook his head. His glasses slid down his nose. He pushed them up and stood with a moan.

Eddie reached across the table and grabbed his arm. "What about a search party? We want to start looking at 8:00 a.m. tomorrow. Can you round up some people to help?"

Graham pulled his arm away from Eddie and held it close to his body. "Yes," he said in a small, defeated voice. "I'll spread the word. I'll have everyone meet at the main parking area."

He walked away. Brad smiled at Eddie. "I see you haven't lost the patented Eddie Fleck charm."

CHAPTER 9

Keeping a foot on the brake, he navigated the back road in the pitch black. He worried as much about running into a deer or a bear as he did sliding off the path. He hadn't planned on getting hung up at the police station for so long.

Being around the police made him nervous, but he thought he covered it. He read people well, and he didn't pick up on the sheriff or his deputy having any suspicions of his involvement in what happened on the racecourse. All in all, it had been a successful day.

Except for the syringe. He swore at himself again, as he thought about the missing hypodermic needle. It had fallen out of his pocket somewhere along the way. Nothing he could do about it, though; he doubted anyone would find it, and if they did, he didn't see how they could trace it to him.

He grabbed the fast-food bag from the passenger seat and pulled a ski mask over his face. The mask was not technically necessary, since his guest would never see another person again, but not letting her know his identity added to her terror and gave him more power.

Using his phone as a flashlight, he unlocked the door and entered more darkness. Black plastic covered all the windows. He felt along the wall until he found the light switch. She cowered in the corner, blinking in the sudden brightness.

"You're awake." He disguised his voice as much as possible.

"Let me go," she said. He took a step toward her, and she drew further into the corner. A chain secured to a steel ring in the floor attached to her handcuffs. He'd given her a three-foot radius and considered it generous. He tossed the fast-food bag at her. It hit her knee and fell to the ground, french fries spilling onto the concrete floor.

"Eat," he said. The room had sparse furnishings, just a table mounted to the wall opposite the woman with a single metal folding chair. A kitchenette butted up against the room. A short hallway led to the bathroom and his bedroom, where a bare mattress lay on the floor.

The woman scooped up the bag and scarfed down the burger and fries. He took a plastic water bottle from the fridge and tossed it at her. She caught it between her body and her hands before gulping it down.

"All the trash in the bag," he ordered. "Bottle and lid, too. Good. Now toss the bag this way."

The bag fell halfway between the woman and him. As he went to pick it up, she scrambled toward him and kicked. He predicted her attack and knocked her feet away. He stood over her and kicked her ribs with his steel-toed boot. She howled. He laughed and moved to the other side of the room where he slumped into the metal chair.

"What do you want with me?" the woman asked. He shrugged. "Let me go!" she shrieked, her voice growing in volume with each syllable. "Let. Me. Go."

He pulled a paperback from his rear pocket and thumbed through the pages until he found his last spot. The woman curled up in her corner and sobbed. He hoped she would break quickly. The women before her had started as fighters but eventually lost their resolve, even becoming catatonic toward the end. This one seemed especially strong; he'd planned on keeping her for about a week, but if she didn't get in line, she wouldn't last nearly that long.

"I need to use the bathroom," she said.

He slammed his book shut and fumbled in his pocket for a key. "Don't try anything," he warned. He drew his boot back as if to kick her again, and she curled her body tighter on itself.

Unlocking the padlock on the chain, he let out another twelve feet and pointed to the bathroom. She stumbled toward it. She stopped when she reached the threshold as if puzzled.

"There's no door," she said. He shrugged again and pointed at the bathroom. She went in and stood in front of the toilet. "At least turn around," she said. He took two steps closer and put his hands on his hips, staring at her.

More tears came to her eyes as she hunched, trying to shield as much of her body as she could as she sat on the toilet. While she sat there, she searched the walls of the bathroom with her eyes. He smiled under the ski mask, knowing she'd been hoping to spot a window.

When she returned to the room, he shortened the chain once again, extinguished the light, and shut himself in the bedroom.

CHAPTER 10

July 20, 2025. Burgess County, Montana.
A contingent of searchers had already gathered when Brad pulled his truck into the parking area near the check-in area. Graham herded them together. He looked refreshed since the day before; determination replaced the anxious expression he had worn in the diner.

Angel stood among the crowd. She, too, looked better off after a night's rest. Brad imagined she would deal with the shock of the day before for quite some time. Lawrence, the volunteer who checked Brad and Shelly in and appeared later at the police station, also joined the searchers. He still looked pale, almost sickly, and Brad was surprised to see him there.

Brad and Eddie were halfway to Graham when footsteps pounded the gravel behind them.

"Hold it right there," Sheriff Yellington said. "What is all this about?"

"It's a search party," Brad said. "We're trying to find my friend."

"Oh no you're not." The sheriff wiped his sunglasses on his uniform shirt, glaring at Brad the entire time. "This is a crime scene, and I need it cleared."

"This whole area can't be a crime scene," Eddie said.

"It can be if I say it is," Yellington answered. "I have a murder to investigate, so head on out of here."

"There a problem, Old Yeller?" Graham said, joining the group.

Eddie leaned close to Brad and whispered, "Old Yeller?"

"Apparently, it's a locals-only thing," Brad said.

"I'm trying to investigate a murder. I can't have all these people running around."

Graham took a few steps closer and settled in between Brad and Eddie. He put a hand on their shoulders. "What area do you need to make off limits? Where the body was found?"

"Yeah," Yellington said. "We need free access and can't have people in our way."

"Look, Randy," Graham said. "They're worried about their friend, and I've got a group of volunteers ready to give up a Sunday to help find her. At some point, the police will have to get involved in this, so you might as well let us give you a head start."

"I don't know," Yellington said. He looked over his shoulder as another police cruiser parked. Deputy Cooper and another officer climbed out.

"We need to look on the other side of the river," Graham said. "Why don't I take the group north to the foot bridge. We'll cross over and search the woods south all the way to where the boat was found and then back up to the ATV. We won't be in your way at all."

The sheriff creased his brow; a frown turned down the corners of his mouth.

"If it was Isabelle, you'd want people out looking," Graham said.

"Fine," the sheriff answered. "Nobody touches the boat or the ATV, understood?"

"Got it," Graham said. He motioned for the searchers to follow him and led the crowd away. Brad noticed Aaron slip in among the searchers. There were around a dozen people in all.

"We're up for a short hike to the bridge," Graham said. "Once we cross the river, we'll fan out and search the woods for any sign of our missing racer. If you see anything that looks like evidence or just looks suspicious, stop where you are and call me over. Don't touch anything."

The group answered with a chorus of yeses and okays, and Graham led them along a gravel path to the north. As the group walked, Aaron made his way through the pack to catch up with Brad and Eddie.

Brad cast a wary eye at him but didn't say anything. Aaron refused to make eye contact.

"I take it you didn't hear anything from Shelly yet," Eddie said.

"No," Aaron grunted. "You guys?"

"Nothing," Brad said.

"You have her phone?" Eddie asked.

"Yeah," Aaron said. He pulled it from a cargo pocket in his shorts.

"Do you know any of Shelly's sign in information?" Eddie asked. "If you can unlock the phone and check her bank account, that would be a huge help."

"I can unlock it," Aaron said. "I'll try her banking app."

Aaron fiddled with the phone as they hiked, muttering to himself with each unsuccessful attempt. "I can only try once more," he said.

"Does she still have that cat?" Brad asked. "What's his name? Milton?"

"Yeah," Aaron said. "It's not long enough for a password."

"His birthday is July 4th, right? She used to make a big deal about Milton sharing a birthday with the country. Try Milton0704."

Aaron stopped walking and thumbed in the password. Brad leaned close to see the screen. A triumphant grin spread across his face as the app unlocked. Aaron scrolled through the account information.

"She's got checking, savings, and a credit card on here," he said. "Savings hasn't been touched in over a month. She used her debit card to buy gas on the way here. That's the last charge on checking; nothing pending. She used her credit card to pay for the hotel. Again, last charge, nothing pending."

The three continued walking. About fifty feet ahead, a concrete pedestrian bridge arched over the Missouri River.

"Good to know," Eddie said. "Searching the woods is still our best first move. Keep an eye on that thing and let me know if any new charges appear."

They stopped at the edge of the bridge, joining Graham in waiting for the rest of the search party. When the stragglers caught up, Graham repeated his instructions not to touch anything suspicious.

"Don't move in a gaggle, either," he said. "We need to go through the trees as methodically as possible, so we're going to spread out with about twenty feet between each person. It's going to be a slow march. Give yourself plenty of time to look to your right and to your left. If the group gets too far ahead of you, let me know, and we'll slow down. Take a moment now to hydrate, and we'll start the search."

Aaron had only brought a disposable water bottle with him. He had no backpack and no supplies of any kind. Brad knew he hadn't come on the trip expecting to spend a day in the woods, but he could have bought provisions the night before.

Brad took the top end of their search chain, making sure he kept Eddie between him and Aaron. Graham positioned himself in the middle of the line of volunteers. On his command the formation moved forward five feet and stopped. Brad searched on each side, staring at every branch. Graham yelled another command, and the group moved forward. Again, Brad looked to each side, hoping to spot something that might point them toward wherever Shelly had gone.

In his heart, he knew it was pointless. The ATV tracks led from the boat to the county road. He had no doubt she had been taken away via the highway. They wouldn't make any real headway in the search until the police got involved. Still, it gave him something to do that felt like helping, and when the sheriff finally backed off his stubborn position, they'd be able to help the police rule out another search of the woods.

Midway through the morning, a volunteer called out that he'd found something. Brad froze in place, and his heartbeat quickened with anticipation. Graham called for him to make his way down the line. Aaron joined him, and they found Graham side by side with Lawrence, the check-in guy.

Lawrence pointed to a low branch on a fir tree where a nylon strip, about two inches by six inches, fluttered in the breeze. It looked like a remnant from a raincoat. It was bright pink and shined in the sunlight.

"Recognize this?" Graham asked. Both Brad and Aaron shook their heads.

"Shelly was wearing a blue moisture-wicking shirt with gray nylon pants," Brad said. "This wouldn't have come from her outfit."

"Did she have a raincoat in her bag?" Graham asked, a hopeful tone in his voice.

"Probably, but I doubt it was pink," Brad said. "Pink isn't really her thing."

"I think her raincoat was blue," Aaron offered.

Graham photographed the fabric with his phone and noted its coordinates in a logbook he carried with him. Brad and Aaron trudged back to their places and waited for the next signal to move forward.

They spent the entire morning hiking through the woods, reaching the canoe at 1:00. Graham called for a break and gathered everyone around him.

"Nobody touches the boat," he said. "We believe Shelly may have ridden in an ATV from here. We're going to follow the tracks to where the ATV is, again nobody touches it, and we'll search the woods around it. Once we reach County Road 15, we'll call it a day and head back in.

The group spread out for lunch along the banks of the river. Eddie had packed an extra sandwich that he shared with Aaron. Brad had an extra water bottle he grudgingly passed along. Some of the volunteers chatted as they ate. Brad kept his back to Aaron and ate in silence.

Graham called for the group to assemble. Brad stood, looking at the river. Sunlight glinted off something in the water. A tingle of anticipation jolted through his body.

"Graham, over here," he called. "I've got something."

Eddie, Aaron, and Graham crowded around Brad, looking at where he pointed in the water.

"I don't like to move anything that might be evidence," Graham said.

"Nonsense," Eddie said. "The police can't do anything with it underwater. Brad, pull it out."

Before Graham could object, Brad fished a plastic wrapped race bib from the water. A rock in the packaging weighed it down.

"The current must have pushed it to the bank here," he said. "I didn't notice it yesterday."

"I take it that was Shelly's race number?" Eddie asked.

"Yeah," Brad said. "This was her bib." He set it on the ground, and Graham took photos from every angle before scribbling in his logbook.

"This confirms that we're on the right track," Graham said. "Let's form up and walk the woods."

For the afternoon shift, Brad moved to the middle of the line, walking on one side of Graham, with the ATV tracks between them. The afternoon passed much like the morning, with the group taking a few halting steps forward while methodically searching the area. Half an hour into the search, Angel called Graham over, but it was a false alarm.

"Bunch of broken branches," he said. "Nothing remarkable, though; probably just a bear foraging."

By the time they could see the county road, Brad's eyes ached from staring into shadows all day. His neck was stiff, and his spirits were broken. He'd had low expectations for the search, but a whole day of looking and not getting any closer to finding Shelly depressed him.

"I see something," a female volunteer shouted as they approached the road. Graham moved toward her, Brad on his heels. Eddie and Aaron tromped behind him. They arrived, and the woman pointed at a wad of duct tape near the road.

"Good eye," Graham said. "It might be nothing, but who knows?" He completed his ritual of photographing and cataloging. Eddie produced a latex glove and a plastic bag from his pack.

"Don't touch it," Graham cautioned. Eddie rolled his eyes.

"You've done a great job leading the search today," Eddie said. "I appreciate all you've done, but we can't leave this here to get moved by an animal or blown onto the road and crushed by a tire. If this has any DNA on it, it could be the thing that gets the police interested in doing their job."

With that, he grabbed the wad and stowed it in the bag. He turned to Brad. "When we get back to the parking lot, we need to have a talk with Mellow Yellow, or whatever they call him."

As they hiked back, Brad talked to Eddie, Aaron, and Graham about his plans for the next day. He wanted to explore from the county road to the highway, searching both shoulders for any sign of Shelly being hidden away and then do the same thing on 287.

"I'm in," Eddie said.

"I am, too," Aaron said. "I'm going to have to get back to the office eventually, but when I tell my boss what's going on, I'm sure he'll give me some more time off."

"What about you, Graham?" Brad asked. "Any chance we can get this intrepid crew to help us out again tomorrow?"

"I'll see what I can do," Graham said. "I'm sure a few folks will be able to help, but it's a workday tomorrow. Like Aaron here, I'm going to have to get back to my office, too."

They arrived at the parking area to find the police cruisers gone. Graham announced that anyone who was willing to search again should arrive by 8:00 the next morning, and they'd drive out from the lot. Then, he offered to accompany the other three to the police station to find the sheriff.

"If it's all the same to you guys, I'm going to beg off," Aaron said. "I'm exhausted, and I don't think I can add much to a police discussion. Let me know if anything changes."

"Suit yourself," Brad said, glad to be rid of Aaron for a while.

At the station, Sheriff Yellington did not look happy to see them. Graham walked him through their finds, and the sheriff scowled the entire time.

"The fabric is probably not related," Graham admitted, "but the race bib definitely is, and the duct tape is a wild card."

"I appreciate the update," Yellington said, though his tone said he did not. "I don't see what I can do with any of this."

"Send the tape to a lab and have it tested," Eddie said. "If this was used on Shelly, there will be trace DNA. Hair, saliva, skin cells."

"Not sure where you were a cop, but around here we follow due process, and we don't waste resources. I have no reason to believe this girl disappeared for any reason other than that she intended to."

"Why would she do that?" Brad asked. He cracked his knuckles and looked down at his fingers. On his left hand, a tattooed letter on each finger spelled out "Truth." On his right hand, more tattoos spelled "Peace."

"You gave me a reason," the sheriff said. "A really good one. If she's in an abusive relationship, that's motive enough to go on the run. All you've found is evidence that she left and didn't want to be followed."

"If someone wrapped duct tape around her, it's pretty good evidence that she didn't leave willingly," Eddie hissed. The sheriff shook his head and looked at the ceiling. "Look," Eddie continued. "You have a murder to solve, right? I bet you anything that the killer has something to do with Shelly's disappearance. Even if they're not connected, the boat and the ATV could have been part of the killer's escape plan. The duct tape could have come from him. That's reason enough to have it tested."

The sheriff reached across his desk and picked up the baggie with the duct tape in it. He held it up to the light and peered through the plastic before dropping it. "Fine. I'll send it in for testing. I need an affidavit to establish a chain of custody. I'll have someone write it up tomorrow. Graham, you okay signing it?"

"Sure."

"It's settled then. Good evening."

The men rose to leave. As they reached the door, Brad turned back. "Sheriff, one other thing. We're going to be searching along CR15 and Highway 287 tomorrow. Getting the search party back together. It would be great if you could spare a few men to help us."

"No can do," the sheriff said, the scowl returning to his face. "We're all tied up with an actual crime to investigate. Good evening."

Brad and Eddie thanked Graham again and bid him goodnight. They climbed into Eddie's Jeep and started back toward the fishing resort. They rode in silence until the rough-hewn arch announced their arrival at the Double T Ranch.

"How well do you know Shelly?" Eddie asked as he drew closer to his cabin.

"What do you mean?"

"The sheriff had a fair point. If Aaron is abusing her, Shelly might have run. How well do you trust that she wouldn't tell you about it?"

"She would have told me," Brad said. "We trust each other. We've been friends for a long time and saw each other through some tough times. There's no way she would have just run without asking me for help or at least giving me a heads up."

"Fair enough," Eddie said. "Time for dinner and some sleep. Here's to hoping tomorrow's search gets us closer to the truth."

CHAPTER 11

The rumble of an engine jolted Shelly awake. She tried to stretch, but the chain didn't give her enough leeway. Instead, she wiped each eye on a shoulder, determined not to give that beast the satisfaction of seeing her tears.

Her stomach gnawed at her. Her breakfast, a bag of stale chips and a bottle of water, had burned off hours before. Raw spots marked her wrists from where the handcuffs rubbed them. Her back and legs ached from sitting on the concrete floor for so long.

The psychological pain was worse than her physical discomfort. She had no idea where she was, she didn't know the identity of her tormentor, and she couldn't figure out why he had taken her. She had no hope of escape. The iron ring anchored into the concrete was far too secure and substantial to pull from the ground. The chain connected to her handcuffs was too heavy to break. Even if she had a hacksaw or bolt cutters, it would take her hours to break through it. Without tools, she was at her attacker's mercy.

The handcuffs were also too strong for her. She had tried pulling them against the metal ring in the ground but had succeeded only in hurting herself.

The door swung open, and a triangle of light spilled into the room. The man slammed the door, plunging her into darkness once more until he flipped on the light. Her head screamed in agony, the fatigue, hunger, and stress combining into a piercing pain at her temples.

"Hungry?" the man asked. He wore a ski mask again, leaving only his eyes and mouth visible.

He tossed a plastic grocery bag in her direction. It struck her chest and slid down her body into her lap. She moved awkwardly with her hands bound and withdrew a sandwich, a bruised banana, and a lukewarm bottle of water.

The bread was stale and chunks of the banana were black and mushy, but she ate every bite of the food. After drinking half the water, she secured the lid on it.

"Nope," the man said. "You are not hanging onto that. Finish it now, put all the trash in the bag, and toss it to the door."

Shelly complied, though her stomach turned. She wanted to space out her hydration more, and she loathed the idea of having to use the bathroom in front of him again.

She finished the final drip, running her tongue around the bottle's opening to make sure she had gotten all she could. She shoved the bottle, the banana peel, and the sandwich wrapper into the plastic bag and threw it at the door. The man scooped it up, turned out the light, and left the room. The click of metal on metal resonated through the space as the deadbolt engaged.

Tears flooded Shelly's eyes again. She wiped them on her shoulders once more. With a foot braced on each side of the ring, she pulled as hard as she could. The ring did not budge. She grabbed the ring and twisted, saying "Righty tighty, lefty loosey" in her head. The ring stood fast.

She changed tactics and attacked the handcuffs again. She tried pulling the chain that connected the cuffs against the metal ring in the ground but did not make any progress. She reversed course and slammed the chain into the ring, hoping she'd hit it at just the right angle to shatter the metal.

Every idea, including bashing the padlock that took the slack out of the chain on the concrete over and over, proved fruitless. When she finished, sweat plastered her hair to her face.

The light came back on, and she blinked in the sudden brightness. Her face flushed from the exertion and the shame of being caught in an escape attempt. The man laughed at her and plopped down in the metal folding chair.

"You're not getting away," he said. "You might as well relax and enjoy your final days."

Terror flooded Shelly. Her hands shook and her knees turned to jelly. While she had known the man meant her harm, he had not verbalized it before.

She tried to calm herself as he flipped through the pages of his book. When she felt like she could stand again, she told him she needed to use the bathroom. The hint of a smile peeked out of the ski mask around the corners of his mouth.

He approached her, moving slowly. She didn't try to attack, remembering how useless it was the night before. He let out the chain and jerked her to her feet. Before she could move toward the bathroom, he stepped closer to her and put his arms around her. He ran his hands over her body.

She swung her elbows at him, but he wrapped his arms around her tightly. She tried to kick, but he smothered the attempt with his legs.

"Careful," he said, his breath hot against her ear. "You're gonna get hurt."

She swung her head back. He dodged, but she struck a glancing blow against his ear. He shoved her forward, and she stumbled into the bathroom. Instead of returning to his chair, he moved closer to the bathroom door. He rubbed at his ear and leaned forward as if he might pounce.

Shelly lifted the toilet lid and vomited, the meager contents of her stomach mixing with bile. She stepped back, but another wave of nausea hit her, and she retched until she dry heaved. She flushed it all away and looked over her shoulder at him. He stepped closer still, his arms crossed over his chest.

Shelly stood in front of the toilet as his eyes bore into her. Finally, she turned, made herself as small as possible, and dropped her pants as she squatted on the toilet. She stared straight ahead, not daring to make eye contact with the monster who held her captive.

She made up her mind to find a way to escape. His intentions were clear, and she didn't plan on letting him succeed.

CHAPTER 12

July 21, 2025. Burgess County, Montana.
Brad woke up angry. He kept replaying the day before in his mind. The smug smile the sheriff wore, Aaron abandoning them to go the police station themselves, and the general hopelessness of the search left him in a rage. He needed to find a gym and go a few rounds with the heavy bag, but he didn't think Broadwood offered that kind of amenity.

He swung his feet out of bed and stretched the kinks out of his back. He appreciated Eddie giving him a place to crash, but three straight nights on the pull-out were taking their toll. He dropped into a plank on the floor, moved into a downward dog, back to plank, and into an upward dog. After banging out fifty pushups, he widened his grip and banged out fifty more.

"That right there is the most exercise this cabin has ever witnessed," Eddie said as he plodded into the kitchen. He dumped coffee grounds into his ancient machine.

When Brad returned from his shower, the coffee was ready, along with toast and Peanut Butter Cap'n Crunch.

"I know you don't like the sugary stuff, but I also didn't know you were staying this long," Eddie said. He held his hands up. "Not that I'm trying to get rid of you. You'll stay as long as it takes. We're in this together."

"I appreciate that, Eddie," Brad said. "I wish we could get everyone else to get behind this search, too."

Eddie offered him a sad smile. "I don't see the sheriff jumping on this case today, if that's what you mean."

Brad didn't reply. He stared into his bowl and chased pieces of cereal with his spoon. When breakfast was over, he refilled his water bottles, made sure he had plenty of protein bars in his backpack, and started to the door. "I'll drive today," he said.

He pulled up to the meeting point to find Graham already waiting. Angel arrived a minute later, followed by three of the other searchers from the day before. Brad explained the plan of searching the roadsides. As he was finishing, Aaron sauntered up. Brad squinted at him but held his tongue.

They carpooled to the county road. Graham took Angel and the three other volunteers in his Ford Explorer. Brad followed in his truck; Aaron brought up the rear in Shelly's Subaru Outback.

Angel joined Brad, Eddie, and Aaron on the south side of the road, while Graham led the others on the north side. Overgrown grass covered the roadside all the way to the tree line. Angel stayed in the grass, while the men spread out in the trees, searching for any sign that someone had come through the area with Shelly.

They kept a cautious pace, and it took them just over an hour to reach the junction with Highway 287. The divided highway ran north and south. They reunited with the other group and confirmed that no one had any new leads.

"I'll take my team north and you go south," Graham said, looking at his watch. "It's 9:30. Let's walk as far as we can until 11:00, and then we'll head back to the vehicles. We can get some lunch, cross the highway, and search the other side this afternoon."

With that, the groups separated. Once again, Angel took the edge closest to the road, with the men further in the trees. As the search wore on, Brad found his frustration with their lack of results rising. He thought about the sheriff saying that escaping Aaron could be a motive for Shelly to run away. He didn't want to believe she could leave without telling anyone, but he'd seen Monica do exactly that.

"This is pointless," Aaron muttered from his position about twenty feet away from Brad. "I should be at work right now."

Brad set his jaw and stormed toward Aaron. "Seriously? Your girlfriend is missing, and you're thinking about work?"

"Chill, Cummings," Aaron said. "This is a job for professionals. We're never going to find her this way."

"I don't see you having any better ideas, Reynolds," Brad shot back. "Your next good idea will be your first. I don't know why Shelly was with you in the first place."

Aaron smirked. "There it is. The truth comes out. All this animosity toward me is because you're jealous that she chose me over you."

"You know that's not true," Brad said. "Our relationship is different."

"That's what the loser always says."

Brad propelled forward in a blur of movement. Aaron blocked his first blow, but Brad followed with a knee to the kidneys that doubled Aaron over. Brad landed a right hook to Aaron's head and moved in for the takedown. He tossed Aaron onto his back and straddled him. Pinning Aaron's arms with his knees, he dealt blow after blow.

"Knock it off," Eddie yelled from behind him. Brad continued to pummel Aaron, thoughts of Shelly and Monica fueling his rage.

A pair of hands gripped him under his arms and threw him aside. Brad lunged forward, but Eddie met him head on. "Stop it," he said. He was out of shape, but he had raw strength that took Brad by surprise. Brad backed away.

"Get me your first aid kit," Eddie said. Brad rummaged in his backpack and threw a nylon bag toward Eddie. Eddie removed some gauze and handed it to Aaron, who stood in Eddie's shadow.

"Get yourself cleaned up," Eddie said. He looked from one man to the other. "I don't care what kind of bad blood there is between you, that kind of thing never happens again. There's something more important at stake here than your feelings about each other. Get it together."

It took Aaron several minutes to wipe the blood from his face. Eddie helped him put a butterfly bandage on a cut above his eye and gave him gauze to stuff inside his nose until the bleeding stopped.

Angel appeared at the edge of the trees, eyes wide and mouth drawn into a tight frown. "Hey, guys," she said. "I'm going to head back to the cars."

Brad checked his watch and noticed his bruised and bloody knuckles. "We might as well head back, too," he said. "We can regroup and come up with a plan for the afternoon."

They arrived at the vehicles a half hour ahead of the other group. Aaron trudged to Shelly's car and popped the hatchback. He opened a styrofoam cooler and removed a sandwich. At least he'd come prepared, Brad thought.

Graham and the other volunteers arrived, and he reported that they had found exactly what Brad's group had: nothing. Aaron came out of the car to join them.

"Whoa!" Graham exclaimed. "What happened here?"

"Just a little misunderstanding," Eddie said. While Brad appreciated Eddie covering for him, he knew Graham would get the full story from Angel on the ride back.

The group sat on and in cars to eat lunch. Aaron returned to Shelly's car. He turned it on to run the air conditioner and listen to music. Brad looked toward the mountains. Clouds had gathered and pushed their way toward the searchers. The air felt cooler.

By the time they finished eating, the steady breeze had turn into gusts, and the clouds grew ominous. Graham talked about abandoning the afternoon's search and making posters instead.

"It's a better use of our time to hang posters in every gas station and shop within fifteen miles of here than to keep poking around in the woods," he said.

"I'd rather keep looking," Brad said. "We know she came through this area. If there's any chance she's nearby, we have to keep the search up."

Before Graham could answer, a bolt of lightning slashed through the darkening sky, followed a second later by a crash of thunder. The sky opened, and rain poured down in torrents. By the time the searchers had taken shelter inside the vehicles, small hailstones clanged off the cars' roofs and windshields.

"Wonder how long this will keep up?" Eddie asked. The rain thickened, erasing all visibility and making driving impossible. Lightning flashed again; ear-splitting thunder followed, shaking the windows on the truck.

"That one was close," Brad said.

They sat in silence for a half hour as rain pummeled the truck. As it let up, Brad got out. The temperature had dropped a good twenty degrees since lunch. He looked around at the leaves that had fallen, matted to the road by rain. He closed his eyes and tipped his head back, letting it bang against his truck. He repeated the motion several times. Whatever evidence of Shelly's movement he hoped to find would be washed away.

Eddie joined him outside. He held his arms away from him, palms up, and caught water droplets as they sprinkled down. Graham came to meet them. Aaron exited Shelly's car, the engine still running, but he didn't come any closer.

"We're headed back," Graham said. "There's not much sense in keeping up the search, especially if there's another volley of rain coming." He motioned toward the mountains, still covered in dark clouds.

"Any chance of getting some help tomorrow?" Brad asked.

Graham shrugged one shoulder. "I don't think so. The crowd's already dwindled, and like I told you yesterday, I have to get back to work."

Brad shook his hand and thanked him for his help. He crossed his arms and watched Graham drive away, taking the remainder of the search party with them. As their taillights disappeared, Brad dropped his arms, turned to Eddie, and said, "Now what?"

"I suggest we talk to the sheriff again," Eddie said. "See if he's feeling any different about Shelly's disappearance now that it's been forty-eight hours and no one has heard from her. Then, we can get some dinner and talk about how much value there is in continuing to look. You're welcome to come with us." He nodded toward Aaron.

"Okay," Aaron said, his voice small and his eyes filled with anger.

As Brad drove back to town, Eddie kept his thumbs busy on his phone. "What's going on?" Brad asked. He rarely saw Eddie that engrossed in technology.

"Just checking in with the office."

"I suppose you need to get back to work, too."

"I told you; we're in this together. All the way to the end."

Sheriff Yellington was gone when they arrived at the police station. Deputy Cooper ushered the three men into his office. "No news on your friend?"

"Nothing," Brad said. "We've been searching all day, and we don't have anything beyond what we found yesterday."

"No one's heard from her?" Cooper asked. "Friends? Family?"

"No," Aaron said. "I checked with her mom earlier, and there's been no word from her."

"She hasn't posted anything on social media, either," Brad said.

Cooper nodded. "Just so you know, the sheriff is interested in this case. He sent the duct tape to the lab for processing, along with the race bib. I don't expect to get anything off the bib, but you never know. We might get lucky."

"Does this mean the sheriff now considers this a missing person case?" Eddie asked, leaning forward.

Cooper stroked his chin and looked up at the ceiling. "I don't think I'd use those words. I'd say the sheriff is putting resources on trying to find her."

"What does that mean?" Aaron asked.

"It means we'll see what the lab turns up. If you give us her photo, we'll circulate it to the other counties and put out a bulletin. We'll question people who might have information to help find her, though at this point, I'm not sure who that would be."

He stood and walked toward the door. Eddie and Aaron followed him. Brad stayed in his chair for another minute before walking out.

"Better than nothing," Eddie said in the parking lot. "Not much better, but at least the lab is looking at stuff. I think we should head back to the lodge and decide on next steps. You coming, Aaron?"

Aaron took a deep breath and blew it out slowly. He ran his hands through his hair. "No," he said. "I'm going back to the hotel. Let me know what you decide."

As Brad drove back to the fishing resort, his anger toward Aaron returned. He really didn't seem that eager to find Shelly. Brad gripped the wheel tighter. If Aaron had hurt her, he better hope there were a lot more people around than just Eddie to stop Brad.

"Ease up," Eddie said. "What'd the wheel do to you?"

Brad looked at his hands, white-knuckled and shaking. He counted to ten and tried to push the tension out of his body. He let up on his grip, but the anger remained. He turned into the resort and pointed the truck toward Eddie's cabin.

"Let's go to the lodge instead," Eddie said. "See if the cook left any snacks lying around."

Brad resisted an eye roll but did what Eddie said. He followed Eddie into the communal dining room. A man and a woman sat at the far end of the table. Brad had to do a double take to be sure he was seeing things correctly.

"What are you guys doing here?" Brad asked.

"We heard you needed some help," Vince Marcotte said as he rose and greeted Brad with a hug.

"We're even waiving our fee this time," Hadley Collins said, a step behind Vince. "Call it the friends, family, and associates discount."

CHAPTER 13

"Eddie called last night and told me what was going on," Vince said. "We closed the agency and left early this morning to get here. From the texts Eddie sent a little while ago, it sounds like there have been no new developments."

"Just that we no longer have a search party," Brad said. "And the police are interested, whatever that means. They're not lending much official support. I can't tell you how glad I am to see you."

Brad looked at the two active partners in the Fleck, Collins, and Marcotte detective agency with a newfound respect. While he knew they'd help if he asked them to, he didn't expect them to close the agency and drive to Montana.

The lodge didn't have a whiteboard, so Eddie procured a roll of butcher paper and a marker from the kitchen, along with a platter of nachos. Hadley spread the paper out on one end of the table and had Brad walk them through the case.

"We have two possibilities," Hadley said, marking up the butcher paper. "One, Shelly left willingly. Motive was to escape an abusive boyfriend. She waited until she saw an opportunity when she was alone, and she bolted."

"I don't like it," Vince said. "You're describing a spur-of-the-moment thing, and this was pre-planned. A boat and an ATV were staged ahead of time."

"There's a dead body near the site of her escape," Eddie said. "Don't overlook that."

"Someone else killed the volunteer," Hadley offered. "Let's stipulate that as fact; Shelly didn't have time to drag someone to the woods, kill him, and then take off before Brad reached the top of the rock. The killer staged the boat and the ATV. Shelly took off on foot, maybe in a totally different direction."

"That's not like Shelly," Brad said, feeling like a broken record.

"Too big of a coincidence," Eddie mused. "I don't like it."

"Scenario two," Hadley said, scrawling the number on the paper. "Someone killed the volunteer—we have to get a name for that guy, by the way—and waited for Shelly. She came down the rock, and the perpetrator grabbed her and ran off to the boat and then the ATV."

"I don't like it," Vince said again. "How did the perp know Shelly would be the first over the rock? Why wasn't there a sign of a struggle?"

"Can't answer the first one," Hadley said. "Maybe she thought the person was a volunteer, and they incapacitated her before she could fight."

Brad looked around the table; the three detectives wore looks of varying degrees of skepticism. "Shelly's been missing for more than forty-eight hours now, and all we have are two bad theories."

Eddie crunched on a chip and stared at the paper. "Let's divide scenario two into two subsets." He crunched again. "One, the perp had a connection to Shelly and specifically targeted her." He raised a hand to cut off the objections. "I know, there's a lot of luck involved. Maybe he was stalking her throughout the race. Yes, I'm assuming that we're dealing with a he. Anyway, he knew that the rock climb created a bottleneck and at some point, Shelly would be there alone, so he set up there."

"I could've come down the rock first," Brad said.

"Maybe he planned to kill you just like he did the volunteer."

For the thousandth time, Brad wished he had gone first. He couldn't see any scenario, short of someone shooting him while he rappelled, where he wouldn't get the upper hand on the perpetrator.

"Subset two is that the perp doesn't have a connection to Shelly, then?" Vince asked.

"Right," Eddie said. "I like that one a little more because it doesn't rely on as much chance."

"What do you mean?" Brad asked.

"Our perp may have decided to abduct someone on the racecourse. Didn't care who. The timing was more important than the victim."

"In which case..." Vince said, letting his voice trail off.

Eddie finished the thought for him. "In which case, we're dealing with a total nut job."

"Let's pursue both subsets," Hadley said. "We'll assume, for now, that she didn't run off on her own. We need to cross check the list of racers and volunteers for any connection to Shelly and see if we can reinterview them in case anyone saw or heard anything that will help."

"I'll contact Graham to get the names," Eddie said.

Brad looked from Hadley to Vince. They both looked deep in thought and determined. He'd seen those expressions many times before. For the first time since Shelly disappeared, he felt a measure of hope.

•　　•　　•

The highest point on the main road provided a vantage point beyond the trees. Parking the car, he peered through the window at the main house on the property, but a hill and the foliage hid the outbuildings from view. He looked through his binoculars.

The house stood as still and abandoned as ever, and the optics did nothing to make the bachelor's shack visible.

Satisfied, he started toward the property. It was a good find, better than the other locations he'd used, but he was getting tired of sleeping on the lumpy mattress. Driving in and out of town every day was getting old, too. He needed to move on from this woman soon. The thought of the kill brought a tingle to his fingers but not strong enough. He couldn't make his move yet; he'd feel it when the time came.

He paused at the house and conducted his ritual walk around. Nothing appeared out of place, and there were no new tire tracks or any other signs of an inhabitant. He continued over the hill and around the bend until he saw the guest house, just visible in the gathering twilight.

He parked the car and waited. Crickets chirped in the distance. It was torture spending time with the woman, knowing he couldn't do anything yet. He had gotten too aggressive the day before, and he needed to control himself better.

A pizza box in the passenger seat had cooled off during the drive, but cold pizza suited him just fine. The woman—well, she'd eat anything he gave her at this point.

He pulled on his ski mask and entered the shack, slamming the door before turning on the light. He locked the deadbolt he'd installed and pocketed the key. The woman cowered in her handcuffs and chain. She looked to have had a rough day; the skin on her wrists rubbed raw from her escape attempts. Her eyes had sunk back into her head, and she looked like a shell of the person he had grabbed.

He unfolded the metal chair and plopped down at the table. He opened the pizza box and held eye contact with the woman for a long moment before scarfing down the first piece. She trembled, as if in fear that he wouldn't feed her this time. He opened a water bottle and took a long draw, maintaining eye contact with her. Then, he ate another piece of pizza.

Finally, he tossed a slice at her. It landed on the ground in front of her, and she scrabbled like a rat on the concrete to get to it. When she finished, he tossed her one more. While she ate, he looked around the guest house. He supposed at one time it had been a cozy spot for visitors, but all the furnishings had been taken out, right down to the concrete floor, which served his purposes perfectly. He'd added the mattress and the table and chair. And, the restraints, of course.

She finished her pizza, and he tossed her a water bottle. She drank it all before putting the cap back on it and tossing it toward the door. She was learning the rules; maybe it wouldn't take much longer after all.

He ate a third slice of pizza while she sat against the wall, her arms hugged around her knees the best the chain would allow. He closed the pizza box. There was more he could feed her, and she looked like she could use it, but keeping her hungry was part of his tactic.

"What do you want?" she asked. The man didn't answer. He narrowed his eyes into slits and stared at her until she turned away. "I can give you my parents' number if you want to make a ransom demand," she offered. Her voice came out raw and raspy. "Or my boyfriend's. I'll do anything. Just let me go."

The tingle crawled across his skin, stronger than before. The stages of victimhood were not unlike the stages of grief, and she had entered bargaining. Depression wouldn't be far behind.

"What do you want?" she asked again, her voice raised and quaking with fear. He stared at her and laughed silently, making sure she saw his shoulders shaking. "I need to use the bathroom." She sounded disgusted with herself.

He moved in to create slack in the chain. She lunged at him, but he easily sidestepped her. He kicked her in the hip, and she yelped. Tears streamed down her face as she limped to the bathroom.

He stood in the doorway to watch her. He didn't find the activity arousing, or even pleasant, but it added to her humiliation and made her understand just how powerless she was.

With her safely locked up again, he went to the bedroom and settled in for the night. He read his novel and listened to her sobs dwindle into whimpers and then into silence. He closed the book, flipped off the overhead light, and closed his eyes when the voice whispered to him.

His skin tingled until he felt like he was on fire. The voice had given him two simple words, words he'd longed to hear since he'd taken her: tomorrow night.

CHAPTER 14

July 22, 2025. Burgess County, Montana.
Brad awoke early, disoriented by his new surroundings. The sound of Vince snoring in the bunk below reminded him that Eddie had commandeered two rooms in the lodge for the detectives' use. Hadley had the room across the hall.

He lowered himself to the ground and crept out of the room, trying not to wake Vince. The smell of coffee and eggs greeted him, and he followed his nose down the stairs. Eddie sat at the bar in the kitchen, working his way through an omelet.

"Hey," he said through his full mouth. "I didn't know when you all would be up, so I ordered breakfast burritos for you. Where are the other two?"

"Still sleeping off a long day on the road, I guess," Brad said. He pulled up a stool next to Eddie and accepted a coffee from the cook.

"What's on the agenda for today?" Eddie asked.

"Hadley wants to go on scene, so she and I are going back to the racecourse. We'll look at the rappelling station, see where the volunteer was murdered, and trace the path from the rock to the road."

"Jerry Smithson," Eddie said.

"What?"

"That's the dead volunteer. I asked Graham last night when I coaxed the volunteer list from him. We can call him Jerry now. Better than Dead Guy, I guess."

Brad cracked a half smile. "What's Graham do around here? He seems to be plugged into everything."

"He's a lawyer. Does a lot of work with ranchers in the area on right of way issues. Kind of looked at as the unofficial mayor. The elected guy is just a figurehead. You want to get things done, you go to Graham. Good morning, sleepyheads."

Brad turned to see Vince and Hadley in the doorway. They settled in with their coffee and burritos, and Brad gave them the plan for the day.

"While they're out in the wilderness, you and I have a bunch of phone calls to make, Vince," Eddie said. He tapped a folder against the counter.

With breakfast finished, Brad and Hadley took his truck to the racecourse. He drove past the parking area and pulled off the road a few minutes later at the spot that would get them closest to where Shelly disappeared.

"What's Shelly's boyfriend's name again?" Hadley asked. "He didn't want to come today?"

"Aaron Reynolds," Brad said. "I didn't invite him." Hadley raised an eyebrow at him, and he said, "I haven't ruled him out as a suspect."

"Eddie explained that Aaron didn't have much of an opportunity, right?" Hadley asked.

"He had as much opportunity as anyone," Brad said. "And a better motive. He actually knows Shelly, unlike anyone else here. He could have gotten the race information from someone ahead of time and used it to plan this whole thing."

Hadley looked unconvinced but said, "Well, if there's a connection between him and someone here, Vince and Eddie will find it."

Brad led them to a trail that skirted the base of the rock he and Shelly had climbed during the race. He explained how they had just pulled into the lead, ahead of G&G, and wanted to put as much distance between them as possible.

"If we had climbing gear, I'd take you up the rock, so you could see," Brad said. "It's not much of a view because of the trees on one side and the rocks on the other, but I had a perfect view of the whole clearing, all the way to the river until it bends around the rocks and disappears. There was no sign of Shelly at all."

"Which means she had to be past the bend in the river by the time you got to the top," Hadley said.

"Exactly," Brad said. "Five minutes, tops. It's not a huge rock, I'd just had an energy bar, and the adrenaline was flowing pretty good."

"Can we assume whoever took Shelly killed the volunteer?" Hadley asked.

"Jerry," Brad corrected her. "And, yes."

"That person had to be staged here in advance," Hadley said. "They wouldn't have known when someone would come over the rock."

"Right," Brad said. "It couldn't have been any of the racers. They wouldn't have known the course, for one thing, unless they had an accomplice. Even so, all the racers were accounted for when they gathered everyone. No one would have had time to take a shortcut back here, kill Jerry, stash Shelly somewhere, and then get back on the course in time to be rounded up."

They turned a corner, and the path led from the trees where Brad found Jerry to the back side of the rock. Brad showed Hadley where they rappelled. They both stared at the rock before turning to get a ground-level perspective on the site.

"This is where I found the body," Brad said, motioning Hadley to follow him. They moved through the trees. The police presence from the previous days had left the ground trampled. The dirt remained spongy from the thunderstorm.

"Not a very good scene for forensics," Hadley said. "Did you notice any signs of a body being dragged through here?"

Brad shook his head. "There was no blood in the clearing, either. I would have noticed if there had been; I was on high alert to find Shelly."

"So, the killer somehow lures Jerry into the woods and dispatches him there," Hadley said. She shuddered at the thought of it. She looked up into the trees, examining trunks and branches as they made their way back to the rock.

"What are you looking for?" Brad asked.

"A trail camera," Hadley said. "Too much to hope for, I guess."

Brad led her to the river. "We have to cross over," he said. "Hope your shoes are waterproof." Hadley shrugged, and the two splashed into the shallowest part of the water, working their way to the opposite bank.

Brad led her to the bend in the river where the canoe had been. "Police must have impounded it," he said.

"How long would it take a boat to get from the rock to here?" Hadley asked.

"Not long. Two minutes."

"You didn't hear it while you were climbing?"

"No, but canoes were designed to cut through the water without making noise. Plus, the rock blocks a lot of sound. The wind was blowing, the volunteers were talking to Gus and Glen below me, and I was focused on climbing. I would have to have supersonic hearing to have picked up the oars in the water."

"And you started up the rock as soon as Shelly was down?"

"Yeah," Brad said. "We gave her a minute or so to start down the rock, and then I began my climb. Whoever took her had to have been ready. As soon as she landed, they grabbed her, dragged her to the boat, and took off."

Hadley stared past him, lost in thought. She shook her head and motioned to start walking again. Brad pointed her a few yards away to where the ATV tracks started.

"What are you thinking?" he asked.

"Just that we're dealing with someone experienced," Hadley said. "None of this seems like the work of a novice. I'll do some research later, see if there are any other unsolved kidnappings that might fit this M.O."

•   •   •

Vince scratched another name off his list. He and Eddie prioritized contacting the race volunteers. There were forty names in all, so they each took half. Midway through his list, all he'd found was that no one was eager to talk about what had happened to Jerry Smithson or might have happened to Shelly. Everyone reported being at their station with no clue anything unusual had occurred until Graham directed them to report back to the check-in station. They had all been with other volunteers who could vouch for their presence far away from the crime scene. No one knew Shelly, Brad, or Aaron, either.

He looked at the next name on his list. Angel Thompson. She was the one who had been sent back to the scene by the father and son team and had called for help.

Vince dialed her number and explained who he was and that he'd just need a few minutes of her time.

"Did your friend ever find his partner?" Angel asked.

"Not yet," Vince said. "That's why I'm calling you. If there's anything you can remember from the race that might help us, I'd appreciate you sharing it."

They walked through the basics of the day: when she arrived, the station she worked, and how she found out about the trouble on the course. Her voice grew quieter when she talked about

Brad telling her someone had died, and Vince wished Hadley had been there. She was always better at keeping people talking.

"The volunteer who was killed was named Jerry Smithson," Vince said. "Did you know him?"

"No," Angel said. "Not all the volunteers were from here, though. People came from the surrounding towns."

"What about Brad Cummings?" Vince asked.

"He's the guy who found the body?"

"Yeah. Had you met him before?"

"No."

Angel didn't know Shelly or Aaron, either. No one had approached her for information about the race.

"I didn't even know what the course looked like or where I'd be stationed until race day," Angel said. "Graham likes to keep things quiet, make sure none of the racers get an advantage on the navigation."

"Last question," Vince said. "This one is subjective. Anything stand out to you as weird on race day? Any volunteers or racers seem out of place? Anyone hanging out at a station they weren't assigned to? Anything you can remember might help."

"I wish I could help," Angel said, "but the day was typical. This is my third year at the race, and it went just like the other two, until the woman was missing."

"Do a lot of volunteers come back from year to year?"

"Yeah," Angel said. "There's a core group you can count on. Maybe half. Then, there are new people who come in each year."

Vince thanked her, ended the call, and crossed her off the list. He stood from his makeshift workstation on the bottom bunk and stretched. His stomach told him it was lunch time, so he headed toward the kitchen to make a sandwich and ran into Eddie on the way.

"Any luck?" Eddie asked, as they settled in at the bar once again.

"Nothing," Vince said. "You?"

Eddie shook his head. "I should be able to finish up calls this afternoon. We can see what Brad and Hadley found this evening and decide if it's worth talking to all the racers or not."

•   •   •

Brad and Hadley hiked the trail the ATV had taken. The sheriff had already impounded the vehicle, so he showed her where it had been abandoned. Brad pointed them through the trees and out to County Road 15.

"We've searched up and down this road. Eddie and I drove the highway, too, but we didn't find anyone nearby with a working camera."

Hadley wandered along the shoulder, staring into the trees and out at the pavement. Brad shoved his hands in his pockets and looked at the ground. He wondered where Shelly was and how she was doing. He prayed she was still alive.

"This case sucks," Hadley declared walking back toward him. "I hope the DNA testing yields something and that Vince and Eddie are having better luck than we are."

A rustling in the trees caught their attention. Brad instinctively stepped in front of Hadley and moved closer to the noise. He scowled as Aaron Reynolds emerged from the woods.

"I thought you were going to let me know the plan for today, Cummings," he said. "You've been ignoring my texts."

Brad shrugged. "I don't have time to babysit you, Reynolds. There are professionals on the case, and your assistance is no longer needed."

Aaron stood stock still, arms over his chest, a glare in his eyes. He did not look like a man who would take no for an answer.

CHAPTER 15

Ten Years Earlier.
September 16, 2015. Chicago, Illinois.
Brad had to hand it to Joe Olivero; the man moved faster than anyone Brad ever fought before. Each time Joe made a mistake and Brad moved in for the kill, Joe used his speed to escape.

Brad landed a few solid punches and kicks in the first two rounds. The bell rang to start round three, and he circled, hands raised in a fighter's stance. As they roved around the ring, movement in his peripheral vision caught Brad's attention.

Joe lunged in with an attack, but Brad knocked him away. With Joe off balance, Brad moved in for a takedown. Just behind Joe, Aaron Reynolds rushed to the ring and slapped the mat. Brad froze in the middle of his move. He looked for the referee to see if he saw it, too.

Pain exploded across Brad's abdomen as Joe rocked him with a powerful kick to the ribs. Brad dropped to one knee. Before he could get his hands up, Joe connected a roundhouse kick to the back of his head. Shocks jolted through his body.

Joe punched his jaw with a left hook, followed by a right cross. A kick to the side of the head sent Brad careening to the ground. The world around him went dark. He felt Joe's body on top of him. The bitter tang of blood filled his mouth.

Something pounded the mat next to him, and Brad tried to turn his head in that direction, certain he'd see Reynolds in the ring, having inexplicably joined the match. A bell rang and the pressure on his shoulders released as Joe got up.

Muffled voices spoke above him. He opened his eyes to a blurry world. He sat up, and someone helped him stumble out of the ring and back to the locker room. Brad dropped into a chair and closed his eyes.

He didn't know how long he slept. When he opened his eyes, the locker room buzzed with activity. Fighters showered and changed. Ring attendants drug equipment in.

Doyle stood in front of Brad. Concern showed on the big man's face. "You okay, Cummings?"

"I don't know," Brad said. "I think so. What happened?"

"Olivero wiped the mat with you." Doyle shook his head.

"Reynolds was ring side," Brad said. His tongue felt thick in his mouth. "He distracted me."

Disgust crossed Doyle's face. "I'll look into that, but that's no excuse. You want to fight in the big times, you have to stay focused."

"It was interference."

"The ref didn't call it. We live by the ref's calls. You know that." Doyle kept a hard stare on him before softening. "You need a doctor. You're in bad shape. Can I give you a ride?"

Two hours and an urgent care bill later, Brad was diagnosed with a cracked rib and a concussion. The doctor ordered him to stay out of the ring for a while and to get clearance from his primary care before fighting again.

The next day, Brad arrived at the gym to retrieve his things. He filled a duffle bag with his gym clothes and towels and handed his locker key to Doyle. As he left the gym, Aaron Reynolds approached.

"Not so good in a fair fight, are you Cummings?"

"That wasn't a fair fight, and you know it."

Aaron sneered at him and lifted his hands. "I don't know what you're talking about."

Brad dropped his bag and took a step toward Aaron. Aaron stuck out his jaw, defiant.

"Forget it," Brad said. "It's not worth it."

"That's what I thought," Aaron said, bumping into him as he passed. Brad winced as Aaron's elbow caught his rib.

"I won't forget this," Brad said. He turned to watch Aaron's retreating figure. Aaron paused at the gym door and faced him.

"I'm petrified, Cummings."

The two men stared at each other, the tension stretching out between them. Brad could think of a hundred ways to inflict pain on Aaron, if his head and side weren't screaming at him.

Finally, Aaron turned and entered the gym. Brad shouldered his bag and started toward his car, hoping he'd never see Aaron Reynolds again.

CHAPTER 16

July 22, 2025. Burgess County, Montana.
Aaron stayed in place, staring at Brad and Hadley. Brad looked back at Aaron's bruised and swollen face. He brushed past Aaron and started into the trees.

"If you insist on coming with us, let's go," Brad said. Hadley scrambled to catch up with him. Aaron's heavy steps cracked branches.

"How good of a look did you get at the ATV?" Hadley asked, stopping where it had been hidden.

"Decent," Brad said. "We weren't allowed to touch anything."

"There's no police tape," Hadley said. "The cops probably searched all they want to. Let's spend some time looking at this area."

She circled the area, hands on hips, staring at the leaves and branches on the ground as if they might spring to life and tell them what happened.

"What are we looking for?" Aaron asked.

"Anything that might help us find Shelly," Hadley said.

"Great," Aaron said. "That narrows things down."

"If you don't want to help, just get out of here," Brad growled.

Hadley put a hand on his arm. "The thing with detective work, Aaron, is that we don't always know what we're looking for until we find it. If you see something that's out of place, let us know, and we'll figure out what it means."

They searched among the trees and branches. Hadley shined a small flashlight into crevices. Brad moved back to where the ATV had been found. The ground was clear, though the branches that had camouflaged it lay strewn about. He tried to put himself in the kidnapper's shoes. Those branches had to come from somewhere before they were on the ATV.

He turned and saw a perfect spot between the trees to stage the branches. He crawled on his hands and knees, moving leaves until he saw the bare ground.

His hand hit something. He grabbed for it among the twigs, leaves, and pine needles and held up a syringe with a hypodermic needle attached.

"Got something," he called, jumping up. He waited for Hadley to get to him, Aaron at her heels. He pointed out where he found it. "This could be huge," he said.

"It could be a druggie getting his fix in the woods," Hadley said.

"You're a real downer," Aaron said. Brad considered taking another swing at him.

"I'm a realist," Hadley said. "I investigate every lead thoroughly, but it doesn't hurt to manage expectations."

Brad held the syringe up, looking at it from multiple angles. He couldn't see any blood on it, but there was a bit of liquid inside. They would need the police to send it to a lab.

Hadley produced a plastic evidence bag to store it in. Brad felt lighter than he had since Shelly had disappeared. He tucked the bag into his backpack and hoped it would bring them closer to finding his friend.

•   •   •

Vince marked the last name off his list. The day had yielded nothing helpful. Every volunteer had the same, useless information. He checked his phone for any updates from Hadley and saw a text: "Back soon. Might have something."

A knock sounded on his door, which burst open a half second later. Eddie filled the frame, waving his list at Vince.

"You find something?" Vince asked.

"No," Eddie said. "That's the problem."

He explained that he had contacted every volunteer on the list except one. Lawrence Lewis's phone was out of service.

"Maybe they wrote the number down wrong," Vince said. He took the paper from Eddie and cracked open his laptop. A search for Lawrence Lewis led to thousands of results, the first page entirely dedicated to George Washington's nephew who bore that name. Adding Montana to the search narrowed it, but there were still a lot of hits.

"We don't know where he's from," Eddie mused. "Could be local here in Broadwood but could be Bozeman or Missoula or somewhere else."

Vince scrolled through the results. He could switch to the agency's background check site, but he needed to narrow it down—without a location, an age, or occupation, the software had no way of identifying the right guy.

"Search for the phone number," Eddie suggested.

Vince opened a new window and logged into a reverse phone lookup the agency subscribed to. He typed in the number, and they waited as the report loaded. "Interesting," Vince said.

Eddie crowded in and plopped onto the bed next to Vince, so they could both see the screen. The phone was registered as prepaid wireless, purchased a week before the race at a convenience store in Billings. They had contact information for the store, but no information on the purchaser.

"I don't like it," Eddie said.

"Lots of people use prepaid phones," Vince countered.

"They just happened to write down the wrong number, which just happens to no longer be in service, and it just happens to be a burner."

"You're getting ahead of yourself," Vince said. "It's probably nothing. First thing is to see if we can find out if Graham has a different number for Mr. Lewis, and we'll go from there. This phone number might not be connected to the case at all."

Eddie did not look convinced. Vince showed him the text from Hadley. "The others will be back soon, and we can compare notes and see what they've got. Then we can go see Graham."

"I hope they have something good," Eddie said. "Because a questionable phone number isn't a lot to show for four people spending a full day searching."

Voices downstairs announced their partners' arrival. Brad introduced Vince to Shelly's boyfriend, Aaron. Vince noticed neither seemed happy to be in the other's presence. They swapped updates on how they'd spent their days. Vince's eyes widened when Brad produced the syringe, and Brad and Hadley were both intrigued by the wrong phone number.

"What'd you say the guy's name was?" Brad asked.

Eddie consulted his list of names. "Lawrence Lewis."

Brad slapped his hands together. "Lawrence. Remember, Eddie?"

Eddie pursed his lips and shook his head. "You're gonna have to enlighten me, bud."

"He was the volunteer they questioned at the police station because he had left the racecourse."

"Seriously?" Vince asked. His heart sped up. "He couldn't account for where he was?"

"According to Graham, it's not uncommon for volunteers to come and go if they're not needed," Brad said. "He worked the check-in desk, so he finished by the time we reached the rock. But there's more. He acted weird when we checked in."

"Weird how?" Hadley asked.

"He had an unusual interest in Shelly. Completely blew me off and couldn't take his eyes off her." Aaron snorted, and anger flashed across Brad's face. "Trust me. It was weird. This has to mean something."

"Could be a different Lawrence," Hadley said.

"Only one on the list," Eddie said, looking through the papers. "I think we need to find out how Graham vets his volunteers and then go to the police with our finds."

"I need to head back to the hotel," Aaron said. "I'm technically on a leave of absence, but I'm still trying to stay caught up when I can."

The group watched him climb into Shelly's car and drive away. Vince thought he heard Brad mutter, "Good riddance." Then, Brad said, "He always disappears right when we're getting somewhere. I'm looking for Shelly a lot harder than he is, and they're supposed to be in love or something."

"Everybody reacts to things differently," Vince said. "Give him the benefit of the doubt."

"I can't shake the feeling that he has something to do with Shelly disappearing," Brad said.

"I keep telling you he didn't have the opportunity," Eddie said. "There's no way he could have pulled that off without someone from the race seeing him lurking around the course or giving him inside information. Let's take our leads and follow up on them. I don't think I should be the one to see the sheriff; he seems threatened by the big city cop."

They decided to send Brad and Hadley, since they could speak directly to finding the syringe. Vince wished them good luck.

"Think there's anything to what he's saying about Aaron?" Vince asked.

"No," Eddie said. "Two things I've learned in this business. One is that when you have a personal history with a case, it clouds everything. I think we both know about that."

"What's the second thing?"

"To never completely rule out a lead, no matter how far-fetched it appears."

•   •   •

Shelly had no idea what time it was or when the guy would return. She feared it was late in the day, and he'd be back any time. He acted odd that morning—not that any of his behavior had ever been normal—but he had seemed jumpy and nervous. She worried a change was coming to their living arrangement.

Hunger fogged her brain. Her wrists ached from the strain she'd put on them trying to break the handcuff chain, and her back and legs hurt from being in the same position for so long. The smell of her body made her sick.

She leaned back against the wall and waited for the tears to come, but none did, either because she was too emotionally exhausted to cry or just dehydrated. She was out of ideas, but something in the back of her head told her that if the man came back, she'd be dead. Or wish she were.

She stared at the handcuffs, wishing she had some trick to get out of them. An attempt at picking the lock with the tip of her shoelace only succeeded in mangling the lace. She wished she had a bobby pin or paperclip.

An idea crossed her mind. She dismissed it as unworkable, but she wasn't in a position to reject ideas. It would be difficult with her hands cuffed, but, fortunately, he had left them in front of her.

She reached inside her shirt and grasped the front of her sports bra with both hands. She pulled with all her might, feeling the fabric stretch against her back. She worried she wouldn't be able to do it in her weakened state, but she kept pulling until she felt a small rip.

Encouraged, she pulled harder. The fabric did not give any further. She yanked, and the bra slipped out of her hands, snapping back against her chest like a rubber band. There was a second approach. She didn't like it because of how vulnerable it would make her if he came in, but she needed a hail mary and had to take the chance.

She worked her shirt over her head and pulled it off until it rested just above her wrists. She grabbed the bra again and repeated the maneuver, her back crying out in protest from moving in ways it hadn't the past few days.

When she had the bra off and at her wrists, she lifted it to her mouth. She found the bottom of the cups, where the wire support was. She bit into the fabric, swallowing back nausea at the acrid, sweaty taste. She bit until she made a hole in the fabric. Using her teeth, she gripped the wire and maneuvered it until an end poked through the hole. She adjusted her grip and extracted about three inches of wire.

The bulk of her shirt and bra on her wrists made the task more difficult, but she bent the wire at a ninety-degree angle. She bent the tip another ninety degrees, so she had a rudimentary Z shape.

She pushed the wire into the hole of the left handcuff. She had no idea what to feel for; she'd seen locks picked on television but had never attempted it in real life.

Something inside the hole gave before pushing the wire back. She pushed harder and felt the give again. She twisted the wire one way, then the other. On her second trip in the original direction, she felt a click and the lock unclasped.

Relief flooded her and the tears finally came. She shook her hand free from the cuff and slid the handcuffs out from under the chain that bound her to the floor. She stood on creaky legs and stumbled toward the wall with the door. She felt along the wall until she found the doorknob. She tried it, but the lock was engaged. She knew it had a keyed deadbolt. She continued groping the wall until she flipped the light switch.

She blinked away the sudden brightness and found the metal table. She braced her arms on it and used her free hand to pick the lock on the right handcuff. It took several minutes, and she had to restart a few times, but she focused on her breathing, pushed aside thoughts of the guy coming back, and worked the wire until the lock sprang free.

She dressed herself again and closed both handcuffs to their tightest positions. She held them in her fist, like a pair of brass knuckles, and took a practice swing. If it came to a fight, they might make up for her disadvantage in size and strength.

She took her first look around the small building. The room where she'd been chained looked like it had been a living room at one time. Directly across from her spot was the table and folding chair the guy used. On the other side of the table, she found the kitchen. It had a sink, a refrigerator, and a couple of cabinets with a small counter. The only windows in this part of the building were by the door and in the living area. Both were covered in black plastic.

Shelly peeked behind the sheeting next to the door and saw the faint light of dusk. She found the latch and unlocked the window. It stuck. She didn't want to disturb the plastic too much because she didn't want to tip the guy off that she'd gotten free, particularly if he came back before she was gone.

She walked past the bathroom with its sink, toilet, and yellowed bathtub. She found the guy's room. Just a mattress and a cardboard box serving as a nightstand. He didn't keep any clothes in the closet. She noticed he'd worn the same clothes every day; she assumed he changed in the morning after he left and again in the afternoon before he came back in.

She looked around the room again. No sign of her backpack anywhere. There was a window on one wall; it, too, was covered in plastic sheeting. She tore a corner away from the wall and looked out. This window faced away from the driveway, toward trees. She tore the plastic down. She examined the window and found that it had a crank that allowed it to open outward about six inches, but it would be useless for climbing out.

As much as Shelly needed to hurry, she also needed nourishment. She had no idea how far from a main road he had taken her, and she might have miles to hike to find someone who could help.

Back in the kitchen, she searched the cabinets and found two cans of beans. In one drawer, she discovered a can opener and a spoon, both covered in a layer of dust. The refrigerator held a bottle of soda. She twisted the cap off, breaking the seal, and drank half of it, letting the sugar and caffeine recharge her. Her stomach roiled at the sudden influx of sweetness. She poured the other half down the drain, rinsed the bottle, filled it with sink water, and capped it. She took the case off the pillow in the bedroom and used it to pack her finds.

She peeked out the front window again. Just before she stepped away, letting the plastic fall back into place, she saw something. She opened it again and looked into the distance. A pair of headlights showed against the dusk.

Just like racing, she had to make a quick decision to gain an advantage on her competition. She grabbed the folding chair and rushed into the bedroom. She held the chair over head with both hands and smashed it into the glass. The window cracked, a spider web reaching from corner to corner. She stepped closer, raised the chair once more, and thrust it into the window.

Glass shards exploded in all directions, nicking her hands and face. She used the chair to knock the remaining fragments of glass to the ground below. She stripped the blanket off the bed and threw it across the windowsill.

She heard a noise outside. She froze in place, listening. The familiar engine sound filled the night. The guy was back.

The light was still on. The guy would know something was up as soon as he opened the door.

With her bundle of items in one hand, Shelly climbed across the sill and lowered herself. Her feet hit the ground below as the front door opened. The guy let out a startled curse. His footsteps pounded toward the bedroom.

Calling on her last energy reserves, Shelly ran. The pillowcase thudded against her thigh with every swing of her arm, but she kept her arms and legs pumping full force. She left the clearing that housed the building and crashed through trees.

She had to slow down to navigate the woods. She heard him hit the ground beneath the window. She needed to put more distance between them.

She slowed to a walk, opting for quiet over speed, and took a zigzag path through the trees. She took random turns, no longer sure of where the building was. After a few minutes, she paused and listened. She heard movement, but it didn't seem close. She continued her escape, moving away from where she thought she heard the sound.

Shelly stopped again after a few more minutes. The movement had grown fainter, and she hoped she had thrown him off her trail. The last bit of twilight had faded to black, and the darkness of the night enveloped her. She moved onward, continuing the path she had started.

She wondered how far from the road she had gone. Part of her wanted to wait a while, retrace her steps, and follow the road the guy had come in on until she found someone who could phone for help.

Another part of her, the part that won out, told her to keep wandering. She needed a different road. It was too risky to go back anywhere near where the guy might be.

Dampness covered her cheeks, and she felt her face to find she had started crying. The emotions of fearing for her life, fighting for her freedom, and not knowing what to do next converged and caught up to her. Despite the inner voice telling her to keep moving, Shelly sat against a nearby tree, drew her knees up to her chest, and rocked until the tears stopped.

She listened for movement but heard none. She didn't see any flashlight beams or hear the sputter of the car's engine. Only the blackness of night, the chirping of crickets, and the buzz of cicadas kept her company. The scent of pine filled her nostrils with each huffing breath.

As silently as possible, Shelly opened a can of beans. She ate every bite and washed it down with half of her water supply. She stored everything in the pillowcase and rose.

Her stomach sank. During her cry, she had lost track of where she had come from and what direction she was going. She had no idea if her next step would take her deeper in the woods or back toward the guy. She took the handcuffs from her back pocket and gripped them tightly as she picked a direction and moved forward.

Another thought crossed her mind as she hiked through the night. Wildlife roamed this area. Deer, bobcats, bears, and mountain lions. No matter; she had to keep moving, had to find a way out of the woods and back to freedom. Fear would not help her do that.

As she turned to move between two trees, she saw a flash in the dark. She couldn't tell how far away it was, but she was certain she saw a pair of eyes.

CHAPTER 17

Brad nosed into the open parking space in front of Detweiler Law, next to a Jeep Grand Wagoneer from the early 1980s. Brad bet it belonged to Graham, and it wouldn't surprise him to learn Graham was the original owner.

Graham met them at the door as the late afternoon sun disappeared behind the mountains, casting a dramatic light over the town.

"Welcome to my firm," Graham said, motioning them past an empty reception desk and into an office labeled Graham Detweiler, J.D. Diplomas on his wall showed he had degrees from Montana State, UNLV, and Stanford. A frame on the corner of the desk displayed a photo of Graham with his arm around a woman, with a lanky young man on the other side of her. Graham looked about ten years younger in the photo.

"Sit down," Graham said as he settled in behind his desk. "Dinner's waiting, so let's get down to business. How's the search going?"

"Slowly," Brad said, "but we think we may have a lead to chase down."

"I hope so," Graham said. "I feel terrible about what happened. The murder is just awful, and knowing one of our racers is unaccounted for makes it even worse. Old Yeller says we might not be able to host the race anymore, but it's been a positive for this area, and I think he'll come around." Graham looked up from his desk and seemed to realize he hadn't met Hadley before. "Where are my manners? I'm Graham Detweiler."

"Hadley Collins," she answered. "Brad and I have been friends for several years, and the past few years, we've worked together at a detective agency in Denver."

"Bringing in the big guns, then?" He smiled at Brad.

"We need all the help we can get," Brad said and immediately felt bad. "That's not a dig at you or the town or anything. Hadley and Vince, our other partner, are experts at solving these kinds of cases."

Graham leaned back in his chair and checked his watch. "So, what can I do for you tonight?"

Brad explained about Vince and Eddie re-interviewing the volunteers and not being able to find one. He told Graham that they researched the phone number, and it was a prepaid phone that had only been in use for a short time.

"It's probably nothing," Hadley said. "Lots of people use those phones for a lot of reasons, but in our line of work, we don't dismiss anything as coincidence."

"We're hoping you can tell us more about Lawrence Lewis," Brad added.

Graham stroked his chin and looked at his watch again. "Unfortunately, I can't tell you anything. I can pull up his application and share what he told us, but he's not a local, and I never met him before the race."

Graham swiveled his chair to face his computer, an old-fashioned tower that rattled and hummed as he searched his files. A moment later, a printer on the other end of the desk came to life and spit out two pages.

Graham looked over the pages before sliding them across the desk. "I shouldn't give that to you," he said. "There's personal information in it. Name, birthdate, address, yada, yada. But, if it helps find your friend, I'll let the chips fall where they may." He shrugged.

Hadley swiped the papers from the desk and read them. "This is exactly what we need," she said. "What kind of background check do you run on your volunteers?"

Graham laughed. "None. You seem surprised? We call that paper an application, but it's really just a way to get contact information from anyone who's interested in helping and make sure any minors get paired up with an adult. This kind of race takes a lot of manpower, and the next volunteer I turn down will be the first."

"Do you check IDs when the volunteers report for duty?" Hadley asked.

Graham laughed again. "Why would I do that?"

Brad wanted to say, "Because one of them might be a psychotic killer and kidnapper," but Hadley jumped in with, "There's no way to verify that someone who shows up on race day is who they said they were on the application?"

"Nope," Graham said. "From where I sit, that's a very low risk." He looked over his shoulder at his degrees, as if implying that of the three people in the office, he was most qualified to assess risks.

"I think I remember Lawrence from the check-in desk," Brad said. "Do you know if that's where he was assigned?"

Graham pulled a file from his desk and thumbed through it. He gave a slow nod. "Yep. Registration and bib handout."

"This has been very helpful," Hadley said. "We will not share this information with anyone outside our investigative team."

"Appreciate it," Graham said. He walked them to the door.

Before they left for the sheriff's office, Hadley phoned Vince and provided him with the personal data on Lawrence Lewis. "Run another check, and call me back ASAP," she said.

Her cell phone buzzed as Brad pulled into the police station. The parking lot sat mostly empty, but a pickup truck with

Burgess County Sheriff emblazoned on the side remained in a stall near the door. He hoped Yellington didn't drive a personal car to and from work and would be in the office.

Hadley put the phone on speaker. "What did you get?"

"Nothing," Vince said. "There's no Lawrence Lewis with that date of birth. We know the phone number is out of service. The address is to a bakery in Missoula. I can run a deed search on it, but I think we know that there won't be any Lewises connected to it."

"Run it," Brad said. "The more we can hit the sheriff with, the better."

They disconnected, and Brad offered Hadley a joyless smile. "It appears the risk of a volunteer showing up with a fake identity is higher than our friend Graham realizes."

The door to the station was locked, but a light glowed inside. Brad banged on the door and waited. He banged again, louder. Still, no one answered.

"I guess we're coming back in the morning," Hadley said. They walked toward the truck, but as Brad reached for the door handle, Sheriff Yellington stepped outside the station.

"I should've known it would be you," he said.

"It's nice to see you, too," Brad said. He introduced Hadley as they ascended the steps. "We won't take much of your time."

The sheriff waved them inside, frowning the entire time, and directed them back to his office. "Let's make it quick," he said as he sank into his desk chair.

Brad removed the plastic bag from his backpack and slid it across the desk. "We found this in the woods where the ATV had been hidden," he said. "We think you should have it tested for DNA."

The sheriff crossed his arms and didn't bother to look at the syringe. "Oh you do?"

Brad shot Hadley a glance that asked for help, and she jumped in.

"Sheriff," she began, "it's highly likely that this syringe is connected to whoever drove that ATV. Even if it has nothing to do with Shelly's disappearance, the ATV is your killer's best means of escape."

The sheriff eased his arms and looked at the plastic bag. "I might be a country bumpkin, but I'm not an idiot. Of course I'll have it tested. But you're getting your hopes up if you think this has anything to do with the murder. It's probably some junkie getting doped up out there."

"Do you have a lot of junkies out here?" Hadley asked.

The sheriff smirked. "You'd be surprised. I'm just saying, don't expect this to lead to anything."

"We've worked enough cases to know that most leads take you nowhere," Hadley said.

The sheriff cocked an eyebrow at her. "What kind of cases have you worked?"

"Murders and kidnapping," Hadley said. "Actually, just the sort of thing you're looking at here."

"Hadley helped investigate a senate candidate in Colorado who was accused of murder," Brad said.

Yellington ran a hand through his greasy ponytail. "I think I heard something about that one."

"I helped her with a case where she located a boy fifteen years after he was kidnapped," Brad said.

"I remember that one. That was you?" Yellington said. "Sounds like you're pretty good at this."

Hadley's cheeks flushed. "We do okay," she said.

The sheriff picked up the bag and held it up to the light. "I'll get this to the lab first thing in the morning," he said. "I'll have someone run it into Bozeman. Anything else come out of your investigation so far?"

Hadley seemed to have charmed the sheriff, so Brad looked at her to continue. She explained about Lawrence Lewis being a fake identity. The sheriff jotted notes while she talked.

"Given that he was one of the volunteers who had left their stations when the body was found, we think he's worth looking into."

"I'll see what we can find on him," the sheriff said. "It won't be easy without any details about his actual identity, but we'll look. Is that it?"

"That's what we have so far," Hadley said.

"We were wondering if you heard anything back from the lab on the duct tape or race bib," Brad said.

The sheriff looked up and to the right as if trying to decide how much to tell them. Finally, he put his palms on the desk and looked at them. "This doesn't go any further than you, understand? I'm not supposed to let civilians in on an investigation, but I'm going to share this with you because it might get you out of my hair." He paused and took a deep breath. "It'll take at least a week to get DNA test results back, but the lab said they won't find anything. The bib and the duct tape were contaminated by the time you found them, so it's not a surprise."

It was what Brad expected, but hearing it aloud deflated him. "Anything from the canoe or ATV?"

The sheriff shook his head. "Afraid not. Unfortunately, that big thunderstorm did a decent job of cleaning the scene, and we couldn't get any prints or find anything to test." He looked sheepish. "Come with me," he said. He shot out of his chair and walked past them and down the hall. Hadley gave Brad a puzzled look, and he motioned for her to follow.

The sheriff led them to a briefing room. It had two long tables with four chairs each and a pair of oversized bulletin boards on the wall. One board held a map of the area with a few thumbtacks in it.

"This is where you found the body," he said, pointing at a red thumbtack. "This is where we found the canoe, and this is where the ATV was. Where have you searched?"

Brad studied the map and waved his hand over an area to the northeast of the red thumbtack. "We've been all through the woods and searched County Road 15 and Highway 287."

The sheriff stepped back and stared at the map as if studying a work of art in a museum. "My team has followed the same path you have, but we're running a day behind you. We spent that first day processing the crime scene, then moved on to search the canoe and ATV areas. We searched the woods north of where the body was found today, but we came up empty. We'll keep up our search tomorrow, moving further north." He pointed toward the left of the map. "Moving west would be a good place to focus your efforts tomorrow if you plan on searching some more."

"Why west?" Brad asked. "We know the canoe and the ATV went northeast."

"Two different scenarios," the sheriff said. "One is that the killer and the girl went off in the same direction. Maybe the killer took the girl. Maybe the girl is the killer. We don't know."

"You can't be serious," Brad blurted.

The sheriff waved for him to be quiet. "We don't know anything at this point. For what it's worth, I think it's a stretch that your friend used this race as a cover to kill some random volunteer. We're not pursuing that line of thinking if it makes you feel any better."

He looked at Brad, who continued to scowl but shoved his hands in his pockets and waited for the sheriff to continue. "So, one scenario is they went in the same direction, together or separately. Scenario two, though, is that one of them staged the boat and ATV ahead of time and left to the northeast. The other one took off through the woods to the north or west."

"The killer would have staged the gear," Brad said. "I just don't see Shelly running off under her own power. She was taken."

"Maybe," Yellington said. "Maybe the killer came out of the woods right as Shelly was arriving. He knew he was caught and tried to eliminate her. She fought him off and ran off to the west. This is rough territory out here. I have no doubt your friend is capable as an adventure racer, but she could have fallen, hit her head, got dehydrated. Any number of possibilities. With the wildlife we have out here, you owe it to her to search that area."

"We'll take that under consideration," Brad said. His phone buzzed in his pocket. He checked the message and saw a text from Vince. "Our other partner ran a deed search on the bakery that phone number led to. No connections between the owners and anyone named Lewis. Looks like the check-in guy picked a name, picked a random address, and added a burner phone number."

"We'll look at it," the sheriff said. "I appreciate you all sharing the information with me." With that, he escorted them outside to Brad's truck.

They returned to the lodge, where Vince and Eddie waited in the common room, adjacent to the kitchen and dining room. The room sported thick pine timbers, an enormous fireplace surrounded by couches, and several trophy trout mounted on the walls.

Brad filled them in on the conversations with Graham and the Sheriff Yellington. "I don't see much point in searching to the west," Brad said, "unless we'll just be sitting around here tomorrow."

"I won't be sitting around," Eddie said. "I'm going to Billings to see if the convenience store has any camera footage that might get us a photo of our suspect. We need to track him down if we're going to get anywhere with this case."

"Good idea," Hadley said. "I have a couple other ideas to pursue." She told them about thinking the work was from someone with experience and that she wanted to research any similar disappearances in the area. "I'd also like to poke around online; he gave an email address on the application. If I can find an IP address for the computer that established that email, I might be able to get us closer to finding this guy."

"What about you, Vince?" Brad asked. "You have any big plans for the day?"

Vince smiled. "Sounds like I'm hiking around in the woods with you."

Brad searched the map on his phone to find a road that led to the area the sheriff wanted them to search. "My thought is that this road is the outer edge of our search, and we work in toward the rappelling station. If Shelly made it out to the road, she would have flagged down a motorist and gotten help. We'd have heard from her by now."

"Sounds reasonable," Vince said. "Is your other friend coming, too? Shelly's boyfriend?"

"We're not exactly friends," Brad said. Eddie snorted. "I'll let him know when to meet us. If he's a minute late, we leave without him."

When they settled in for the night, Brad lay awake in the top bunk long after Vince started snoring. As much as he hated to admit it, the sheriff had a point. Shelly could have had reason to run in the opposite direction they'd been searching. But, finding her out there after that many days wouldn't be good news.

He'd never had a personal connection to a case before. He understood the drive behind Hadley and Eddie in cases that had struck close to them. He was just as determined to find Shelly. They'd had a good day, with a couple of decent leads. He hoped Hadley and Eddie would come up with something the next day, and that he and Vince would not.

CHAPTER 18

He cursed at himself as he wandered through the woods. It had been more than an hour since the girl ran off. She didn't get much of a head start on him, but the dark, the density of the woods, and the sheer size of the space combined to keep her out of his grasp. Discouraged, he trudged back toward the guest house.

His prey had never escaped. He surveyed the inside of the house, at a loss for how she did it. The chain and the O-ring remained in place, but the handcuffs were nowhere to be found. She'd either picked the lock or broken the chain. In spite of the circumstances, he was impressed that she'd been able to do it.

The building wouldn't be hard to sanitize in the morning; he'd load the furniture in the back of his truck and dump it far away. He could wipe down the entire place in a matter of minutes. He could still smell her; the sour mixture of body odor and fear permeated the place. They couldn't match DNA to a smell, though. He'd make sure everything was clean, that there was no physical evidence to link him or her to the guest house. Setting the place on fire crossed his mind, but he didn't want to draw any unnecessary attention to the place.

He should have killed her that morning, but he felt like nighttime was best for that. He flexed his fingers and imagined wrapping them around her neck, his grip getting tighter as she cried out her last whimpers.

A check of the cabinets in the kitchen and under the bathroom sink revealed nothing useful. Back at his truck, he retrieved a headlamp, which he secured around his forehead, and a handful of zip ties, which he shoved in his pocket, before setting out again.

He skirted the outside of the tree line until he saw a place where the branches had been freshly snapped off. He entered the woods at that point, looking for any further signs of his quarry.

It didn't take long for the signs to disappear. She'd been careful and hadn't left a trail. He paused and listened. Far away, an owl hooted. If he strained his ears, he thought he could make out the sound of the river in the distance. No other sounds betrayed her.

According to the maps, the woods went for miles. If she kept running from the house, she'd get lost in the trees at some point. She was hungry and tired and would want help. The road would call to her. She'd come back toward him eventually, and he'd be ready. He'd finish what he came to do, but he'd take his time with it for the extra work she was creating.

•   •   •

Shelly's pulse pounded in her temples. She took another drink of water, but her mouth instantly dried out again. She'd definitely seen something watching her. She didn't think it was human. That both scared and comforted her.

She wished she could bathe somewhere, get the stench of the last few days in the dungeon off. She realized she had no idea how long she'd actually been locked up. She thought it had been three or four days, but she didn't know how long she'd been knocked out. The thought of being out cold and under the power of that demon sent a wave of nausea though her. She closed her eyes and waited for it to pass.

Opening her eyes, she ground her teeth. She had a problem to solve, and the odds were stacked against her. Unfamiliar terrain surrounded her, with only a can of beans and a third of a bottle of water to her name. Someone who wanted to kill her was in the woods, and she was on another creature's home turf. She wished she could reach Brad for help; she immediately wondered why she thought of Brad before she thought of Aaron. Knowing that line of thinking would not help her current situation, she closed her eyes and held her breath as she listened to her surroundings. She hoped to hear a road or a river, but she had no such luck. She had to make a decision with the data that she had.

A road lay behind her, but there was also a maniac back there somewhere, and she would not let him capture her again. If she maintained her current direction, she'd eventually intersect with the point where she saw the eyes. She hoped they belonged to a deer or an elk, but she knew it could be something much more dangerous.

Shelly stared at the stars above, more than she ever saw in Chicago. She wished she'd learned something about navigating by stars, but she'd never had a need. They always carried a map and a compass during the races.

Wanting to put more distance between herself and the maniac, she pivoted forty-five degrees to her right and set off, trying to move quickly without making noise. She kept her ears open for movement behind her, but aside from the occasional hoot of an owl or a cricket's chirp, silence enveloped her.

She kept a watchful eye to her left, wondering if she would see an animal again. She wished for more moonlight. One wrong step in the darkness could have disastrous results.

She wanted to whistle while she hiked, so she could avoid surprising any bears, but she couldn't risk giving away her position. She walked in silence. Though her body ached, it felt good to stretch her muscles after spending so many hours in the same position. Her stomach rumbled, and she told herself she'd estimate another fifteen minutes and then stop for more beans.

The ground took a slight incline. She kicked a rock or tree root and flailed forward. She crashed into a tree, a pine branch slashing against her cheek, before she regained her balance. She felt a welt form under her left eye and told herself to be more careful. Before moving again, she listened, wondering how far back the creep was and if he had heard her near fall.

She looked around her. A flash of movement to her left caught her eye. She couldn't tell how far away it was in the darkness. She worried it was the guy, and she gripped the handcuffs in her fist.

The movement blurred by again, too quick and graceful to be human. Based on the size and shape, she guessed it was a mountain lion. A second later, a noise that sounded like a combination of a hiss and a whistle confirmed it.

Shelly told herself to stay calm and not make any sudden movements. The animal called out again, but it sounded more like a scream. Shelly turned another forty-five degrees to her right and sprinted up the rise, dodging trees as she went. Loose gravel slipped under her shoes as the trees thinned out.

She looked over her shoulder to spot the predator. Seeing nothing but trees, she turned her head forward in time to see that she had reached the top of the rise.

She skidded to a stop, hanging onto a delicate balance. Gravel slid behind her. She turned and found herself face to face with the big cat.

It lunged. She didn't know if the next scream came from her or the mountain lion.

CHAPTER 19

Shelly swung the pillowcase in a wild, looping arc. The can of beans gave it weight, and her frightened rage helped her deliver a furious blow. The cat growled as it stumbled. It lunged at her again. She screamed and swung the beans once more. She connected again and kept the cat at bay.

She backed up a few steps as she gathered her courage for another swing. She still held the handcuffs in her left fist. As the cat pounced at her, she swung the pillowcase. It connected with the mountain lion again, but she hit its side, rather than the head. Unfazed, the predator barreled forward and snapped at her leg.

Miraculously, she got out of its way. She stumbled backward, nearly tipping over the other side of the rise. As she regained her balance, the cat continued its assault.

It snapped at her leg again, catching her just above the ankle. Pain surged through her body as the beast's teeth clamped into her. She hit it with the pillowcase, but at close quarters, she had less leverage and could only land a glancing blow.

She kicked with her free leg, but the lion would not let go. It swiped at her, the claws whizzing through the air with frightening speed. She screamed as the paw raked across the knee of her free leg.

Images of the cat dragging her corpse through the woods swirled through her mind. Adrenaline took over, and she leaned into a blow with her left hand, catching the animal in the eye with the handcuffs. The force of the blow jolted through her arm and rattled her teeth, and the cat let go.

Despite the searing pain in her leg, she leaped forward, landing on the animal's back and taking it to the ground. It whipped its head left and right in a frenzied attempt to bite her.

Holding a handcuff in each hand, she looped the chain across the cat's throat and pulled as hard as she could. The cat growled and hissed. She slipped off its back to her side and gripped the chain as hard as she could. The fall gave her more leverage, though the cat rolled onto her.

The mountain lion's thrashing slowed as she choked it. Finally, it stopped moving. She gave the chain a final yank before letting go of the handcuffs and rushing away. After thirty feet, she turned to see if the cat had moved. Her chest heaved and sweat soaked her clothing. Blood ran down both legs.

The mountain lion remained motionless at the spot of their fight. Shelly crept closer and snatched the pillowcase before backing away. The animal did not stir. Convinced she had killed it, she tried to estimate its size. It was difficult in the dark, but she would put it at around four feet long. It probably weighed fifty pounds. She didn't know if that made it an adult or a juvenile. She feared a cub's mother coming for it, or other mountain lions being drawn to the carcass.

Shelly climbed to the top of the ridge. She reached in the pillowcase for her water, and her heart sank as her hand came away soaked. The plastic bottle had broken during the fight, the last of her drinking supply gone.

She examined her injuries the best she could in the low visibility. The cut on her knee seemed deep. Blood flowed from it freely. Ripping a strip off the pillowcase for a bandage, she wrapped it as tightly as she could.

The puncture wound above her ankle didn't bleed as much, but it hurt more than anything she'd felt before. She bound it with the remainder of the pillowcase. She hiked another hundred yards away and found a place where she had good visibility of anything coming.

She cracked open the last can of beans. When she was finished, she left both empty cans, the broken water bottle, and can opener behind. She shoved the spoon into a pocket on her sleeve, thinking she might find some use for it.

She stood, but before she could take the next step forward, she grew lightheaded. She listed to her right. Her foot slid out from under her on a patch of gravel and she tumbled over the rise, sliding headfirst down the bluff.

•   •   •

Shelly awoke in the gray light of pre-dawn. Her dry lips cracked when she opened her mouth to yawn, and her shoulders shrieked in protest as she stretched. A dull ache engulfed the rest of her body, except for the mountain lion wounds. They pierced her as though the big cat still had a hold of her.

She needed water. She needed food. She needed a doctor. She couldn't get any of those things staying there.

She forced herself into a seated position and checked her bandages. They were brown and crusty, but no new blood seeped through. She took off her trail runners. She could wiggle and feel all her toes, so she had good circulation.

With her shoes back on her feet, she selected a rock that weighed around two pounds and carried it with her. She didn't relish the idea of carrying any extra weight, but she wanted something she could use as a weapon should the need arise.

Just let the creep who took her show up, and what she did to the mountain lion would look like pet sitting gone wrong. She didn't like the idea of killing an animal, but knowing that she did what she had to do to survive gave her confidence to start walking.

The sky in front of her tinged with pink and orange as she walked. The bite wound seared hot with pain when she took the first step, snatching her breath away. She calmed herself and moved forward a few steps. "You can do this," she said aloud, her voice a scratchy whisper. "One step at a time."

Soon, the sun peeked over the horizon. She felt comfort in knowing which direction she was moving. The terrain and the trees told her the guy hadn't taken her too far east; they were still along the Rockies somewhere. That didn't exactly narrow down the possibilities of where he had held her.

She had to stop to catch her breath frequently. Her slow pace discouraged her, but she had no choice but to keep moving. Staying still meant waiting for death. If she kept going, even at her turtle's pace, she'd at least have the opportunity to find help.

• • •

He secured a tarp over the bed of his truck, covering everything from inside the guest house, including the garbage from his hasty cleanup. He felt certain the girl would never be able to lead the cops to this place, and even if she did, they wouldn't find any evidence that led back to him. If the owners ever came back, they'd think a squatter had occupied the place. He hadn't gotten his kill, but he would elude capture.

He took the dirt road back to the gravel road that eventually led to a paved road. He stayed on two laners that wouldn't have speed traps. Not that he was going to speed. He kept both hands on the wheel, eyes on the road, and seat belt buckled, following every traffic law he could remember.

The road took him north, further away from Broadwood, until he found a gas station with a diner attached. He parked on the back side of the building, away from the road and prying eyes. He slipped on a Yellowstone T-shirt and pulled a matching ball cap down to his eyes. A pair of sunglasses completed the ensemble and made him look like a tourist.

At the counter, he ordered the day's special—biscuits and gravy with a black coffee—and found a booth in the back. He kept his head down and his sunglasses on. If the woman behind the counter thought it was odd, she didn't say anything when she brought him his order.

He ate slowly, giving his body a much-needed rest. After spending a fruitless night searching for the girl and a morning emptying the bachelor shack, fatigue consumed him. He wondered where the girl went. He still couldn't fathom how she had escaped. He would do better next time.

As he finished eating, the server brought him a refill of coffee in a to-go cup. "You look like you can use one for the road," she said. He wondered if it was something she said to all her customers. Maybe she was just being friendly; maybe it was a not-so-subtle hint that she was tired of a lone guy occupying an entire booth.

He paid cash and exited through the gas station. On his way out the door, he saw her take her station behind the cash register. His fingers tingled in anticipation.

He pulled the truck around to a pump. It was pre-pay or credit card. He wasn't going to leave an electronic trail, so he went inside. His heart pounded.

She looked just like the last girl. Same height. Same build. Same blond hair. Same blue eyes. He eyed her name tag. Ronda.

"Fifty bucks on pump three," he said, shoving the cash across the counter.

She took the money without giving him a second look, and he went outside to fill the tank, thinking about her the entire time. He thought about her as he drove north to the place where he could get rid of the junk under the tarp.

He spoke her name, enjoying the taste of it on his lips. He uttered it over and over like an incantation. He knew he'd be returning to that gas station, and he knew he would get his kill after all.

CHAPTER 20

July 23, 2025. Burgess County, Montana.
Aaron showed up right on time, to Brad's disappointment. The two rivals dressed alike, wearing tactical pants and long-sleeved T-shirts. Brad had used the lodge's laundry the night before. He hoped he wouldn't need to a second time.

Vince came downstairs wearing a pair of faded blue jeans, one of his standard polos, and a pair of mud-spattered hiking shoes. He volunteered to drive, so Brad left his keys behind for Hadley, in case she needed to follow up on any leads in person.

"Good morning, guys," Vince said. The two muttered their greetings and followed him to his Subaru. Brad sat in the passenger seat to navigate, so Aaron climbed in the back.

They spoke little as they drove, other than Brad's directions for the frequent turns they had to take to cut around the woods and reach the western edge they had earmarked. Halfway there, Vince spoke up.

"I know you guys are frustrated and anxious, but we're doing the right thing," he said. "The biggest cases I've worked on got solved because we chased every lead and played it like a numbers game. You get enough leads, and something will pan out. Hopefully, we'll generate another lead or two today."

"Thanks, Dad," Aaron said, sarcasm dripping from his voice.

Brad opened his mouth to tell him to shut up, but Vince spoke first, never taking his eyes off the road. "I'll let that one slide, sport, but there's only one person in this car who's been shot at by the Taliban, and that does something to a guy. Keep pushing me, and you'll find out."

Brad smirked. He'd seen Vince exasperated before, but he couldn't imagine his mild-mannered partner getting violent with anyone.

"Sorry," Aaron mumbled.

When they reached the spot Brad had identified, Vince pulled as far onto the shoulder as he could. They retrieved their backpacks from the cargo space, and Brad checked his cell phone. The single bar of service exceeded his expectations.

"Brad, you're the lead on this search," Vince said, and Brad noticed he cast a sidelong glance at Aaron as he spoke. "What's the game plan?"

"Let's spread out," Brad said. "There's only three of us, so there's going to be some gaps. I'd say thirty feet between us. We'll walk the woods as far as we can. We'll find an alternate route back, so we can cover more ground. We're looking for any sign of someone who didn't belong in the woods coming through here."

He dropped a pin for their location, stored his phone in his cargo pocket, and headed into the woods, Vince to his left and Aaron to his right.

Forty minutes into their walk, Aaron called that he had something. Vince and Brad scrambled to join him. He stood in front of a trampled area between two trees. "Someone's been here," Aaron said.

They circled the area. Five yards away, Brad spotted debris: beer cans, insect repellent, candy bar wrappers, and a lighter. "Looks like a camp out," he said. "The spot you found is probably where they had their tent." The remnant of a plastic garbage bag hung on a tree and fluttered in the breeze. "Must have left their trash behind, and something got into it. Let's keep looking."

It served as a stark reminder for Brad that they were in the wilderness. Whatever had foraged for food among the campers' trash could still be out there. "You talk to Shelly's parents lately?" Brad called out.

"I can't talk when I'm looking," Aaron replied.

"We need to make some noise," Brad said. "We don't want to scare any animals into reacting badly."

Aaron didn't answer, and Brad wondered if he'd heard him or if he was just being stubborn. "I talked to her mom yesterday," Aaron finally said, his voice filled with melancholy. "I guess she called the sheriff and gave him an earful, but he's only interested in looking for Shelly if it will help him find his killer."

"That's a little short-sighted," Vince said. "I'd bet anything that the killer and the kidnapper are the same person."

They made small talk as they searched. Vince told Brad he'd missed an intake appointment at the agency. "Sounds like an interesting case," Vince said. "This old guy is trying to track down his granddaughter. Apparently had a falling out with his son, and he's never met his grandchild. He wants to write her into his will, but he wants to meet her first."

"How much is he leaving behind in the will?" Brad asked.

"A lot," Vince said. "He's a rich, old guy."

"Rich clients are the best kind."

"You've been hanging around Eddie too long."

They didn't find anything else during the morning's search. The sun beat down from overhead, shining in patches through the trees. Brad called a break for lunch and declared they'd move further south for the search on their return route.

After lunch, they started walking again, moving south until Brad directed them to spread out and resume searching. As they walked, Brad kept thinking about what would have happened if he had gone up the rock first. Shelly was the best person he knew. It wasn't fair for this to happen to her.

"We're wasting the day," Aaron complained. "There's nothing out here."

"That's helpful," Vince offered. "That makes it more likely that Shelly and the killer departed on the same route. We already believe that, but maybe it will help convince the sheriff. There are no wasted days in an investigation."

Brad waited for a sarcastic rejoinder from Aaron, but he held his tongue. Maybe Vince's combat line had put him in his place. He wondered how Hadley and Eddie were doing. He hadn't heard anything from them. A check of his phone revealed that he still had one lonely bar and no text or phone notifications. He double checked their distance to the pin from earlier.

"We're about half an hour out," he said.

As Brad shoved his phone back in his pocket, it buzzed. He looked at the screen and didn't recognize the number. Ordinarily, he'd reject those calls, but since Shelly had disappeared, he'd answered everything, telling more than a few people he didn't need to update his car warranty.

"Hello," he said.

"Brad? This is Sheriff Yellington."

"Hey, sheriff. What's up?" Brad looked to each side and saw Vince and Aaron closing in on him.

"Where are you?"

"I don't know exactly. We're a few miles west of the racecourse. We've been searching that area like you suggested."

"Who's we? Is Aaron Reynolds with you?"

"Yeah, he's here. What's going on?" Brad's voice came out more urgent, almost commanding the sheriff to feed him information.

"I'm north of you. I'm going to send you a location. I need you to get here as quickly as you can."

"Why?" Brad asked. "You gotta tell us what's happening." He nearly shouted the last line.

"We found a body," the sheriff said. "A woman. We need to see if Reynolds can confirm the ID."

Brad dropped the phone and stumbled to the nearest tree, bracing himself on a branch for support. Aaron must have heard what the sheriff said because he froze in place as the color drained from his face.

Vince picked up the phone, said something to the sheriff, and clicked off the call. He looked from one man to the other. "Look, guys, we don't know anything yet. Take a minute, catch your breath, and we'll go together."

Aaron shook his head, "I can't do it."

Vince put an arm around him in a brotherly gesture. "We're right here with you. This might be the worst thing you'll ever have to do, but we have to go. Do it for Shelly. If it's her, we can start looking for justice for her. If it's not, we keep looking. You can do this."

Aaron nodded, his head barely moving. The three stayed close as they made their way back to Vince's car.

CHAPTER 21

Eddie found the gas station on a quiet road north of Billings. He stretched while he filled the Jeep at the pump. With his Denver PD badge in his back pocket, he proceeded inside. A customer stood at the counter, apparently a regular. He and the clerk discussed the intricacies of Montana versus Montana State football. While they talked, Eddie found the coffee station and loaded up the biggest cup he could find. He took two donuts from a case because he saw no point in having bad gas station coffee without a donut to go with it.

The guy at the counter started toward the door, then turned back to face the cashier. "I'm telling you, Ted, we need to figure out how North Dakota State is always good. We oughta be able to do the same thing here." Ted gave his head a wistful shake; the customer waved and exited. Eddie brought his purchase to the counter.

Ted rang up the items, and Eddie pointed to a rack of cell phones behind the counter. "You get much business for those phones?"

Ted thought it over and nodded. "Yeah, I sell one or two a week. Got phone cards to refill the minutes, too. You want one?" He turned, reaching for the closest model.

"Actually, I'm interested in someone who bought one of those phones here about a week and a half ago."

The cashier faced Eddie again, concern etched across his face. "Look, mister, I don't know what you're involved in, but keep me and my store out of it."

Eddie put both forearms on the counter and leaned in. Lowering his voice, he said, "The thing is, Ted, your store is already involved. I'm looking for a guy who disappeared. He gave the police in Broadwood a phone number we traced to a burner that he purchased here. Let me get the details."

Eddie reached into his back pocket and produced his detective badge. He flipped the cover open, making sure Ted got a good view of it. Eddie guessed Ted wouldn't know the difference between an active badge and a retired one, and he wouldn't look close enough to see that it was from Denver, rather than Montana. He slid a paper from under the badge and pushed it across the counter to Ted.

"That's the date and time he made the purchase. Are you able to look that up and see if he paid with a credit card?"

Ted stared at the badge for a long moment before turning his attention to the paper. "Who did you say you're with again? A cop from Billings came in yesterday, looking for the same information. Said he was doing a courtesy visit for the Burgess County sheriff."

Eddie closed his badge and returned it to his pocket. "I'm with a private group. You could say we're running a parallel investigation."

"Why don't you just get your information from Burgess County?"

Eddie straightened himself, leaning back from the counter. Ted was spooked, and Eddie needed to reel him back in, or he'd made a long drive for no good reason. "My team is not working directly with the sheriff. We have a different angle we're looking at." Ted's eyes told Eddie he was losing him. "I ran dozens of investigations just like this one during my time with the Denver PD," Eddie said, deciding to come clean. "I retired to be a fly-fishing guide up here. Thought my detective days were over. Now, a friend of a friend has disappeared, and we think Mr. Burner Phone has something to do with it. I need to track him down, so we can talk to him. When there are two parallel investigations going on, my time as a cop tells me it's best for each side to independently verify information."

Ted relaxed, but he made no move to find any information for Eddie. They stared at each other in an awkward game of chicken.

"It would help us a lot," Eddie said. "The sooner we can track down my friend's friend, the better. We don't know if she ran off with someone or if she's lost in the woods, and we're worried about her. There won't be any trouble with the police, here or in Broadwood, I can promise you that. They'll never hear anything from me about getting the guy's information from you."

Ted's face softened, and Eddie knew he had him. "I looked up the info for the Billings police," Ted repeated. "The guy paid with cash."

"Do you keep the footage from your camera?" Eddie asked, pointing to a security camera mounted above the counter.

"Yeah. The guy had a hat on and kept his head down; can't really get a good look at him from that camera. I can show you the video from the outside camera."

He took Eddie to a cramped office-storage room combo behind the register. A gray window gave a gauzy view of the store, and Eddie realized the mirror he saw behind the counter was a two-way job.

It took Ted a couple minutes to call up the footage of the exterior camera on an ancient laptop that whirred and clicked as it ran. Eddie counted himself fortunate that the computer ran at all.

"Here it is," Ted said. He turned the screen for Eddie to see. They watched as a well-built man in a ball cap and sunglasses approached the building. Eddie asked Ted to pause the video. Then, he had Ted back it up a few frames and they used slow motion to watch him approach. Ted paused it when the guy looked up.

"Not great," Eddie said, "but it's better than nothing. Any chance I can get a copy of the video?"

Ted nodded, accepting a flash drive from Eddie. A few minutes later, the video was copied, and Ted handed the drive back.

"You don't know the guy?" Eddie asked.

"Never seen him before, as far as I can remember," Ted answered.

Eddie thanked him, and they returned to the register. Eddie completed his purchase, returned to his Jeep, and called Hadley.

"Can't you just send me the file now?" Hadley asked.

"Nope; it's on a flash drive," Eddie said. "You should've seen the guy's computer. Belongs in a museum."

Hadley gave him instructions to stop at an electronics store in Billings to purchase an adapter, so he could connect the drive to his phone. "No sense in wasting three hours for you to come back," she said. "I can start hunting the guy down while you drive."

•   •   •

Hadley hung up from her call with Eddie. She thought about texting Brad to see how he was doing, but she decided they'd reach out to her if they had an update. They probably didn't have good service where they were anyway.

She turned her attention back to her research while she waited for Eddie to send the video. She had not found any similar disappearances near Broadwood. She opened a mapping app on her laptop and had it draw a 300-mile radius from Broadwood. That reached almost to Miles City, Montana, in the east, and pulled in parts of Wyoming, Idaho, and Canada.

She recorded the boundary coordinates and went back to her crime database. If someone had disappeared within the circle she'd drawn, it would show up, assuming the disappearance had been reported to the police.

She received more hits than she cared to sift through. The first three were children who had been taken by a parent during a divorce, triggering amber alerts. She opened the search filters and selected a victim age range of sixteen to forty. She guessed they were dealing with a much narrower range, probably twenty to early thirties, but she didn't want to miss someone who was on the border. She set the victim's gender to return results on missing males and females; again, she thought they were dealing with abducted women only, but they didn't have an official profile on their suspect, so she proceeded with caution. She asked for unsolved crimes only; if she didn't get anywhere, she could go back and look at the solved cases to see if any perpetrators had gotten off on a technicality or were free on bail while they awaited trial.

She ended up with four results, three women and one man. The male was a nineteen year old who had disappeared while hiking alone at Yellowstone National Park. Similar to Shelly in that he was doing an outdoor activity, but he had gone out alone, while Shelly was part of a group activity. It didn't feel like a similar disappearance to Hadley; she noted the case as a maybe and moved to the female victims.

Rebecca Grossman was a thirty-nine year old from Missoula; she had disappeared four weeks earlier. She was going through a rancorous divorce from a man she accused of physically abusing her. Similar to Shelly, Hadley thought, if you bought the idea of Aaron being abusive. They had no proof of that beyond Brad's hunch. Rebecca had reported to work at a bank, where she served as a loan officer, made a large withdrawal from her savings account, and driven away at lunchtime. No one had seen her since. Not exactly like Shelly; Rebecca's disappearance seemed premeditated.

Next was Kiersten Lewis, a twenty-two-year-old bartender in Helena. She did not have any romantic entanglements but had had a falling out with her parents, who she lived with. She hadn't been seen in two weeks, though her credit card had been used in Oregon since her disappearance. The database entry hadn't been updated in more than a week, and Hadley wondered if the Helena police decided she had left on her own and stopped pursuing it.

The third woman was Victoria Owens, a thirty-year-old geologist from Pocatello, Idaho. She had worked a full shift at a mining company before returning home. Neighbors found her garage door wide open, her car parked in the driveway, and tire tracks cutting through her front lawn. No one had seen her in sixteen days. No texts or phone calls to friends. No credit card charges or withdrawals from her bank account.

Hadley clicked the thumbnail photo of Victoria to enlarge it. Like Shelly, she had blond hair and blue eyes. Her height was listed as five foot six, and she weighed 115 pounds, giving her a similar body type to Shelly.

Hadley plugged Victoria's information into a background search and found her social media profiles. She opened Instagram. Victoria had shared a lot of photos of cats and horses. Mixed in among the animal photos, Hadley found a few selfies, which she compared to their photo of Shelly. They looked like they could be related. Not twins, probably not even sisters, but maybe cousins.

Next, Hadley opened her map and looked for Pocatello. It was south of Broadwood on Interstate 15. Hadley felt a chill as she traced the route from Pocatello to Broadwood, noting that the interstate and state highways created a path to U.S. 287, the highway that connected to County Road 15 and the racecourse.

If they had a serial perpetrator, he had easy access to both locations within a few hours of each other.

Her phone buzzed with a text message from Eddie. He'd finally sent the video, along with a picture of a chocolate donut. She shook her head as she moved the video from her phone to her laptop.

The camera quality was lacking, and the guy disguised himself well. In one frame, he looked up, and she grabbed a screen capture and cropped it tight to show only his head and shoulders. She sent that photo to her phone and texted it to Brad. "Does this look like the check-in guy?"

Not knowing if Brad had cell service or not, she moved on to the next phase of her search. She opened KryptoSearch and fed the image into it. The sunglasses would obscure some of the facial recognition software, but she hoped he showed enough chin and cheekbone structure to yield a few results.

The search came up empty. She switched to deep search mode, scanning cached web pages and deleted social media profiles. Krypto gave her three hits—deleted profiles from two dating sites and a cached page from a now-defunct message board.

The message board picture looked just like the guy in the security video, right down to a ball cap and sunglasses. The site was dedicated to BMX racing; according to the profile page, the user, LikeMyBike2206, had replied to three posts. None of the reply links were active. She moved on to the dating profiles.

The first one did not resemble the photo. The face had the same basic structure, but something about the picture seemed off. Too thin in the shoulders and neck. She zoomed in on the dating profile picture and saw the hint of a tattoo peeking out of the neckline on the guy's shirt. She compared that to the security photo; the image grew too grainy when she zoomed in, but she didn't see any sign of a tattoo.

The second profile could have been the guy. No hat or sunglasses; he had blond hair and blue eyes. He had the same pale skin in both photos and the shoulders and neck looked similar. No tattoos.

She scanned the profile, looking for any information she could glean. The name was listed as Corey Henderson. His hobbies included hiking, fishing, and BMX racing. He said he lived in Garrity, Montana. Hadley found it on the map: forty-five miles south of Broadwood on U.S. 287, right along the route one would take to get to Pocatello, Idaho.

She ran a background check on Corey Henderson in Garrity but didn't get any results. She'd be surprised if the guy used his real name. She scribbled some notes about him and turned to her next task, cracking the IP address he used to register as a race volunteer.

Whoever Lawrence Lewis really was used heavy-duty IP masking and encryption. Hadley found her way into the email server that hosted his address, but she couldn't pinpoint his exact address. She hoped to get access to his messages, but that was blocked as well. She stretched, cracked her knuckles, and opened her decryption app. She fed in as much information as she could about the email address and the date and time the registration was received.

The screen dimmed as the program worked its magic. It could take minutes, sometimes hours, to get results. Hadley had no idea how close to his IP address she would get. She grabbed her phone and Brad's keys. The cook at the lodge was a nice guy, and he'd gone out of his way to make his unplanned guests feel welcome, but Hadley didn't want to impose on him that day. She'd go into town to find some lunch and hope that when she got back, she had something more she could work with.

She got comfortable in Brad's giant truck, laughing at how out of place she seemed behind the wheel of that behemoth. With mirrors adjusted and the radio turned down, she put it into drive. She'd barely made it down the road when her phone rang.

She picked up, instantly recalling all the lectures she'd given Vince and Brad about distracted driving. The rules didn't apply when she was on a case.

"Hadley," Brad panted on the other end. "We have an update."

CHAPTER 22

Seven Years Earlier.
September 14, 2018. Chicago, Illinois.
Brad pulled the platter of nachos from the oven, added a few dollops of sour cream, tomatoes, and green onions and surveyed his masterpiece. Satisfied, he carried the plate into the living room and set it on the coffee table in front of the television. A knock at the door sounded, and he bounded across the living room to let Shelly in.

She wore a vintage Jim McMahon jersey and offered Brad a six-pack of Leinenkugel's as she entered.

"Just in time for kickoff," he said. "The others bailed, so it's just the two of us today. Hope that's okay."

"More food for me," Shelly said. She slid onto her spot on the couch while Brad found the Bears game.

Watching the games together had become a tradition over the past two years. They met when Brad started dating Daphne, Shelly's roommate. It was a case of opposites attracting at first, but eventually Brad, whose pastimes involved a lot of loud people and various feats of strength, and quiet, book-loving Daphne realized they were just too opposite and broke things off.

In contrast, Brad and Shelly had gotten along great. Toward the end of his relationship with Daphne, Brad found himself hoping Shelly would be home when he visited their apartment;

conversation with her flowed much more easily than with his girlfriend.

By the time Brad and Daphne broke things off, Shelly started dating a guy named James. He worked out at the same gym as Brad, but they didn't know each other well. Brad and Shelly hung out when James wasn't available, but once Shelly and James broke up, Brad found they were locked into a friend zone that they both found comfortable and neither wanted to change. They continued to hang out and watch sports and made plans to team up for an adventure race just outside the city later that fall.

At halftime, with only a couple of sad-looking chips remaining on the platter, Brad opened his third beer and turned down the volume on the television. The time had come to share his news with Shelly.

"You know how my uncle hasn't been doing very well?" Brad asked. His father's brother lived in Colorado and had been battling stomach cancer for more than a year. Uncle Doug never married and didn't have children of his own, so he treated Brad more like a son than a nephew.

"Yeah," Shelly said. Concern clouded her eyes. "Did something change?"

She meant "did he get worse," Brad thought, but asked it in the tactful way he had come to expect from her.

"No, not really," Brad said. "He doesn't think he has a lot of time left. He wants me to visit him in a couple of weeks, so I'll be gone for a long weekend."

Shelly looked confused before she smiled. "As serious as you seem, I thought you were going to share some kind of major thing. We'll miss a game. No big deal."

"It's a little more than that," Brad said. "He owns a commercial lab service north of Colorado Springs. A little town called Monument. He wants me to come check out the business with him, and if I like it, it's mine."

"Wow," Shelly said. "That's great." Her voice went up at the end like she was asking a question. The comment hung in the air between them.

"So, anyway," Brad said, "it's not really something I can just own and give to someone else to manage. It's a hands-on business. He wants me to move out there and learn from him while he's still able to run things."

"Wow," Shelly said again. Her voice held no trace of enthusiasm. "That's a big change. Are you sure that's what you want to do?"

"I guess I'll know for sure after I visit, but it's a huge opportunity for me. He thinks there's a big future in that kind of lab. People willing to pay out of pocket for tests that their insurance company won't cover. It's already profitable." She looked like she wanted to say something. The truth was, she would be the biggest reason he'd miss Chicago. Their friendship meant more to him than any other he'd ever had. "I never looked at being an EMT as a long-term career," Brad said. "I thought maybe MMA held a future, but that didn't pan out, and it's hard to get a foothold in the personal training world—too much competition. I'm twenty-five, and if I take this offer, I'll have a chance to be set up for a long time."

"Will you enjoy it?"

Brad shrugged. "Maybe. I have a degree in biology, so this is at least somewhat related. Game's starting up again."

He turned the volume back on the television, and they pivoted away from the conversation to become engrossed in the Bears once more. Midway through the fourth quarter, he noticed Shelly becoming more interested in her phone than the television.

"What's going on?" he asked during a commercial break.

Shelly blushed and tilted her phone screen away from him. "A guy I've been talking to. He wants to make plans for later."

"Another Prince Charming coming to sweep you off your feet," Brad teased. Since her breakup with James, Shelly had gone on a string of first dates but not many seconds.

"Actually, you might know this one," Shelly said. "He used to fight MMA, too. Aaron Reynolds. Ever hear of him?"

Brad put his drink back on the coffee table and turned toward her. "Reynolds? Seriously?"

"You know him?"

"Yeah. He's bad news. Stay away from him."

Shelly let out a nervous chuckle. "You really are like a big brother sometimes."

"I mean it. I know some things about him."

"What kind of things?" Shelly asked, the concern back on her face. She waved Brad off. "No, don't tell me. I don't want to know. I need to make my own decisions, just like you're doing. I told him I'd meet him for drinks later tonight."

Brad wanted to spill his guts, to tell Shelly all about Monica and how Reynolds was partially responsible for his MMA career ending. Instead, he held up his hands. "All I ask is if there are any red flags, you run. There are plenty of other guys out there."

"And I'll have dated them all within the next year at the rate I'm going," Shelly muttered.

They finished the game without much more conversation. When it was time to leave, Shelly gathered her things, and Brad walked her to the door. She looked like she might cry.

"This isn't goodbye, you know," he said.

"I know. But it will be, eventually."

"I'm coming back for the race next month no matter what," Brad said. "If we like it, we'll do some more. Anywhere in the country; we find a race we like, we conquer the course together. Deal?"

"Deal."

He held out his hand for a fist bump. She gave him one before sliding into an awkward side hug and leaving.

Brad flopped back on the couch and looked for another game. He tried not to think about Shelly getting mixed up with Reynolds. Even if Brad moved to Colorado, he'd make sure to come back to Chicago frequently enough to keep an eye on her and help if things went south.

CHAPTER 23

July 23, 2025. Burgess County, Montana.
Vince's little Subaru juddered along the gravel road. Brad felt every rut and dip and wished he had brought his truck instead. He checked the location the sheriff had sent him and pointed ahead.

"Our turn's coming up," he said. Other than directions, they'd ridden in silence. No words were appropriate words for the task at hand.

Vince slowed to a near stop and made the turn onto an even narrower dirt road. They didn't get far before Yellington flagged them down.

"Pull off here," he said, pointing to an area just off the road. Vince complied, and they climbed out of the car.

"We walk from here," Yellington said. "We have a mess of cars down at the house, and I'm only allowing official vehicles in. Who's this?" He pointed his chin toward Vince.

"I'm Vince Marcotte," Vince answered. "I'm a private detective who works with Brad back in Denver."

"Great, another one," the sheriff said. He turned his back on the trio and walked along the road. Brad, Aaron, and Vince fell in behind him.

Two minutes later, they arrived at a log cabin, nestled into the surrounding pines. It looked small; Brad guessed it was two bedrooms at the most, more likely one. A wide, steel building stood across a clearing from the cabin. A pair of garage doors covered the further two-thirds of the building. The third closest to the men had a standard door and a bank of windows.

"We found the body in here," the sheriff said, gesturing toward the steel building. "Looks like it was at one time a combo garage and workshop. No sign of occupants here or in the cabin. Power is still on, so this place could be a summer home that the owners didn't come back to this year. We're looking into ownership now."

Brad heard the sheriff's words but didn't process them. His thoughts were on Shelly alone. Deputy Cooper emerged from the cabin and walked across the clearing to join the group outside the garage.

"They're going through it inch by inch," the deputy said. "So far, they're not coming up with much, but if there's any evidence in there, they'll get it."

"Good," Yellington said. "Crime lab on the way?"

"Yes sir," Cooper said. "Should be here in the next thirty minutes."

The sheriff turned back to Brad, Aaron, and Vince. "Strictly speaking, we should send the body to the morgue and have you go there for the identification. But, given what this looks like, we'll need to send it to Bozeman, and it's more efficient to have you do it here."

"What does it look like?" Aaron asked, his voice thin.

The sheriff ran his hand through his ponytail. He pulled a pack of gum from the breast pocket of his uniform and shoved two pieces into his mouth. "Promised my wife I'd quit smoking," he said. He rolled his eyes. "Occasions like this, I need a cigarette. But, if she even catches a whiff of smoke on me, that body in there won't be the only one." Brad's eyes widened at the sheriff's insensitivity; Vince and Aaron must have had similar expressions because the sheriff gave a nervous chuckle and apologized. "I don't know how to be anyone but me, and I'm blunt. Sorry if that offends you." He locked eyes with Aaron. "To answer your question, it looks like a murder. Young woman who fits your friend's description. Body is naked, wrapped in plastic, and shoved in the freezer. No visible wounds except for bruising around the neck, so my guess is we're looking at a strangulation."

He shoved his gum wrappers in his pocket and looked at each of them in turn. He ended on Vince. "You ever meet Shelly?" Brad was surprised the sheriff remembered her name. Vince shook his head. "Then you'll wait out here. Fewer people in there the better. You two: I'm going to have you put on booties and gloves. Don't touch anything. Don't go anywhere except with me. If you think you're going to be sick, you let Coop know, and he'll get you out here. We're still processing the scene, and I don't need you yacking all over the place."

They put on protective gear and went inside. Brad followed with Aaron close behind and Deputy Cooper bringing up the rear. Three police officers in coveralls, booties, gloves, and ball caps buzzed about the building, taking pictures, recording measurements, and shining lights into shadows. Brad figured they must have the entire police force there and possibly borrowed manpower from another county.

The third of the garage they entered had a table saw, a lathe, and stacks of wood. A pegboard covered one wall with hammers, wrenches, levels, and tools Brad couldn't identify hanging over every inch. A shelf next to it held sandpaper, wood glue, and a pile of rags.

The first vehicle bay sat empty. Tire tread marked the concrete floor. The next bay didn't have room for anyone to park. It held a drill press, a planer, an enormous worktable, an antique stereo, complete with a turntable and stack of vinyls, and, in the back corner, an upright freezer. It stood at least eight feet tall and was four feet wide.

The sheriff led them to the appliance. On the ground outside of it was a plastic-wrapped body. Brad's stomach roiled and bile rose in his throat. He located Deputy Cooper, just in case.

The sheriff kneeled on the concrete next to the plastic. He unfastened the tape holding the wrap in place over the victim's face. Brad's knees wobbled. He'd seen plenty of terrible things during his time as an EMT in Chicago, but it had never been that personal before.

He felt movement next to him. Aaron had edged away from the body and angled himself to face a different direction. Brad wished he could do the same; the idea of the corpse on the floor being Shelly repulsed him, while at the same time held him in an inescapable grip.

The sheriff stared up at the two men. "You gonna be okay?"

"Yeah," Brad said, surprised by how steady his voice came out. Aaron didn't answer.

The sheriff moved the plastic. Brad felt his world crumbling as he looked at the blond hair and pale skin. The sheriff moved the sheeting down an inch, revealing the forehead. He kept inching it down, and the eyes, nose, cheeks, lips, and chin came into view.

Brad kneeled next to Yellington to get a closer look. He dropped from his knees to his butt and exhaled.

"It's not her," he said. "That's not Shelly."

"You sure?" Yellington asked.

Aaron moved in between them, peering down at the dead woman's face. "He's right," Aaron said. "That's someone else."

He sat on the ground next to Brad, an arm propped on Brad's shoulder. It was the closest the two of them had ever been in contact without trying to knock the other one out.

The sheriff pulled the plastic over the woman's face and affixed the tape. "Gentlemen, thank you for coming out here. Sorry to take you away from your search," he said. "Coop, get these guys out of here, and they can be on their way. And tell

Barton to bring in a gurney, so we can get the victim ready for transport."

Aaron sprang to his feet and offered a hand to help Brad up, a gesture that caught Brad off guard. He waved Aaron off. "I'm good," he said.

They followed Coop back through the garage and outside where Vince waited. Vince's eyebrows shot up as soon as he saw the men, and Brad said, "Not Shelly." That brought a smile to Vince's face.

The deputy insisted on walking the men all the way to Vince's car and watching as Vince turned it around on the narrow road and started back the way they came. Brad gave Vince a rundown of what they saw inside the garage.

"Way too soon to know if these are related," Vince mused.

Brad didn't answer; too many thoughts swirled around his head. On one hand, more victims would mean the potential for more witnesses, security cameras, or some other type of evidence to find the killer. It also made nailing down a motive difficult; they could be dealing with a psychotic whose only motive was to kill. That meant Shelly was in danger—if she was still alive. They needed to find her fast.

He looked in the backseat where Aaron stared out the window. He wondered if his rival was having the same thoughts. "You okay back there?"

Aaron faced forward for a second before looking back out the window. "I've never been that close to a dead person before," he said. "I've been to funerals, but that's different, you know?"

Brad didn't answer; he understood Aaron's sentiment entirely. He didn't get a full night's sleep the first few months he was on the job in Chicago. Seeing trauma up close and personal took a toll.

He pulled his phone from his pocket and dialed Hadley's number. "We have an update," he said as soon as she answered.

He told her about the sheriff's call and about the woman who wasn't Shelly.

"Where did they find her?" Hadley asked. Brad could feel the excitement in her voice.

"About thirty minutes north of Broadwood."

"Near 287?"

"Yeah. Not right off the highway or anything. There were dirt roads we had to go down. It's a wonder Vince's car held up."

"Hey," Vince said. "This car has lived through more life and death action than that truck of yours."

"Anyway," Brad continued, "287 is the closest major road to where we were."

"Call the sheriff and tell him to look at Victoria Owens from Pocatello, Idaho," Hadley said. "There's a good chance that's the victim."

Brad listened as Hadley explained about her morning of online searches and identifying a case that seemed similar to Shelly's disappearance. "I haven't gotten far with tracking down Lawrence's real identification, but I have reason to believe he also went by the name Corey Henderson," she said. "More on that when you get back."

Brad repeated the story for Vince and Aaron before calling Yellington back. The sheriff answered on the fourth ring.

"Sheriff," Brad said. "We have the name of a possible victim. Victoria Owens from Pocatello. She went missing a couple of weeks ago under suspicious circumstances."

"I'll have one of my men look at that as soon as we can," the sheriff answered.

"Thanks," Brad said. "Did you get anything back from the lab yet? Results on the syringe I found?"

"Too soon," the sheriff said. "Even if they put it in as a rush job, it's days, not hours, before they can get us results."

"Are you sure?" Brad asked. "I used to..." He let his voice trail off.

"You used to what?"

"Nothing," Brad said. Yellington would not react well to Brad bringing up his past experience running a lab. "Just let me know if you hear anything."

"You'll be my first call," the sheriff said, and Brad didn't think he'd ever heard more sarcasm in his life.

Brad thanked him and ended the call. Vince took the exit for the Double T Ranch. A cloud of dust down the dirt road announced the presence of a vehicle in front of them. They arrived at the lodge just as Eddie exited his Jeep.

"Not a bad day, gentlemen," Eddie said. He brushed crumbs off the front of his shirt. "I got video of a potential suspect."

"Hadley filled us in," Brad said. The four went inside and found Hadley in the common room, her feet propped on an ottoman and her laptop balanced on her legs.

"Any luck?" Brad asked.

Hadley shook her head. "Nothing. There's definitely no Corey Henderson living in Garrity. But, the only reverse image results I'm getting from the photo point back to Corey Henderson. It's an endless loop." She closed the laptop with a clack and moved it to the couch beside her.

The men sat down, Brad and Vince on either side of Hadley, and Eddie and Aaron on a facing sofa. Brad talked Eddie through the sheriff finding a body.

"I'm sure it's Victoria Owens," Hadley interjected.

Eddie stroked his chin and looked at the ceiling. "I hate to say this, but I don't have a ton of confidence in our local law enforcement. Hopefully, they have a decent medical examiner who can see if this victim was injected with a syringe."

"Good thinking," Brad said. "If the syringe I found is positive with Shelly's DNA and we find that one was used on the other victim, that's a stronger connection between them than we have now."

"What we have are a whole lot of ifs and maybes," Vince said.

A somber silence settled over the room, the joy of potential progress evaporating in the face of just how much work was still ahead of them to find Shelly.

"What do we do now?" Aaron asked.

"You guys look like you've had a rough day," Hadley said. "I say we call it a day and regroup in the morning. Maybe the sheriff will have more information and be willing to share it with us. I'll keep plugging away on online research and see if anything helpful comes up."

"More ifs and maybes," Aaron said.

"Welcome to being a private detective," Eddie answered.

CHAPTER 24

Shelly couldn't go much further. While she hoped she might encounter someone during her day of walking, she also had to admit the small amount of ground she'd covered decreased those chances. Injuries and dehydration slowed her, and she had to stop for frequent rest breaks. Gone was the girl who confidently flew past obstacles during the race.

She wondered how Brad was doing and if he was still looking for her. He would be, she decided. Brad would search until he found her, dead or alive.

Aaron, too. He'd grouse and grumble, but he would search, practicing the lecture he would give her when she was found.

Pain radiated through her leg, and she needed to stop again. Her face felt warm. She hoped it was the late afternoon heat getting to her, but she worried about infection. She wondered what diseases mountain lions carried.

The path she followed led into tree growth, but a game trail sprouted off its side. The idea of following a path made by animals did not appeal to her, but she liked the idea of fighting through brush and branches even less.

She followed the trail up a hill and decided she would stop on the other side of the rise, no matter what. She took solace in knowing that if she lay down in the wilderness and never woke up, she would die on her terms and not at the hands of some crazy killer.

Dropping to her hands and knees, she climbed the final ten feet to reach the top of the hill, where she collapsed on her stomach. She wanted to roll to her back, but she lacked the energy for even that.

A breeze drifted over her, providing some relief from the heat. A familiar noise sounded nearby, but she couldn't place what it was. The sound repeated, and Shelly drew herself to her knees, looking around for any flashes of movement.

She heard it again and turned her head. About a hundred feet from the bottom of the hill stood a cabin, and a loose screen door banged its frame when the wind stirred.

Hope soared through Shelly. Forcing herself to her feet, she dragged herself down the hill and to the cabin. As she got closer, she saw how small it was. She cautioned herself that she didn't know what type of person might be on the other side of the door, but she had reached the point of getting help or dying alone.

She banged on the door and waited. She banged again. Rather than knock a third time, she tried the handle, which turned in her frail grip. She swung the door open and stepped inside.

"Hello," she called. She could barely hear her own voice. "Anyone there?"

The cabin was little more than a walled-in patio. There was no one there. A cot occupied one corner, and a pot-belly stove stood in another. Not far from the stove, an old-fashioned wash basin stood on a rickety stand with a primitive-looking drain leading to the outer wall.

She looked around for a light switch but didn't find anything. She searched a footlocker near the cot, hoping to find food or, better yet, a bottle of water. It held a musty blanket and a pair of rubber boots.

She rolled the blanket up and set it at the head of the cot. Using the blanket for a pillow, she lay down, thankful for the measure of comfort being off the ground provided. She closed her eyes and drifted off.

When she awoke, darkness had set in. She double-checked the door to make sure it was securely closed. It didn't have a lock, but she just wanted to keep the wildlife at bay. A bear could find its way in easily, even with the door closed, and that's probably why there was no food left behind, but she doubted a mountain lion or bobcat could force the door open.

Shelly stripped off her shirt, pants, shoes, and socks, letting fresh air touch her skin for the first time since before the race began. She lay back on the cot in her underwear and tattered sports bra. The night had brought cold, so she covered up with the scratchy blanket and drifted off once again.

When she first heard the voices, she thought she was dreaming.

CHAPTER 25

July 24, 2025. Burgess County, Montana.
"Let's put the cooler inside and then hit the water," a deep voice said. "We can get the other stuff later."

Shelly definitely was not dreaming. Footsteps crunched on the gravel path. She threw her clothes on, wincing as her ripped pants met the pillowcase bandages. Her eyes searched the room as she laced up her trail runners. She needed something to fight with and settled for a rubber boot from the footlocker as the door swung open.

A man filled the frame. He wore shorts and a long-sleeved fishing shirt, a wide-brimmed hat atop his head. His gray-streaked beard reached halfway down his torso.

Shelly let out what she thought of as a shriek, but what the man probably heard as a whimper. She lunged at him and swung the boot. The pain from the bite wound overcame her as she planted on that leg, and she crumpled to the floor.

The man stepped toward her, and Shelly swung the boot at him again. He backed up and held his hands up. As he did, a teenaged boy stepped around a cooler in the doorway and stood next to the man.

Shelly struggled to regain her feet. The man and the boy couldn't have looked more shocked to find her in the cabin if she had been a black bear curled up on the cot.

"Are you okay?" the man asked. "You look like you need help."

The boy stood closest to the door. Shelly flung the boot at him. When he reached to knock it away, she sprang forward and vaulted the cooler. Her right foot caught it as she went over, and she fell to the ground in a heap, putting pressure directly on the bite wound. Her scream echoed throughout the valley.

"Stay here," the man told the boy. He rushed around the cooler and stood near Shelly. "Ma'am, I'm not going to hurt you," he said. "My name is Everett. That's my son, Noah. This is our cabin you've been staying at."

Shelly pushed herself into a seated position but didn't try to run. She lacked the strength to move. If Everett and Noah wanted to hurt her, she had no way to escape them. Tears welled up, and she blinked them back, causing the world in front of her to go blurry.

"There's a road close by, and my truck is there," Everett said. "We can get you to the hospital."

Shelly realized the offer was sincere, that this stranger really wanted to help her. The tears came back in a deluge, cutting trails through the dirt caked onto her cheeks. She couldn't speak, so she nodded.

"Noah, get our guest some water from the cooler," Everett said, and Shelly heard noises behind her. "Grab her a sandwich, too, and we'll head to the truck."

Shelly accepted the water from Noah and drank the entire thing without taking a breath. The cool liquid spread throughout her body as she gulped it down. Noah fetched a second bottle.

Noah was probably fourteen years old. He was just shorter than Shelly and wiry. He watched as she nibbled at the sandwich, daintily at first, before taking bigger bites. When she had eaten half of it, she asked if they could take her to the truck.

With the uneaten sandwich half in one hand, she put an arm around Everett's shoulders, and he helped her down the path, around a bend, and up a shallow rise to a red Ford pickup. Fly fishing rods, waders, and the largest tackle box Shelly had ever seen were in the bed.

Noah opened the back door to the extended cab, and Everett lifted her into the seat. She sat sideways with her legs propped up. The engine rumbled to life, and Everett set off down the road at a moderate pace.

"What happened to you, anyway?" he asked.

Shelly didn't know where to start. "I was taken," she said. The tears started all over again, and Shelly had a hard time going on. She managed to choke out, "From the race at Broadwood."

They reached pavement, and Everett sped up. "Noah, dial 911 on this thing," he said, passing an ancient cell phone to his son. Noah dialed and handed it back.

"This is Everett Hearst," the man told the dispatcher. "I'm driving toward Burgess County Hospital with a woman who looks to have some wildlife injuries." He lowered his voice, but Shelly still plainly heard him continue, "She's in bad shape. Said she was taken from the Broadwood race." He paused a moment before asking for her name. She told him, and he relayed it to the dispatcher. "Name's Shelly Cantwell. We'll be there in about twenty minutes; make sure they've got a doctor ready."

He tossed the phone back to Noah and mashed the accelerator further down. The road noise grew louder as the truck picked up speed. "Thank you," Shelly said. She wasn't sure he could hear her, but she didn't have enough voice to go any louder. Instead, she settled back into the seat, finished her sandwich and water, and said a silent prayer of gratitude.

•   •   •

He showed up at the gas station in his second car, a white Toyota Camry. He'd doctored the stolen plates with electrical tape, changing a C into a D and a 3 into an 8. It wouldn't hold up under scrutiny, but it might fool traffic cameras or witnesses.

He pulled behind the building once again, so he could see the two spots marked for employees. A Chevy pickup from the day before occupied the first slot. The second slot sat empty. He gazed at the building and didn't see any security cameras. He didn't know if Ronda would be on shift or not or which vehicle she drove. If the Chevy was hers, she'd already be inside, and he'd have to come back later.

Unlike his previous work, he hadn't planned this abduction, and his heart thrilled with the excitement that brought him. All the ways the whole affair could go wrong would it make it that much more spectacular when it worked out. He saw this instance as a change in his methods. Gone were the days of watching and waiting, carefully plotting each move. The exhilaration of operating in the moment provided a new addiction.

He checked his rearview mirror and spotted a Saturn sedan that had seen better days approaching the station. After snapping on his rubber gloves, he grabbed his ski mask. His palms sweated under the gloves when the car grew close enough for him to see Ronda behind the wheel.

He pulled the mask in place and kept his head turned away, so she wouldn't notice. When he saw her nose into the spot with his peripheral vision, he popped his trunk and slipped out of the car as she cut her engine. She never looked his way. His entire body tingled with electricity. He was catching all the breaks he needed.

"Ronda," he said as she stepped out of her car and toward the station. She stopped and turned. He sprang forward, sliding over the hood of the Saturn to grab her. She tried to run, but he caught a handful of her hair and pulled her back. He slapped his right hand over her mouth as she started to scream, cutting it off before it was little more than a gasp.

He wrapped his left leg around her legs and pulled her toward his body with his right hand, still clamped on her mouth. He pulled the syringe from his pocket. He would not lose it this time; there would be no repeat of the incident in the woods.

Before he could get the needle to her neck, she bit his fingers hard enough to draw blood. He pulled his hand away—just for a second—but it was long enough for her to shove him backward and bolt.

She shrieked as she ran. He lunged after her and caught her before she had taken more than three steps. A punch to her throat cut off her air for a few seconds, and the next scream died in her throat. He scooped her up and thrust her into his trunk, stabbing her in the neck with the syringe and thrusting the plunger down.

He slammed the trunk shut, jumped in the driver's seat, and peeled out. The other employee came around the corner, and he nearly ran her over. She jumped out of the way, looking from his car to Ronda's before running inside.

Ronda's kicks and punches clanged inside the trunk but grew weaker by the second. He kept the gas pedal down and got onto Highway 287. Tossing the ski mask to the floorboards, he pointed the sedan north going just over the speed limit, trying to blend in with the other traffic as much as possible.

Fifteen minutes after the kicking and screaming from the trunk subsided, he found an exit that promised no services. It led to a quiet road. He followed it until he was out of sight of the highway and then pulled over.

Ronda's bite had shredded his right glove. The blood had stopped oozing out. He grabbed a roll of duct tape from the passenger seat, put his ski mask back on, and returned to the trunk.

He opened it quickly, ready to restrain her if she tried to escape. The drug had done its job, though. He looked at the beautiful woman now in his possession, and the electricity returned to his body. He caressed her cheek with his gloved left hand, then ran his hand through her hair.

He remembered that he hadn't gotten away with anything yet. He looked around. Still clear. He put a strip of duct tape over her mouth before taping her wrists together behind her back. He did her ankles, too, just to be safe.

He got back in the driver's seat and shoved his gloves and mask inside the center console. He turned the car around and pointed it back to the highway. He needed to go south, back past the gas station, but he didn't dare retrace his steps. There were probably cops at the station already. He didn't know how good of a look the other clerk had gotten, but if she pegged his car as a white Camry, he'd get stopped for sure.

Instead, he continued north. There was a two-lane road he'd find a few miles ahead. From there, he could head west and take a series of two-laners, dirt roads, and county roads until he got to his place in the woods south of the station. He could stash the girl inside, hide the car in the garage, and switch back to his truck.

He rolled down the windows and breathed in the mountain air. His heart slowed to its normal rate, but his hands kept tingling. The universe had given him a second chance, a do-over after letting one get away. He wouldn't fail again.

CHAPTER 26

The phone call woke Brad from a coma-like slumber. Forgetting where he was, he rolled over to grab the phone and tumbled out of the top bunk. He caught the frame with his hand and kept himself from completely wiping out. The phone continued to ring from the charger across the room. Brad snatched it and answered the call without bothering to look at the caller ID.

"Is this Brad Cummings?" a female voice on the other end asked.

"Yes," Brad said. "Who is this?"

"This is Gina Taylor, I'm a nurse at Burgess County Hospital," she answered. "Shelly Cantwell asked me to call you."

"You talked to Shelly?" Brad half-screamed. "When? Where is she? Is she okay?"

Despite Brad's animation, Gina maintained an even voice. "Mr. Cummings, Ms. Cantwell is here at Burgess. She asked that you and Aaron Reynolds come see her."

"Is she okay?" Brad repeated.

"I can't give you any details about her condition," Gina said, "but I can tell you she's well enough to talk and she's aware of where she is."

Brad thanked her, ended the call, and dialed Aaron's number. He put the phone on speaker and started dressing in his clothes from the day before.

"Yeah," Aaron said.

"Shelly's been found," Brad said. "Get over to the lodge now, and we'll drive out together."

"Wait, what? Where is she? Is she okay?"

"She's at a hospital. I'll get the address while you're on your way. The nurse didn't give me any details other than that she's there."

"How'd the nurse get your number?"

"I don't know. Shelly asked her to call me."

Aaron didn't answer right away, and in the ensuing silence, Brad felt a twinge of satisfaction knowing that Shelly hadn't asked for her boyfriend.

"I'm on my way," Aaron said. The call ended.

Brad raced downstairs and found Vince, Eddie, and Hadley in the kitchen drinking coffee. They were all laughing, but the merriment abruptly stopped when Brad stepped into the room.

"You okay?" Vince asked.

"I'm fine," Brad said. "It's Shelly. She's in the hospital. We need to get going."

All three detectives spoke at once, shooting questions at Brad. "What hospital?" "Is she okay?" "How'd you find her?"

"Slow down," Brad said. "She's at Burgess County Hospital. She's talking and has her wits, but that's all I know."

"How'd they find her?" Vince asked.

"No idea," Brad said, his frustration with all the questions growing. "Eddie, you know where the hospital is? You can drive."

"Actually," Hadley said, elongating the word in the way she did when she was about to disagree with him. "Maybe I should drive. It might help to have another woman there. No offense, Eddie."

"None taken," Eddie said as he refilled his mug. "My testosterone will be put to better use in Garrity with Vince."

"I'm lost," Brad said. "I thought Garrity was a dead end."

"I did a lot of online searching last night," Hadley explained. "The IP address Lawrence Lewis used to register for the race pinged through a bunch of different locations, but the tracer I used told me it most likely originated somewhere near Garrity. The online dating profile for Corey Henderson mentioned Garrity, and now the IP tracker thinks his computer was there, too. There's a Garrity connection."

"What are you two going to do?" Brad asked.

"Visit Garrity," Eddie said. "It's not that big of a town. We'll ask around, see if we can find someone who knows Corey Henderson."

"Or Lawrence Lewis," Vince added.

Tires crunched on the gravel outside, and brakes squealed. Seconds later, Aaron burst into the room, looking bewildered. "What's going on?"

"I told you everything I know," Brad said.

"Boys, you both need to breathe," Hadley said. Vince handed her his keys. "Come on. I'll drive. I have the directions on my phone." Brad and Aaron obediently fell in line behind her.

It took forty-five minutes to reach the hospital, but Brad thought he could have done it much faster. He stopped giving Hadley driving suggestions after her second glare. The hospital looked like new construction. It stood four stories high with plenty of windows. They went inside and made their way to the front desk. Brad explained who they were, and the woman behind the desk nodded earnestly.

"We've been waiting for you," she said. She dialed an extension on her desk phone. "Pete, the Cantwell visitors are here."

They huddled around the desk waiting for their escort. The clacking of dress shoes on tile moments later announced Pete's arrival. "Hi, I'm Pete Dawson. I'm an administrator here. I'll be taking you up to the fourth floor."

The trio introduced themselves as they walked. Brad asked how Shelly was doing while they waited for an elevator.

"You can ask her yourself in just a few minutes," Pete said.

"How did she get here?" Aaron asked.

Pete offered a smile that wasn't quite apologetic. "I'm going to let Ms. Cantwell or the police tell you that part of the story. My part begins with her arrival here a few hours ago, and I can assure you, she's been given top-notch care the whole time."

After a short elevator ride, Pete led them down a linoleum-lined hallway with harsh fluorescent lights. Burgess County lacked the buzz that hospitals in Chicago and Denver had. One nurse sat at a station in the center of the ward, a bank of monitors behind her, most of them dark. The only other people were at the end of the long hallway. A pair of uniformed police officers stood outside a patient room. Pete greeted them as the group approached.

"The doc's in with her now," the first officer said. He had broad shoulders and a buzz cut on his square head. His name tag read Torres. The second officer, a lanky red head whose name tag read O'Brien, stood silently.

Pete knocked on the door before opening it a crack. He must have gotten the go-ahead because he entered the room, leaving Brad, Aaron, and Hadley with the two officers.

"Can you tell us what happened?" Hadley asked, always in detective mode. O'Brien looked to Torres who shook his head. Before either could say anything, the door opened and a short man in a white coat came out. He was bald, except for a tuft of gray hair above each ear, and he wore thick glasses.

"I'm Doctor Carlisle," he said. "Come on in."

He ushered the three into the room and closed the door behind them. A matronly nurse in black scrubs with lightning bolts all over them scribbled in a chart. Shelly lay in the bed, her head elevated. An IV tube ran from her left arm. Bruises covered her face, and she looked frail. She smiled when she saw Brad and Aaron.

"I'm glad…" Brad started and trailed off. Relief at Shelly being alive, anger at whoever took her, and worry that she was seriously injured combined in a tidal wave that took his words away.

"What happened?" Aaron asked, stepping forward and taking Shelly's hand.

"I don't remember," Shelly said. "I was climbing the rock. The next thing I remember is being chained up in a room." Tears streamed down her cheeks, and the nurse approached the bed.

"You don't have to talk if you're not ready," she said, casting a wary eye at Aaron and Brad.

"It's okay," Shelly said. "There was a guy who kept me there. He wore a ski mask. I never saw his face. Barely heard him talk. I figured out how to pick the lock on the handcuffs, and I escaped. Then, a man and his son found me and brought me here."

"She skipped the best part," Doctor Carlisle added. "She fought off a mountain lion while she was wandering in the woods."

Brad raised his eyebrows and stared at Shelly, who offered a weak smile. She turned to the doctor. "How long will you keep me?"

"Don't know," he said. "Depends on how well you respond to the IV fluids. We cleaned the lion wounds, but I want to watch them to make sure there's no infection. If all goes well, we might be able to release you tomorrow."

Shelly gave a slow nod and turned back to Aaron. "Did you bring any of my clothes from the hotel?"

Aaron shook his head. Brad noticed the disappointment in both Hadley's and the nurse's faces as they stared at him, as if questioning how he could be so clueless and inconsiderate. For a second, Brad actually felt sorry for him.

The door burst open, saving Aaron from any additional scorn. Sheriff Yellington walked in. He wore civilian clothes, and his long hair was free from its ponytail, hanging over his shoulders. Worry etched his face.

"Sorry it took me so long," he said, though Brad wasn't sure if he was addressing Shelly or the hospital staff. "Had another call to respond to." He surveyed the room, nodding at the occupants. "I need to take a statement from Ms. Cantwell. Doc, you can stay, but I'd like everyone else to leave."

"Can Brad stay?" Shelly asked. Aaron's face flushed red again.

Yellington looked at the ceiling and wrinkled his brow. "Yeah, I guess that's fine, if he can stay quiet. Just him and the doctor. The others have to go."

The nurse returned the chart to its holder at the foot of the bed and led the way out of the room, Aaron and Hadley on her heels. The sheriff commandeered the one chair in the room. He moved it bedside, so he could look Shelly in the eye. Brad and the doctor stood on the other side of the bed.

Yellington went through preliminary questions, establishing her name, confirming her address and date of birth, and verifying that she came to Broadwood for the adventure race.

"You were racing with Mr. Cummings here, but you traveled in with Mr. Reynolds. Is that correct?"

"Yes," Shelly said. "Aaron and I drove from Chicago, and Brad came up from Denver."

"That's quite a drive from Chicago," Yellington said. "Why not fly?"

Shelly looked at Brad before turning back to the sheriff. "Things had been tense between Aaron and me," she said. "We thought taking some extra time for a road trip together might be good for us."

"Tense how?" Yellington asked.

"Just normal couple stuff," Shelly said. "We saw the relationship going in different directions. Aaron was ready to settle down, you know, long term. I wasn't sure. That kind of spilled over into other things, and we were arguing a lot."

"Did the arguments ever get physical?"

"No," Shelly said. She looked back at Brad, who took a small step away from the bed.

"Do you remember the guy who checked you in at the race?"

"Kind of," Shelly said. "I remember getting the race bib."

"Had you ever seen him before?"

"No. If he had been someone I know, I would have remembered that."

"How was his behavior when he was checking you in?" the sheriff asked.

"I don't remember," Shelly said. "I just remember checking in and getting the bib."

"He seemed very interested in Shelly," Brad said. The sheriff shot him a look that clearly said to shut up. Brad took another step back.

"What do you remember about the race?" the sheriff asked.

"Not much," Shelly said. "I remember the bike ride. That's where the yellow shirts passed us. We caught them on the run, and then we did the rock climb. That's the last I remember from the race."

The sheriff moved into questions about the place where she was held. Shelly couldn't tell him how long it had taken to get from the race to the house or how long it took her to get from the house to the ridge where the mountain lion attacked her. As she described the kidnapper terrorizing her and watching her use the bathroom, rage formed a knot inside Brad's stomach. He would find the guy, and if he got a hold of him before the sheriff, he'd deliver a heaping serving of justice himself.

The sheriff moved into questions about the escape. Shelly impressed Brad with her description of picking the lock on the handcuffs, finding food and water, and using surprise to evade her attacker.

"He was wearing the ski mask when you escaped?" Yellington asked.

"Yes," Shelly said. "I never saw him without it."

"What can you tell me about the outside of the house where you were held?"

Shelly closed her eyes. When she opened them, she wore a blank expression. "I didn't get a good look at it. I was running for my life. The front looked out at a road. The back window I climbed out of led to the woods. Lots of pine trees with some oak mixed in."

"Do you know what direction you escaped in?"

Shelly shook her head. "I zigzagged a lot. I didn't want to be easy to follow. Based on where I saw the sun rise, I think I was moving east."

The sheriff had her describe the inside of the house again, guessing at dimensions. "It wasn't big," Shelly said. "It wasn't furnished. There was just the folding table and chair, the mattress, and a cardboard nightstand. The guy didn't keep any clothes in the closet."

"If we took you back to the woods and tried to retrace your steps, do you think you'd be able to help us find the place?"

"Not any time soon," Dr. Carlisle said. He crossed his arms over his chest. "Sheriff, I'm not releasing her until she's physically cleared, and with the patient's consent, I'd like to have a full psych eval done, too. She won't be leaving before tomorrow, and the next day is more likely."

The sheriff put his hands on his hips, and the two men stood as if in a staring contest, neither backing down. Without taking his eyes off the doctor, the sheriff continued, "Doc, I understand your concern. I need her to help us as soon as possible. There's been an event today that gives us a bit more urgency."

Brad stepped back to the bedside and let the anger that had been building inside him erupt. "Where was the urgency when we told you Shelly was missing?" he shouted. "You didn't investigate anything involving her unless we served it to you on a silver platter. Now you have the audacity to ask for her help? If she hadn't outsmarted the kidnapper, she'd probably dead right now, and you'd be at least partially to blame for it." Sweat beaded on his brow, and he cracked his knuckles. He looked at the peace and truth tattoos on his fingers while he seethed.

The sheriff jutted out his chin. "Maybe you're right, but I have limited resources, and I have to prioritize. Nothing we can do about that now, but I do need Ms. Cantwell's help to find where she was held and see if there's any evidence that will help us find this guy."

"And I'm telling you, it's not happening before tomorrow at the earliest and probably later than that," Dr. Carlisle said. He maintained a calm authority that said the sheriff was in his jurisdiction and would follow his rules. Brad wanted to hug him.

"I don't think I can help much, anyway," Shelly said. "Everything looked the same out there, and my brain was foggy from the dehydration and pain."

"You know where the father and son found her, right?" Brad asked. "She thinks she came from the west, so we search from that location west until we find a little house with a broken window. My team will help. We can start this afternoon."

The sheriff flipped his notepad shut without acknowledging Brad. "Doctor," Yellington said, a tone of mock deference in his voice, "when you examined Ms. Cantwell did you find any sign of a hypodermic needle being used on her?" The doctor looked surprised by the question, and the sheriff continued, "We have reason to believe the kidnapper drugged her. Are there any wounds consistent with a drug being delivered via needle?"

The doctor moved to the sheriff's side of the bed and pointed to a place on Shelly's neck. "This bruise is older than the others. We think most of the bruising came from her fall down the bluff, but this one looks consistent with needle usage."

"Can you test to see what substance was used?"

The doctor shook his head. "We've done some routine lab draws and urinalysis, but those results won't show a sedative from almost a week ago. If she'd been regularly drugged, we might pick something up, but a fast-acting, short-term sedative would have exited her system days ago."

"That's all I've got," the sheriff said. "If it's okay with the doctor, I'll send the others back in."

"Is it okay with you, Ms. Cantwell?" Dr. Carlisle asked.

She nodded. "I can talk for a few more minutes, and then I need to get some sleep."

"Mr. Cummings, a word with you," Yellington said. The sheriff led the way out of the room, followed by Brad and the doctor. O'Brien and Torres remained in the hallway, but there was no sign of Aaron or Hadley.

"I'll catch you guys up in a minute," the sheriff said to the officers. He led Brad a few feet away. The doctor continued down the corridor without looking back. "I shouldn't tell you this, since you're a civilian, and especially not after that outburst in there."

"Sorry," Brad said, looking at his shoes. He didn't mean it; he guessed the sheriff could tell that, too.

"We won't know anything for sure until we get the DNA on the syringe back and see if it's a match for Shelly," the sheriff said. "I think we're dealing with a serial kidnapper and murderer here. The victim we recovered yesterday had a similar needle mark on her neck. Same M.O. We confirmed the victim's identity as Victoria Owens. Just like your partner thought."

Brad met the sheriff's eyes and saw the most urgency he had from the lawman up until that point. He wished the sheriff had reacted the same way when he told him Shelly had been kidnapped. "Any leads?" Brad asked.

The sheriff shook his head. Before Brad could ask his next question, Hadley and Aaron appeared in the corridor. Hadley hoisted a shopping bag. "We picked up a few things for Shelly from the store down the street." Brad tried to signal her with his eyes that they were having a serious conversation. She thrust the bag into Aaron's hands. "Aaron, why don't you go in and see Shelly?"

He went through the door with a skip in his step. Brad quickly filled Hadley in on what the sheriff had told him.

"Right now, our best suspect is Lawrence Lewis, or whatever his real name is," the sheriff said. "We got a photo of him from the store where he bought the cell phone, so thanks for that information. Identifying him is priority one right now. I can have a small team start the search from the fishing cabin she slept at, going west, like you suggested, but I need most of my resources elsewhere right now."

"Why?" Hadley asked. "What's going on?"

The sheriff exhaled a long sigh and seemed to deflate in front of them. "Another woman is missing."

CHAPTER 27

Eddie exited the convenience store carrying two bottles of Diet Coke and a bag of pretzels. He hopped into the Jeep and handed a drink across to Vince. Eddie opened his, the hiss cutting through the silence in the vehicle, and swigged down half of it before saying, "No luck."

Vince smiled at his old partner. "You miss this don't you?"

"Nope."

"Come on. There's at least part of you that would rather be hunting down bad guys than fishing."

Eddie chomped a handful of pretzels, producing an impressive array of crumbs. "Let's see," he said, and more crumbs flew out of his mouth. "On the one hand, I could burn a day showing a picture of someone who may or may not be connected to a crime to people who have no idea who he is. On the other hand, I could spend the day wading through pristine water with the mountains in the background, the sun on my back, and the opportunity to catch my own dinner. Nope. Don't miss it at all."

They had visited the post office, a small restaurant bustling with the morning breakfast crowd, and the gas station, and they had nothing but a pair of drinks and a bag of pretzels to show for their efforts. Vince believed identifying Lawrence Lewis/Corey Henderson was the key to solving the case. There was too much smoke for him not to be their primary suspect. Unless they found a fingerprint or DNA from him somewhere, the police wouldn't be able to match him to his real identity, and that was only if his fingerprints or DNA were on file somewhere.

Their best hope of figuring out who this person really was, finding him, and discovering if he was involved in Shelly's kidnapping and Victoria's murder was to find someone who recognized his photo.

Eddie pointed the Jeep toward a church down the street. "Garrity Lutheran is our next stop," he said. They pulled into a gravel parking lot with a dozen spaces. Vince's phone rang. He put it on speaker, so Eddie could hear Brad and Hadley's update, as well.

Brad filled them in on Shelly's story, giving them the timeline from when Shelly disappeared to the father and son finding her at their fishing cabin.

"After you guys get done at Garrity, come join the search," Brad said. "We want to find the place where Shelly was held."

"Got it," Eddie said. "Not sure how much more we can do here. There aren't a ton of businesses, and I don't really want to go door to door. We're at the church now. We'll try there, the hardware store, and a burger joint I saw a sign for. We can head toward you after that."

"Send me your location," Vince added.

"There's one other thing," Hadley said. "Another woman is missing. She appears to have been kidnapped at the gas station where she works north of Broadwood. A coworker heard her scream, but by the time she got outside to see what was happening, a white sedan almost ran her over. She didn't get a make or model, and the security cameras don't work."

"Great," Eddie said. "Another dead end. I'm getting sick of this guy."

"There was blood at the scene this time," Brad said. Vince looked at Eddie and raised his eyebrows. "Not a lot, and the cops don't know if it's from the woman or the kidnapper, but it's at least something."

They ended the call, and Vince and Eddie approached the church. It was a small, A-frame building with a steeple on top and stained-glass windows. The paint peeled from the siding, and the steps groaned and shuddered as the men walked up. The front door was locked, which wasn't surprising for mid-morning on a Thursday.

They walked around the building and saw a one-story extension built onto the back, extending straight out from the church proper. There were a half dozen doors, most of them marked as classrooms, but the one on the end said it was the church office. Vince tried the knob, and the door swung open.

They walked into a waiting area with the lights out. Behind a reception desk, light spilled out from underneath another door. The door opened and a thin man with jet black hair stuck his head out. He fumbled on the wall for a light switch before greeting his guests.

"I'm Don Schaefer," he said. "I'm the pastor here. How can I help you?"

Vince explained who they were and what they were looking for. The man nodded along, though his eyes grew more concerned the further into the story Vince got. Vince flipped to the photo of Corey Henderson from the dating profile.

"This is the man we're trying to identify, and we think he has roots in Garrity," he said. "Have you ever seen this man before?"

The reverend took the phone and studied it closely. He brought it close to his face until it nearly touched his nose. He zoomed in on the face. Then, he handed the phone back. "Sorry, I don't know that man."

Vince took the disappointment in stride. He hadn't expected much. He flipped to the next photo, from the convenience store outside Billings. "Here's a different photo. We think it's the same man."

Schaefer held the phone up to his nose again. "Sorry," he said, as he handed it back.

Vince thanked him, and they headed back outside. Eddie drove to the hardware store and then the burger place. They had the same results at both. The owner of the hardware store didn't know him. The manager at the restaurant had all the employees and a couple customers gather round. None of them could identify the mystery man, either.

"That's it," Eddie said. "No one around here knows the guy."

"It was a long shot," Vince said.

Eddie put the Jeep on the main drag running through Garrity. It would meet Highway 287 just outside town, and they could go north to meet up with the others. He slowed as they came to the end of the town and stroked his chin.

"What's up, Eddie?" Vince asked.

"Let's check out this school," Eddie said. "Guy in the photos is young. If he lived around here, even if it wasn't in the actual city limits of Garrity, he probably went to a local school."

"Good thinking," Vince said, not wanting to put a damper on any idea since they were desperate. He didn't say that it would be a better idea if it wasn't the middle of summer.

Eddie pulled into the parking lot, which stood empty aside from a minivan parked on the opposite end. Vince followed Eddie, and they approached the front doors to the school. A sign above the entrance read "Garrity Secondary School," and a smaller sign proclaimed that it served grades 7-12.

Not surprisingly, the door was locked. Vince spied an intercom call button nearby and pressed it, but no one answered. Eddie shrugged and continued walking, staying close to the building. He peered inside windows. Vince hoped Eddie had his detective's badge with him in case someone saw them and called the police.

They found another set of doors on the side of the building, but they were also locked, as were the doors on the back end.

They continued to the final side of the building. A path led from the building to the sports fields and a maintenance shed.

"There's a light in here," Eddie said, peering into a window of the school. Vince beelined to the door and tried it to no avail. He rapped on the door several times and waited. No answer.

Eddie took his keys from his pocket and used them to bang on the closest window. A moment later, the door swung open, and a man in jeans and a faded Garrity Secondary School T-shirt appeared. He looked the two detectives up and down and slid a hand into his pocket. Probably grabbing his cell phone, Vince thought.

"Hi, my name is Eddie Fleck." Eddie didn't step toward the man and kept his tone friendly. "This is my partner, Vince Marcotte, and we're helping investigate the disappearance of a woman from Broadwood last week."

The man's expression turned serious. "From the race?"

"Yes, sir," Eddie said.

"It's Maurice," the man said, stepping forward and shaking Eddie's hand. He had leathery skin and the ropy muscles of a man who made his living doing manual labor. "I'm the facility manager at the school here, which is a fancy way of saying I clean up messes and make sure everything keeps running."

Eddie chuckled. "Sounds like you're a busy man. We won't keep you long. The woman who disappeared has been found, but we're trying to track down a suspect in the case."

"It was an abduction, then?"

Eddie shot Vince a sideways glance. Vince didn't know how much information was public, but they had come this far with Maurice, so Vince shrugged, and Eddie continued. "Yes. We're private investigators. We've been sharing information with the police, but we're not law enforcement. Just to be transparent."

"Appreciate it," Maurice said. He took off his ball cap, revealing wispy gray hair, and wiped his brow.

"One of the people the police talked to used a fake name. We're trying to track down his real identity, so we can ask him some follow-up questions. We're wondering if you could help us find someone at the school who might recognize this man. He may have attended here a few years ago."

Eddie thrust his phone forward, and Maurice accepted it. Like Reverend Schaefer, he held the phone close to his face. He nodded slowly. "Come with me," he said, motioning toward the building.

He pulled a massive key ring from his pocket and flipped through keys until he found one for the side door he had just come out of. He held it open and ushered them inside. The door clanged shut behind them, and Maurice led them through the darkened hallways until he reached the library. He held the door open and motioned for Vince and Eddie to follow.

Maurice flipped on the lights. A nearby table held a display of books on Montana history and geography. The back wall proudly proclaimed, "Garrity Reading Hall of Fame" above a list of student names and the number of books they read during the previous school year. Maurice headed toward a large desk, which had a poster plastered to the front featuring kittens peeking around stacks of books.

Maurice rummaged in the desk and came back holding an index card. "Let me see that photo again."

Eddie handed over his phone, and Maurice squinted at it. He put the index card over the top of the photo, blocking out Corey Henderson's hairline. Maurice nodded and said, "You came to the right person. I'm not too good with names, too many kids here to keep up with all of them, but old Maurice doesn't forget faces. I've seen that kid before. Wait here."

He left them at the desk and disappeared into the stacks in the reference section. Vince cocked an eyebrow at Eddie, whose expression clearly said not to get his hopes up. Maurice muttered to himself from the aisle of books. A couple minutes later, he came back with three yearbooks.

"If this is the kid I'm thinking of, he was kind of a strange bird," Maurice said. "Kept to himself. Didn't get involved in any extracurriculars. He was only here for his senior year. I think he graduated in 2019."

He spread out yearbooks from 2018, 2019, and 2020 on the librarian's desk. He cracked open the 2019 edition and flipped to the senior photos before stepping aside. Eddie and Vince crowded together and examined the fresh-faced kids in tuxedos and formal dresses.

They made it to the third page before Eddie told Vince to flip back. "Third row," Eddie said.

The third row had five pictures, three males and two females. Vince focused on each of the males and shook his head. "I'm not seeing it," he said.

"Middle photo," Eddie said.

Vince looked closer, and his eyes widened as he realized the resemblance. The kid in the photo was skinny, wore glasses, and had a mop of unruly blond hair. They were looking for an athletic-looking guy with short, dark hair and no glasses.

"Hand me that card," Vince said. Just like Maurice, he covered up the hair. He pulled up the photo on his phone and compared the two.

"Zoom in," Maurice said, rummaging through the desk once more. He produced a magnifying glass and handed it to Vince. Vince held it up to the yearbook photo, taking a close look at the eyes behind the glasses and the facial structure.

"I think we have our guy," Vince said.

Eddie looked over his shoulder and agreed. "Look at the name. Corey Holgate. Same first name, same last initial."

"What can you tell us about this kid?" Vince asked. He used a scanner on his phone to take an image of the page before shooting several close-up photos.

"Not much," Maurice said. "It's like I said. Family moved here right before his senior year. Always seems like a raw deal to me when folks do that to their kids. Anyway, they lived outside of town. Not sure where, exactly, and he kept to himself at school. I probably never said two words to him. Like I said, though, old Maurice doesn't forget faces."

"Can we take the yearbook?" Eddie asked.

"No sir," Maurice answered quickly, as if he'd anticipated the question. "If the police come asking, the principal can turn it over to them. You'll have to rely on your friend's photos."

They thanked him repeatedly on the walk back to the main door. Maurice let them out through the front of the building and walked outside a few steps with them.

"You don't know if the family is still around, do you?" Vince asked.

"No. If it doesn't happen in the walls of this building, I wouldn't know about it."

Vince thanked him again and followed Eddie to the Jeep. He retrieved his laptop from the backseat. Using his phone as a hotspot, he searched for Holgates in the area. He grew frustrated as he watched the activity wheel on the screen spin so slowly the motion was barely perceptible.

"Cell service sucks out here," Vince said. "I need an actual internet connection if I'm going to make any progress." He closed the laptop and slid it back into its case.

"I'll drop you off at the lodge," Eddie said. "It's on the way to where we're supposed to meet the others."

"Brad will be mad if I don't come searching with you guys," Vince mused.

"We don't have time to waste. Divide and conquer, I say. They're out there looking for a needle in a haystack, and you might get actual, actionable data from your searches. Make sure you see if they have any other properties in their name. Particularly the one they found the body at yesterday."

Vince tapped out a text message to let Hadley and Brad know the new plan. He attached one of the photos he'd taken of the yearbook picture. Looking at it again, the resemblance was easier to pick out. The guy had put on some muscle since graduating, lost the glasses, and cut and dyed his hair. It was an effective disguise, particularly if he wasn't well known in the community. Unless someone had a set of before and after photos, they'd never give Corey Henderson a second look as Corey Holgate.

"That's our guy, Eddie," Vince said.

"One hundred percent," Eddie agreed. "I missed it at first, but there was something about the way he held his head and the look in his eyes. Those photos are of the same person. Identifying him is one thing, though."

"Finding him is another," Vince said.

"You've got your work cut out for you."

Vince had to agree.

CHAPTER 28

Brad waved Eddie over to join the search party. The sheriff's warning that there would be limited resources came true. Eddie's arrival brought the group up to eight people—two of the sheriff's men, three Montana state troopers, and Brad, Hadley, and Eddie.

"Did you pass the name to the sheriff?" Eddie asked.

"Yeah," Hadley said.

"What did he say?" Eddie asked.

"He said, 'I'll look into it,'" Brad answered. "Typical Old Yeller response."

"Any news from the hospital?" Eddie asked. "Did Shelly remember anything else?"

"Nothing new," Brad said. He explained that Shelly's mother and sister would arrive that evening and that Aaron was still at the hospital, although Dr. Carlisle was being a stickler about visiting hours. "If we find a location that fits Shelly's description, one of the officers here will send pictures to an officer at the hospital and get Shelly to look at it. It was Yellington's compromise with the doctor."

Deputy Cooper put his pinky fingers in his mouth and whistled. The rest of the searchers gathered around. Joining Cooper from the sheriff's office was Greg Stanley, a young cop with a goatee and a lanky frame. The state troopers were all clean cut with starched uniforms and polished boots. The state ran a tighter ship than the county, Brad noted. All three looked to be in their mid-twenties with muscular builds. Blake Farmer had dark hair and a scar just above his left eye. Jake Gebhardt was the tallest of the three and also had dark hair. Sam Bender was the shortest with hair so blond it was almost white and the bluest eyes Brad had ever seen.

"Our objective this afternoon is to find the location where Ms. Cantwell was held," Deputy Cooper said. "We'll spread out and work our way through the woods slowly. Based on the victim's description of the place, it could be an abandoned outbuilding on someone's property, but some of this area belonged to the military before it was turned back to the state. It could have been an old bunker or some other facility the state never tore down. Bottom line, keep your eyes open, and if you see a structure, let us all know."

"Any concern that the kidnapper might be using the location again with his new victim?" Eddie asked. Trooper Gebhardt nodded at the question and peered at Cooper.

"We don't think so," Cooper said. "He'd have to be pretty dumb to come back to a site where a victim got away, but your point is well taken. If you see any sign of a lurker, let law enforcement know." He stared at the three private detectives as he said it.

"Watch out for wildlife, too," Gebhardt added. "Deer won't be a problem, but you don't want to surprise a bear or a bobcat."

With that, the group proceeded into the woods, stretching the distance between each member as far as they could while still being able to communicate. The fishing cabin where Shelly had spent the night was in a valley near the river. They proceeded west from there, moving in and out of trees. They walked for more than two hours without seeing anything.

They reached the base of a hill that would take them out of the valley when Trooper Bender announced he had found something. Brad froze in place. To his right, he saw Eddie do the same thing. They waited for several minutes before word passed down the line that Bender had found the remnants of a can of beans.

Brad's spirits immediately lifted. Shelly had eaten after the mountain lion attack. They were on the right trail.

They climbed the hill. Eddie lost his footing on the steep, rocky terrain a couple of times. Brad thought he might have to give him a hand, but Eddie stuck with it and made it to the top.

Once they were out of the valley, the trees grew denser. Brad immediately understood why Shelly said she wouldn't be able to find her way back to the building. It was hard enough to see during the day, and she had fled in darkness without a specific destination in mind.

They walked for two more hours. They still had plenty of daylight, but Cooper said they would have to turn around soon to get back to their vehicles before night. They agreed to search for another half hour before calling it a day.

Just before their time ran out, Eddie said, "Brad, I see something." Brad broke the rules and ran to join Eddie. Through the trees, he spied a clearing ahead of them. Eddie pointed toward the back side of the clearing, and Brad noticed the edge of a building, nestled back among the trees.

"We've got a building," Brad shouted, his heart pounding. He had been ready to write the day off, but a new energy surged through him.

The group gathered, and as they walked around the building, they saw broken glass glinting in the late afternoon sun. Cooper motioned for Brad, Eddie, and Hadley to stay back.

"Law enforcement goes in first," he said. "Greg, is the front door the only entrance?"

"Yeah, Coop," Officer Stanley shouted back.

Cooper drew his weapon and stood by the back window, while Stanley and the state troopers entered the building. The sounds of their feet scuffing the floor and shouts of "Clear, here!" rang through the woods. It took them less than a minute to declare the building free of people.

"Check this out," Trooper Gebhardt said as Cooper and the private detectives joined them inside. He pointed at a steel post drilled into the concrete floor with a ring attached to its top. "This must be where he had her chained."

"Don't touch anything," Cooper cautioned. "Let's exit carefully. I'll take pictures, and we can see if Ms. Cantwell recognizes the place. Stanley, find out who owns this property."

Cooper took pictures and texted them to Officer O'Brien, who was still at the hospital with Shelly. While he worked, Brad, Hadley, and Eddie ventured further away from the shack. They rounded a corner and found the main house. Two of the troopers, Farmer and Bender, walked around it, checking doors and shining flashlights into windows.

"Doesn't look like anyone's been here," Farmer said.

"It's a great set up for a deranged kidnapper," Brad said. "If this house has been empty for a while, no one would notice someone using the guest house."

"The guest house is hidden from the road, too," Hadley said. "We almost didn't see it, and we were out here looking for it."

A truck rattled down the gravel road. A police officer rolled down the window and asked, "Is this the place?"

"Need to go a little further," Bender answered. "I'll show you."

"That's the tech to process the scene," Farmer explained.

Bender hopped in the truck and directed the other cop to the guest house. Farmer and the others followed and found Deputy Cooper waiting outside the little building.

"He's not going to find anything," Cooper said, gesturing toward the tech's truck. "The whole place stinks of bleach; looks like it's been wiped down."

"Any word from Shelly?" Brad asked.

Cooper nodded. "Yeah. She says this is the place. She recognized the steel post. Here's your ride. I'll stay here while he processes the scene."

A van crept toward the group. Brad exchanged glances with Eddie and Hadley. Eddie shrugged as if to say there was nothing more they could do there. They piled into the van with the state troopers and Officer Stanley. The driver took them around a series of roads until they reached the spot where they'd started searching. The drive took more than an hour, but it was still faster than hiking it.

Back at the lodge, they reunited with Vince to see how his searching had gone. "Just one property in the Holgate name," Vince said. "I have an address on a Lydia Holgate. I think she's Corey's mother. Found an obituary for Lydia's husband, Simon. He died about two years ago."

"Anything on the property where they found Victoria?" Hadley asked.

Vince said, "Got a name of the property owner. No connection to Victoria or the Holgates. Or Ronda. Not much on the property you guys just came from, either. Have an owner's name but, again, no connection to any of the other people or places in this case."

"Did you share any info with the sheriff?" Eddie asked.

"Yeah," Vince said. "I talked to someone in his office. They already had the names of the property owners, but they hadn't found Corey's mom yet."

The four sat in silence. They had made plenty of progress, but they still felt a long way from apprehending Corey Holgate. If he was even the right guy. Brad checked his phone for any messages from Aaron or Shelly and went back to the room to call her.

As Brad stood, Eddie said, "Just a second. I talked to my cousin Trent a little while ago. This has been a slow week at the resort, you know, so it's been fine for us to use this as our headquarters. He has three different couples coming in on

Monday, though, so I'm going to have to get back to my official duties as river guide."

"And this place is going to transform back to a vacation resort, I assume?" Hadley asked.

"You got it. I have room in my cabin for one, but two of you will need to find a place to stay in town."

"Or we get the case wrapped up by then," Vince said.

"I like your optimism, kid," Eddie said.

"In all seriousness, I think we have to move fast," Vince said. "Something tells me Ronda doesn't have much time."

CHAPTER 29

He returned to the house just after dark. He hated to use a place he'd used before, but he hadn't taken time to scout another location. It didn't matter. They wouldn't stay long. After what happened with the last one, he wanted to kill quickly and move on. Maybe he'd burn the house when he finished, starting with the basement and the other body.

He wished he could strangle her and be done with it. Euphoria jolted through him and goosebumps covered his flesh as he thought about feeling the last breath choke out of her. Unfortunately, the timing wasn't right; she wasn't ready. She hadn't come to terms with her fate yet.

He pulled on the ski mask and grabbed the grocery bags from the car. Unlike the other properties he'd found, this one had been abandoned for more than a year. It still had running water, but the power had shut off long ago. He stepped inside and lit a battery-powered lantern. He held it up in the kitchen and looked out the pass-through bar to see her in the dining room where he'd left her.

She struggled against the ropes binding her to a ladder-back chair. He took no chances with her, tying a rope around her torso, as well as one around each leg. He duct taped each ankle to a chair leg for good measure and cuffed her hands behind her back. Just in case she tried to pull any Houdini nonsense, he'd wrapped the cuffs in duct tape, too.

Liquid had puddled at the base of the chair where she'd soiled herself. He seethed at the sight and smell. She drew back in the chair as he approached, nearly tipping it over. He backhanded her across the forehead, and a stifled scream rose from behind the tape.

He tore the tape from her legs and set to untying the ropes. She trembled as he worked the knots. As soon as the last coil of rope fell from around her, she bolted sideways. He caught her by the hair and jerked her down. She hit the ground with a thud.

He grabbed her arm and pulled her to her feet. With the lantern in one hand, he propelled her toward the bathroom. He set the lantern on the counter and fished the key to the handcuffs from his pocket. As he freed her hands from the tape and restraints, he saw that he would need a different solution for keeping her subdued; he didn't want to go through this routine every time he took her to the toilet.

"Take off your dirty clothes and clean yourself up," he instructed, keeping his voice low. She didn't move until he raised his hand and stepped closer. She moved away from him and took off her shoes, so she could remove her pants.

"Kick the shoes my way," he said. She complied, and he tossed the pair into the hallway to deal with later.

She lowered herself onto the toilet, covering as much of her body as she could. When she finished, she started to pull up her panties, but he told her not to.

"Those are dirty, too. Leave them here."

She sobbed as she stood, tugging downward on her shirt. He grabbed her arm again and led her back to the kitchen. He pulled a bag of cleaning wipes from a grocery sack and told her to clean up her mess in the other room. Under his watchful eye, she obeyed.

He took her back to the kitchen and grabbed a pair of sweatpants from a bag. "Put these on," he said. She snatched them, and he thought he recognized gratitude in her eyes as she dressed. Her dinner that night would consist of a protein bar and a warm sports drink. He handed them to her and watched as she ate and drank.

He made her sit on the floor while he had his dinner—a sandwich, a bag of chips, a cookie, and a cold soda. Then, he led her back to the bathroom. When she had finished, he took her to the closest bedroom. It had a full-size bed along one wall. The wrought iron headboard had vertical rails spaced every six inches across its length.

He shoved her onto the bed, and she sobbed again. As he approached, she kicked him in the chest with both feet. He dropped the lantern. In the darkness, she slipped past him and took off down the hall.

He sprinted after her. She flailed as she ran. She reached the front door, twisted the knob, and jerked. Her sobs erupted into full-blown wails when the door didn't budge. Just like at the last house, he had installed a deadbolt that required a key to unlock.

He rabbit-punched the back of her head, and her forehead slammed into the door, giving a satisfying thwack as it struck wood. He grabbed her arm and twisted it behind her back. She screamed, and he used his free hand to push her chin upward until her mouth closed. He kept clear of her teeth, remembering what had happened that morning.

He cuffed her wrist as soon as they reached the bedroom and threw her onto the bed. She started fighting again, but he sat on top of her, immobilizing her with his knees. He looped the handcuffs around one of the rails and secured the free end to her other wrist.

She spit at him, the hot liquid spattering across his face. He punched her in the cheek, and she cried out in pain. He wanted to hit her again, but he controlled himself.

He moved from the bed and stood in the doorway. He held the lantern high to light the room. Blood and tears matted her hair to her face.

"If you scream, I'll tape your mouth shut again," he said. "I don't want to hear a sound from you."

He collected the trash from the other rooms—her clothing and shoes, the used cleaning supplies, and the wrappers from dinner—and shoved all of it into an empty grocery bag. He'd dispose of it in the morning.

He took the bedroom next to the girl's. He lay on a twin bed. Her cries crept through the thin walls. He scrolled through the news on his phone. He saw a headline about Ronda earlier, and she was all over the news that night. Nothing in the stories indicated the police had a suspect or knew he'd taken her well south of where they were searching.

Another headline caught his attention. He clicked the story, and his stomach flipped when he saw that they had found Victoria Owens' body. He'd never even known her name, but the photo was unmistakable. The story mentioned another woman being found at a fishing cabin north of Broadwood. According to an anonymous source, the police believed all three women had been taken by the same man.

His heart pounded, and his fingers tingled. He'd found taking a woman to be almost as exhilarating as killing her. Eluding the police gave him a new sense of achievement. They wouldn't find him. He'd make sure of it. He had some business to attend to the next day to prepare for his escape. When he returned, he'd strangle Ronda and be on his way. Maybe head south to Texas or Oklahoma. Maybe east, to the Carolinas. Wherever he landed, he'd be well established with a new look and ID while the police continued scouring the Montana woods for any sign of him.

The thought gave him the greatest feeling of satisfaction he'd ever experienced.

CHAPTER 30

July 25, 2025. Burgess County, Montana.
Aaron arrived at the lodge early. Brad found him in the common room while the others were in the kitchen eating breakfast.

"I thought you'd be at the hospital," Brad said.

Aaron didn't look up from his phone. "Not today," he said. "Shelly's mom and sister got in last night, and the doctors and nurses are always coming and going. Only so much space in that little room."

The excuse seemed flimsy to Brad, but he thought better of pressing the issue any further. "When do you head back to Chicago?"

Aaron finally looked up. "Sunday. Couldn't get an earlier flight. I was going to drive Shelly's car back starting tomorrow, but she wants her sister to do it. They might go back together if the doctor thinks she can handle a long car ride."

They sat in silence, the apparent awkwardness between Aaron and Shelly adding to the already-awkward nature of the two men's relationship. Brad looked toward the kitchen.

"Hungry?"

"No thanks," Aaron said.

Brad helped himself to coffee and toast while the detectives discussed their plan for the day. Vince hadn't heard from the sheriff regarding Mrs. Holgate, so he wanted to reach out to her directly.

"I'm trying to run down more information on Corey," Hadley said, pointing to her laptop. "I gotta tell you, though, it hasn't been easy finding anything."

Eddie stood over a map of Montana, where he'd circled places related to the case: Broadwood, the house where Victoria's body was discovered, the house where Shelly was kept, and the gas station where Ronda had been abducted.

"What do you think, Eddie?" Brad asked. "Should you and I drive the corridor between these locations and see if anyone knows anything about Corey Holgate?"

Before Eddie could answer, Sheriff Yellington stomped into the kitchen, Deputy Cooper behind him. Aaron stood five feet back, looking on. The sheriff hurled a rolled-up newspaper onto the counter. Brad grabbed his coffee mug just before the paper sent it flying.

"Who's been talking to the press?" Yellington demanded. His face flushed, and his eyes filled with anger.

Brad unrolled the newspaper. The front-page headline read, "Possible Serial Killer Holds Burgess County in a Death Grip."

"Bit of hyperbole in the headline," Eddie noted. The sheriff did not look amused.

Brad scanned the article, which described the disappearance of Ronda from the gas station and the discovery of Victoria Owen. A few paragraphs down, he saw Shelly's name. The article mentioned that both she and Victoria had been stabbed in the neck with a syringe, citing "a source familiar with the investigation." That same source reported Victoria's cause of death as strangulation and said the police believed all three crimes were related. The article ended by saying police had not recovered any physical evidence from the crime scenes involving Victoria or Shelly.

"I don't know how they do things in Denver, but around here, we don't go out of our way to make things harder than they have to be," the sheriff growled. "It's bad enough that we can't find any trace of the killer. Now, my office is tied up taking phone calls from other reporters and mothers who are scared out of their minds that a psychopath is on the loose."

"Calm down, man," Eddie said. The sheriff wheeled on him, hands balled into fists. Hadley stepped between the two.

"Sheriff, we understand where you're coming from," she said. "Trust me, no one here would ever involve the media in a case without getting police clearance first. That's not how we operate." The sheriff released his fists but did not look convinced. "We worked a case with the FBI once where we knew about a raid on a compound in advance, and we never said a word to anyone. If the FBI can trust us, you can, too."

The sheriff picked up the newspaper and looked at it before tossing it down again. "That true? You really worked with the FBI?"

"A couple of times," Vince said.

"We want to solve this case as much as you do," Brad added. "Maybe more. It's personal for me. Trust me, we aren't sharing information with anyone except you."

The sheriff blew out a sigh and plopped down on a bar stool. Vince got him a cup of coffee. When the sheriff seemed to have calmed down, Vince asked if he'd gotten the message about Lydia Holgate.

The sheriff looked at each person in the room, starting with Brad and ending with Aaron, who had joined them at the kitchen bar. "No one here talked to that reporter?" They answered in a chorus of nos. "Okay, then. I located Lydia, and she's agreed to an interview. If I really can trust you, it might not be a bad idea for one of you to sit in on the interview with me."

The sheriff's sudden change of heart shocked Brad. His expression must have said so, because the sheriff continued, "I wouldn't have the name without you guys, and if she starts asking questions about how we tied her to this mess, it might help to have someone who did the digging in the room."

"When's the interview?" Vince asked.

"Nine," the sheriff said. "I'm headed there as soon as we wrap up here."

"You should go, Vince," Brad suggested. "You and Eddie identified Corey, and you did all the online searching that found Lydia's name."

"Sounds good," the sheriff said. "Let's go."

"Before you leave, I have one other idea," Hadley said. The sheriff looked at his watch and motioned for her to speak. "Since you're getting calls from the media and the public, maybe you can get them to help you. You could share a picture of Corey Holgate and ask anyone who has information about where he is to call it in."

"Nope," Yellington said. He started for the door.

"Why not?" Hadley slid off her stool and stayed a half-step behind him. "We could look for a year and not find him. You need more eyes and people who might know him to help."

"First, the photo we have of him is crap," Yellington said. "I put that out there, anyone who's seen a dude in a hat and sunglasses will call it in. Second, I don't even know that he's our guy. I agree that the check-in volunteer, Lawrence what's-his-name, is suspicious since he gave a fake ID. That doesn't mean he has anything to do with any of these cases because we don't have proof that he and Corey Holgate are the same person. I'm not about to pull the yearbook photo and put it out there and potentially ruin some kid's life based on the hunch of a private detective. We do this through solid police work."

Hadley crossed her arms. Though Old Yeller towered over her, Brad could tell she wasn't going to back down.

"First," she said, "you don't have to announce him as a suspect or issue any warnings about him. All you have to say is he was a volunteer at the race who might have information about Shelly's disappearance and the police need assistance locating him." The sheriff looked back at his deputy, who stared at his shoes and offered no help. "Second," Hadley continued, "we don't have to use the yearbook photo, and we don't even have to give out a name. We can work with the gas station photo."

"Which is crap," the sheriff repeated.

Hadley returned to the bar, popped open her laptop, and motioned for Yellington to look over her shoulder. Deputy Cooper followed. Brad crowded in, as well, eager to see what Hadley had cooked up. She navigated to a photo editing application and opened a file. The gas station photo appeared but without the hat and sunglasses.

"Where'd you get that photo?" Yellington asked. "Have you all been holding out on me?"

"No," Hadley said, the hint of a smile in her voice. "There's a lot you can do with photo editing and artificial intelligence these days. I combined the gas station photo with the dating profile picture to show what Holgate would look like without a hat or sunglasses."

The sheriff peered closer before stepping away. "Can't use it," he said. "This is a doctored photo. If this even is our guy, there's no way this would hold up in court."

Hadley angled the laptop so it still pointed at the sheriff. "We're not taking it to court," she reasoned. "We're putting it out in public to get leads on where a suspect—person of interest, that is—might be. You've used a sketch artist before, right? Consider this a high-tech, composite drawing by an automated police sketch artist."

The sheriff turned to Cooper again for support. Cooper shrugged. "She's got a point, Randy. If you want to find out why the guy gave you a fake name, this might be the best way to find him."

"I swear, these machines are making us obsolete," the sheriff muttered.

"If Holgate had anything to do with these crimes, you have to turn over every stone to find him," Hadley said.

"Fine," the sheriff said. "We'll do it. But stop saying Holgate. You have some very thin, very circumstantial evidence that ties Lawrence Lewis to Corey Holgate. Apparently, we have a leak in the investigation somewhere," he gestured toward the newspaper, disgust filling his face once more, "and I don't want a name who might not have anything to do with this getting out to the public. Maybe I'll feel different after I talk to the mother. Speaking of which, it's time to go."

The sheriff stomped toward the door. Vince grabbed a notepad and his phone and followed him. After they left, Cooper smiled at Hadley.

"You'll have to show me how you created that picture," he said. "That's pretty cool."

"It's easy," Hadley said, settling onto a stool. She opened the original picture from the gas station, prepared to demonstrate.

"Not right now," Cooper said. "Can you send the new picture to me, though?" He slid a business card across the counter to her. Then, he turned to Brad and Eddie. "I'm going to need some help tracking where we get tips from when this goes out. Our force isn't exactly the same size as Denver's."

"We'll go with you," Brad said, and Eddie nodded. "Reynolds, you up for a field trip?"

Aaron looked like he just wanted to go back to bed and sleep until his flight later that weekend, but he nodded. "Yeah, I'll go."

"Picture is sent," Hadley said. "I'm going to stay behind and keep researching. Let me know if you get anything else to work with."

•   •   •

Vince climbed into the passenger seat of the sheriff's Dodge pickup truck. It was black with sheriff's department markings on the outside and a light bar on top. Inside, a communications suite intruded into Vince's space. He positioned himself to avoid pressing any buttons and buckled in.

Yellington took them north, toward the town of Dunwood and the county hospital where Shelly was. Vince watched out the window as they passed acres of woods with businesses tucked into the side of the highway at irregular intervals. Billboards and homemade signs advertised fishing and hunting guides.

"You're responsible for the entire county?" Vince asked.

"That's what they tell me," Yellington said, eyes on the road.

"That's a lot of area. How big is your department?"

"Not big enough," Yellington said. "Of course, we don't get a lot of crimes of this magnitude. We've had our fair share of meth labs, but from what I hear most of rural America has the same problem. The rest of our calls are domestic violence and trespassing. Occasional shoplifter. All the big stuff goes to other agencies."

"Like what?" Vince asked.

"Illegal hunting or poaching goes to Fish and Wildlife. State troopers take the big car accidents and anything that crosses county lines. We've even had DEA come up to take some of the meth cases. Most days, my job is downright boring, the way I like it. This past week has been something else."

Vince stole a glance at the man and noticed the bags under his eyes. His skin had an unhealthy pallor to it. Vince suspected he wasn't eating or sleeping the way he should. Like the rest of us, Vince thought, and he wondered if he looked as tired as the sheriff.

They drove through Dunwood, past a bar and a church. The sheriff turned onto a smaller road that vanished into the hills and trees. He turned onto a narrow street that was little more than a gravel path. It seemed like every place they visited during this investigation involved a road like that one. Hadley was right: they could search for a year and not come across every hiding place in the woods.

The sheriff made one more turn onto a short driveway that led to an old shipping container that had been converted to a house. An aluminum awning next to the house served as a carport, offering cover to a beat-up truck with rust patches and a cracked windshield.

The sheriff parked behind the truck and cut the engine. "Listen," he said. "When we go in there, I'll do the talking. If you have a follow-up question to anything, look at me before jumping in. I'll give you the go ahead if it's okay to proceed. Got it?"

"Fair enough," Vince said.

The sheriff beat on the front door, and a petite woman in faded jeans and an equally faded tie-dye T-shirt answered the door. She had curly brown hair that frizzed in the humidity.

"Lydia Holgate?" Yellington asked.

"That's me," she said. "Come on in."

Based on the condition of the roads they took to get there and the looks of the truck outside, Vince expected to find a sparsely furnished home in a state of general disrepair. Instead, Lydia led them into a clean, bright space. The door was situated in the middle of the structure. To the left were two bedrooms, with a recessed third door between them. Vince assumed it was the bathroom. Lydia took them to the right and into the living room. A leather sofa faced a fireplace with a flat-screen television mounted above it. Matching chairs and a loveseat faced each other on either side of the couch. Beyond the living room, Vince spied a small kitchen with granite countertops and stainless-steel appliances. A wide-board hardwood floor ran throughout the entire structure. Skylights provided plenty of natural light, with floor lamps and wall sconces accenting the space.

Lydia sat on the loveseat, curling her legs underneath her. The sheriff and Vince each took one of the chairs opposite her, and the sheriff made introductions.

"We were surprised to find you in Dunwood," Yellington said. "We thought you lived further south, in Garrity."

"We rented a place outside Garrity for a year," Lydia said. "We thought if we were closer to the school, it would be easier for our son to get involved in extracurricular activities, but he never did. We moved up here to be closer to Simon's work right after our son graduated."

"Your son is Corey Holgate," Yellington said. "Is that right?"

"Yes," Lydia said. The sheriff asked if he lived at the house with her, and she shook her head.

"Anyone else live here?"

"No, not since my husband died."

The sheriff nodded and consulted his notepad. "We've had a hard time locating your son," he said. "Can you tell us where to find him?"

Lydia frowned. "I'm afraid not. He went to Texas right after graduation and worked for an oil company for a couple years. Not sure what he did for them, but it sounds like it was dangerous, and they paid him well. We encouraged him to come back up here and go to school, but he wasn't interested in college. He found a place outside Missoula and did odd jobs around there. I haven't seen him since Simon died."

Vince scribbled notes as she talked. He shot the sheriff a glance, but the sheriff didn't look his way. Instead, Yellington asked the next question, "As far as you know, is he still in Missoula?"

"Oh no," Lydia said. "After Simon died, he moved back to Texas. I think he's doing oil work again." A beep emitted from the kitchen, and she hopped up. "Coffee's ready. Cream and sugar?"

"Black is fine," the sheriff said.

"A splash of cream for me," Vince said.

Lydia busied herself in the kitchen, and Vince looked around the room. A few framed photos adorned the mantle above the fireplace. He walked to it and looked at the pictures. There was one of the family and two individual shots of Corey—his yearbook photo and another of him wearing a cowboy hat. In that photo, he looked much more like the yearbook Corey than the one posing as Lawrence Lewis, though Vince could see the resemblance.

Lydia returned with a tray of coffee and a package of chocolate chip cookies. "I know it's early for sweets," she said, glancing at a clock across the room, "but there's nothing better than a cookie with your coffee."

With refreshments served, they jumped back into the interview. Yellington took the lead again. "Does the name Lawrence Lewis mean anything to you?"

Lydia furrowed her brow. "No. Nothing."

"Corey never went by the name of Lawrence or Larry or anything like that?"

"No," Lydia said.

"Anyone in the family named Lawrence or Lewis? Maybe someone's maiden name?"

Lydia shook her head. "What's this about?"

The sheriff unfolded a piece of paper from his shirt pocket and set it on the coffee table between him and Lydia. It was the gas station picture. "Do you recognize that man?"

Lydia picked up the paper and studied it. She nodded slowly. "It looks like Corey, but it's hard to tell for sure with the hat and glasses."

"Vince, do you have the other picture? The one your friend put together?"

Vince opened a text message from Hadley and tapped on the photo. He passed the phone to Lydia.

"This is the same photo but altered to remove the hat and sunglasses. Is that Corey?"

Lydia stared at it for a long minute. "I don't know," she said. "It does look like him, but his hair is different."

"That picture was taken outside a gas station in Billings," Yellington said. "The person in the photo went inside and purchased a prepaid cell phone. He registered as a volunteer for an adventure race in Broadwood, using the phone number for the cell phone purchased at the store. We know the volunteer at the race is the person in this picture."

"And Corey was the volunteer?" Lydia asked.

"That's the thing," the sheriff said. He leaned forward, elbows on his knees, and lowered his voice to a near whisper. "The volunteer said his name was Lawrence Lewis, but there's no record of a Lawrence Lewis his age in the area. The address he gave us was bogus, and the phone has been deactivated. We believe Corey was the volunteer. Now, why would he lie to me and the race organizer about who he is and where he lives?"

Lydia drew further back into the loveseat. "I don't know," she said. "Maybe it's not him."

The sheriff moved forward in his seat, so close to the edge Vince thought he might fall off. He ran his hand through his ponytail and continued. "A woman disappeared from the race. We've found her, but now another woman is missing, and it looks like the two cases could be related. I need to talk to anyone who might have any information about what happened at the race, so it's crucial that I find the person who called himself Lawrence Lewis, and all signs point to it being your son."

He let the statement hang in the air. Vince looked at him, eager to ask questions in a friendlier tone. He feared they were losing Lydia. The sheriff saw him but shook his head. He leaned back in the chair and crossed his legs.

"Ms. Holgate, I need to know where we can find your son," the sheriff said.

"I told you," Lydia said. "He's in Texas. Now, if you're done here, I have some other things to attend to."

"We're not done," Yellington said, not making a move.

"When's the last time you talked to Corey?" Vince blurted. The sheriff squinted at him through angry eyes.

"I don't know. A month or so ago. He doesn't get to talk much while he's away working."

"How do you talk to him?" Vince asked. "Does he call you, or do you call him?"

"He usually calls me," Lydia said. "Sometimes, I call him."

"Can you always get through?" Vince hoped they had just scored a break.

"He doesn't always answer," Lydia said, "but I can leave a voicemail for him."

"Can I get the phone number you use?" Vince asked. "And is it the same number he calls from?"

"Yes, it's the same number," Lydia said. She withdrew her phone from her jeans pocket and read the number to them. "I still don't see how Corey could have anything to do with this. He's in Texas." She looked at the picture again. "I don't think that's him at all."

"It would help us if we could clear that up with him," Yellington said. "If you talk to him again, will you ask him to call me? You have my number."

Lydia said she would, and she stood, motioning them toward the door. The sheriff stood and let her usher them out of the house. They'd barely made it out of the driveway before the sheriff scolded Vince for interrupting the interview.

"We have a phone number for Corey now," Vince said. "I didn't think you were going there, and it looked like we were going to lose her. If he uses this phone regularly, it's his non-burner."

"Which means?"

"We can find out where calls have been made from, possibly a billing address. It gives us a foothold for locating Corey."

The sheriff stopped the truck and grabbed his notepad. "I'll call it into Deputy Cooper and see if he can start working on a warrant."

"Sounds good," Vince said. He didn't tell the sheriff he'd already texted the number to Hadley, and she'd track down every bit of data they could get related to the phone while Cooper was still filling out forms.

"You ask me, this is a waste of time," Yellington added. "Mrs. Holgate isn't convinced it's even her son in the picture. If we had any other leads this would go to the bottom of the list."

Vince disagreed. Lydia couldn't reconcile the son she knew with someone who would use a fake name, lie to the police, and show up in Montana when she thought he was in Texas. That affected her perception of the photo. To the sheriff, he simply said, "Maybe so, but if we rule out Corey Holgate as a possible ID on Lawrence, then we know to keep looking. Progress, right?"

The sheriff grunted and pointed the truck south on Highway 287.

CHAPTER 31

The Burgess County Sheriff's Office was not staffed for a high-profile case. Besides Deputy Cooper, there were only two other officers present, a dispatcher named Warren—Brad wasn't sure if that was his first or last name—and Officer O'Brien, who had been at the hospital. While the phones weren't ringing off the hook, calls came in at a steady clip.

Cooper's first order of business had been to publish a BOLO, or be on the lookout, for the person they believed was Corey Holgate. He didn't include a name or suggest they suspected Corey of anything. The notice simply said he "might have information related to ongoing cases in Burgess County." Cooper sent the notice to the office's media contacts in the region, as well as other sheriff's offices throughout the state.

With that done, he set up a war room in the conference room. He showed Eddie, Brad, and Aaron the state map on the wall with markings for each of the crime scenes and locations they knew about. He pointed to a phone at the center of the table.

"When Warren gets a call that has a tip about Holgate, he'll route it back here. Write as much information as you can on this form and mark the location on the map."

"Got it," Eddie said.

Cooper left them, and the three men settled into chairs around the table. For the first hour, they didn't take any calls, and Eddie passed the time by telling the younger men stories about fish he'd caught at the resort. Brad had never gotten into fishing, not physical enough for him, so he struggled to understand how Eddie could get so excited by the prospect of landing a trout, especially since he did it pretty much every day.

"Is this what it's like to be a cop?" Aaron asked.

"Sometimes," Eddie said. "There are days when it's wall-to-wall excitement, but that usually means someone else has had an awful day. Trust me, this is better."

"What do you do these days, Reynolds?" Brad asked.

"Accountant," Aaron said. "Not exciting, but it pays the bills."

"Still fighting?"

"Now and then. Not as often as I did before. I'm the old man at the gym now. Tell you the truth, though, I miss it. I haven't worked out in a week."

The phone chirped, and Eddie took the call. He scribbled down information but didn't ask many questions. He hung up and shrugged. "One of the volunteers from the race. Said he recognized the picture as the check-in guy."

The phone rang again, and Brad took a turn answering. It was another volunteer from the race. Brad logged the information, thanked the woman for her call, and flopped back into his chair. "Tell us something we don't know," he said.

They didn't get a call for another half hour. Brad answered it again.

"Hey, I think I saw the guy in the picture you all put out," a man said. Brad took his name down as Jared Sherman and asked where he saw the person of interest.

"In Stanton," Jared said. "It was Sunday or Monday. I work at a gas station, and he filled up his car and bought a pizza."

"What time was that?" Brad asked.

"Probably around 8:00 or 9:00."

"How did he pay?"

"Cash," Jared answered. "I remember because he wasn't pleased about having to prepay. I told him if he used a credit card, he could pay at the pump."

Brad walked through the rest of the form with him, confirming that the shopper didn't have anyone else with him, he didn't say anything that would indicate where he was going, and Jared didn't see what kind of car he was driving.

"Does your station have security cameras?" Brad asked.

"No," Jared said. "Not much of a need out here."

Brad took his phone number and relayed the information to Eddie and Aaron. Aaron found Stanton on the map and added a marker for it. Eddie stood at the map, hands on his hips, deep in thought. Finally, he looked at the younger men and said, "Look, there's a pattern."

He pointed out Broadwood on the map. "Almost everything else has happened south of here," he said. "Shelly was kidnapped here and taken south. She ended up wandering through the woods all night and came out further north, where the fishermen found her and took her to the hospital even further north, but the house was south of Broadwood. Victoria Owen was taken from Pocatello, way south, and kept at a house not all that far from where Shelly was held. Stanton is south of Broadwood, too. My hunch is that Corey Holgate lives somewhere around Stanton. He finds empty or abandoned houses to hold his victims in, and he can stay close to home."

Brad turned that over in his head. It made sense. Shelly said her kidnapper left every morning and came back late in the evening. He must have had somewhere else to go in the area. Maybe a job or maybe he had a house. He could have even rented a motel room while he waited to decide when to kill his victims. If Eddie was right, the police could narrow their search considerably.

"Seems flimsy to me," Aaron said. "This guy could be anywhere. For all we know, he took Ronda to Canada. Or killed her already and is on his way to Mexico. My guess is we'll never see him again. I'm just glad Shelly's okay."

Aaron stared at his phone screen, and Eddie gave him a withering look. Brad pulled up Stanton on his cell phone and searched for motels near it. There weren't many, but there was a place further south on 287 that looked like it would accept cash payments. Brad pinned the location. When they wrapped up at the sheriff's office, he and Eddie could stop by and see if anyone there recognized Corey Holgate.

●　　●　　●

He counted his money and chastised himself for getting that low on cash. He peeled off a few bills to handle the morning's expenses and shoved his wallet into a backpack. He tucked the bag into the passenger seat of his truck and went to the motel office to turn in the key. It was an old school bronze key attached to a paper disk with the room number on it. The television only pulled in half the channels it was supposed to; the shower ran two temperatures, freezing and scalding. He wouldn't miss the place.

The owner wasn't in the office, which suited him fine. He'd used the motel during the day, sleeping somewhere else at night. He didn't want to answer questions about that odd arrangement, if the owner had even noticed. He slapped the key on the counter and went back to the truck.

He drove south a few miles to a gas station he knew sold kerosene. After paying in cash, he loaded three full jerry cans into the back of the truck and pictured the flames consuming the house, perhaps spreading to the nearest trees. Everyone would freak out, and with the focus on containing the blaze before it became a full-fledged wildfire, he'd slip away unnoticed. All the evidence of his crime would burn in the fire, and the police would spend months trying to find him.

He looked at the newspaper in the front seat of the truck. The police knew the three women were connected, but they didn't have a clue who was behind it. He was winning the game, but he couldn't elude them forever. He'd make his move that night.

He stopped in a drugstore, keeping his hat pulled low and his sunglasses on. An employee near the front door asked to help him, but he waved the kid off and continued down the aisles. He picked up a bottle of sleeping pills and a box of latex gloves. Thinking the purchase too memorable, he added a bottle of vitamins and some toothpaste. He stopped in the snack aisle and grabbed a bag of tortilla chips and some chocolate-covered pretzels. He added a gossip magazine when he got to the register, hoping he'd added enough miscellany to cover his necessities.

Back in the truck, his stomach growled. He'd skipped breakfast. The woman had been a fighter that morning, trying to run when he took her to the bathroom. He didn't feed her or give her water as a result. Instead, he left her chained facedown on the bed, a strip of duct tape running over her mouth and across her blond hair. He'd tied her legs to the foot of the bed to limit her movement. She could thrash around all day, for all he cared, really tire herself out. Maybe he wouldn't even need to drug her when he returned that evening to end it.

A diner across the street advertised a weekday brunch special. He went inside and took a spot at a back table. The aroma of pancakes, sausage, and eggs cooking on a flat-top griddle filled his nostrils, and his mouth watered. A man, woman, and two kids occupied a booth on the other end of the establishment. The younger of the two kids, a toddler, held the parents' attention with his crying, while the older girl colored in a kids' menu. They didn't look up when he came in.

The waitress stopped at his table, and he ordered a sausage, egg, and cheese biscuit with a side of home fries and a coffee. The waitress wore a strange look as she stood by his table. Probably wondering why he had his sunglasses on. Let her wonder.

A television at the end of the bar played a national morning news show. The hosts blabbered on about finding the best deals on back-to-school shopping and even had a guest expert to tell viewers how to save the most money. He didn't know how one became an expert on back-to-school shopping and found himself getting annoyed with the program.

The waitress brought his meal, still looking at him in a way that made him uncomfortable. He turned his body in the booth, looking away from her. She left, and he dug into breakfast. It was the best food he'd had in a while, and he savored each bite.

He thought about his financial situation. He'd saved up money from the crappy part-time job he had helping a local rancher do grunt work. It involved a lot of lugging heavy stuff and shoveling stables, but the rancher paid him in cash, and his hours were flexible, which allowed him time to go back and forth between the motel and the house. He'd burn through that money quickly, though. He needed to purchase a new vehicle, so he could navigate the back roads to Texas unnoticed. After he finished with the woman, he had to curtail extravagances like a breakfast out. He could sleep in the car and save money on hotels.

"Anything else, dear?" The waitress interrupted his thoughts.

"No," he said, looking away. "Actually, if you have a to-go cup of coffee, I'd appreciate it."

She disappeared behind the counter and came back a couple minutes later with a styrofoam cup, steam wafting from the plastic lid. She slid a piece of paper onto the table. "You can pay at the register when you're ready. No rush."

He lingered a moment longer, knowing he'd have time to kill before he needed to go back to the house. He didn't want to spend a minute longer with the woman than he had to, and he liked to kill them in the evening.

He sauntered to the register, and the waitress came from the back and accepted the check and a twenty. He glanced at the television as it switched from national to local news. His heart dropped. Two pictures of him filled the frame. On the left, he wore his hat and sunglasses, the same ones he had on in the diner. The photo on the right showed what he looked like without them. He wondered where anyone had gotten those photos.

"I'll just run to the back and get you some change," the waitress said. She backed away from the counter, eyeing the family at the other table cautiously. If they noticed anything amiss, they didn't react.

He started to tell her not to bother with the change but kept quiet. Since he had started killing, he had learned that when situations came up unexpectedly, the most important thing was to make a decision and live with it. He never dwelled on the consequences of those decisions, never tried to think about long-term implications. The key was to change the situation in his favor at that moment, and the future could sort itself out.

He dashed around the counter, noticing the father from the other table look up as he did. He pushed his way through the swinging door with the round window at head height and assessed the kitchen. To his left, a cook in a greasy apron sweated behind the griddle. To his right, the waitress stood among shelves filled with dry goods and held a cordless phone in her hand.

He sprinted at her, and she screamed. The cook started toward them. The man snatched the phone from the waitress. He disconnected the call and smashed the device into her face. She cried out again.

He turned as the cook arrived. The cook was tall and stocky but soft in the middle. The cook took a swing, which the man easily sidestepped. As the momentum of the punch turned the cook the other way, the man stepped into a punch of his own, drilling the cook's unprotected jaw. The cook staggered, and the man used a quick kick to sweep his leg out from underneath him.

The cook hit the ground in a heap, and the man kicked him in the head.

The waitress started for the door. He grabbed her from behind, clamping his hand over her mouth. He kept pressure on her chin, so she couldn't open her jaw and bite him like Ronda had done.

He dragged her away from the supplies and into the cooking area. He spied a set of knives on a counter next to the griddle and grabbed the biggest one. The woman kicked and thrashed. The man glanced at the door. No one watched. If the family had been frightened by the waitress's screams, they would probably take off and call the police when they were a safe distance away. It would take a minute or two to collect the kids, buckle them in the car, and go. He needed to move fast.

He stabbed the knife into the woman's neck and jerked it out. Blood spurted, and he repeated the movement two more times. He dropped her. He ran to the cook and gave him the same treatment.

He spied a sink in the back of the kitchen, but even though he was a red, sticky mess, there was no time to waste cleaning up. He grabbed a stack of towels. A steel door stood in the corner, past the sink. He kicked the release bar to push it open and burst into the daylight. He exited to the back of the property, where two vehicles were parked, probably the employees' cars. A dumpster sat next to the cars. He rushed to the corner of the building and peeked out. He didn't see anyone, so he crept along the side of the diner and peeked around the next corner. A station wagon peeled out from the parking lot, scattering gravel in its wake. They'd probably gotten photos of his license plate, but he could solve that problem later. The most important thing was to keep moving.

He slid inside the truck, throwing the knife onto the passenger floorboard. He cranked the engine and took off, not thinking about where he was going. He almost sideswiped another truck as he pulled onto the street, eliciting a flurry of honks.

He slowed down and mopped blood from his face and chest with the stack of towels as he drove. He turned toward the highway and headed south.

A police cruiser screamed past him going north, lights flashing and siren blaring. His heart nearly stopped. He took the next exit and wandered through side roads. He found a dirt road that led to a pond. He parked under an oak tree and climbed out of the truck. Seeing nobody around, he dipped one of the diner towels in the pond water. He stripped out of his clothes and sponged away the cook's and waitress's blood. He mopped up the inside of the truck, too, cleaning blood from the steering wheel, driver's seat, seatbelt, and floorboards. He found a change of clothes in his backpack.

He pulled a shovel from the back of the truck and dug a hole for his clothes and the towels. He threw the truck's plates in, too, but kept the knife. He covered the hole and installed his last set of spare plates on the truck. He had planned for contingencies. Everything would be okay. He just needed to get back to the house unnoticed, finish with the girl, and hit the road for Texas. Everything else would take care of itself.

He slid behind the wheel and turned the key. The truck sputtered but did not start. He slapped the dashboard and tried again. Again, it sputtered but would not turn over. He took the key out of the ignition before slipping it back inside and trying once more.

The engine didn't even sputter. He got an empty click, like dry firing a rifle. He cursed the truck, his bad luck, the waitress, and the family of four. Popping the hood, he looked at the engine. Corrosion covered the battery cables, clamps, and battery posts.

He found a wrench in the back of the truck and loosened the cables. Using a pocketknife, he scraped the clamps as clean as he could. He set to work on the battery posts next. When he finished, he struck the positive terminal with the blade of the knife and a spark emitted.

Hopeful, he reattached the cables and closed the hood. He slid back into the driver's seat and gave the key a go. The truck coughed like an old man, gave a stronger pull, and finally turned over. He put it in gear and retraced his tracks back to the highway. He needed to finish the girl, burn the house, and get out of the state. It couldn't wait any longer.

He turned north and continued driving until he saw police lights in the distance. He immediately pulled off the road. The newspaper headline in the front seat mocked him; at that moment, he didn't hold anything in a death grip. Everything was slipping from his grasp and spiraling outside his control.

He made his decision. He crossed the median and turned back to the south. There were other routes to get back to the house and get the job done.

CHAPTER 32

Hadley plugged the phone number into a search window and waited for the results. She chose a more powerful site than standard phone lookups, but it was not, strictly speaking, legal. She could get information in minutes that the police would take days getting a warrant to track down. Nothing she collected could be used as evidence in an eventual prosecution. Normally, she'd work through the process and get clean information the authorities could do something with. They had a ticking clock, though, and none of them knew how much time Ronda had left. That changed the equation.

The report completed, and she entered her credit card information to purchase the full rundown. She opened the document and scrolled through the pages, skipping the legal disclaimers at the front and scanning for information that would be useful.

The phone belonged to Corey Holgate, which did not surprise Hadley. The Texas number and billing information did not surprise her either. She kept scrolling; the first two pages had surface level data that did not matter to Hadley. She went deeper and found what she was looking for.

She pulled up a table of calls from the previous billing cycle, which cut off a week before the race. Corey didn't make many calls with that phone, but there was one to his mother. The report showed that it originated in western Montana. She couldn't get specific tower information from the report, but Corey had not been in Texas when he last spoke with Lydia.

She scrolled further, hoping to find something that showed he had been in Idaho when Victoria had disappeared. He had no calls from that date, but a week before, his mother had called him. They had a short call, less than a minute, but the report data showed his end of the call pinged against an Idaho-based tower.

"You never counted on us finding your mother," Hadley said to the computer screen. "And you never thought she'd give up your phone number. Now, we've got you."

Her own phone buzzed with a text message from Brad. He asked her to research properties within a fifteen-mile radius of the town of Stanton, Montana.

"Try to find something that's vacant or abandoned," the message instructed. Hadley sent him a thumbs up. Energized by the cell phone data, she navigated to a property search for Burgess County.

She found plenty of records for houses within that radius, but she didn't know how to determine what was vacant. The property records showed ownership changes, but they didn't show sales listings or pending sales. She called Vince.

"That phone number was golden," she told him, recounting what she had found. "Maybe the sheriff can get someone to go back out to Mrs. Holgate's place and see if she has any additional information about her son."

"I'll ask," Vince said. "We're almost at the sheriff's office now. I'm going to check in with the other three. What's up?"

"Brad thinks the area around Stanton, Montana, has potential for finding Ronda. It's between Broadwood and Garrity, and it's close to where most of the action has been. I'm trying to find properties that fit the profile of the other two kidnappings. How do I locate vacant properties in the records database?"

"You can't," Vince said. "There's no public data available that would show that."

Hadley's energy for the task slipped a few notches. "What do I do, then?"

"First, we're looking for a place in the woods, away from a development. So, look for lot sizes with at least a couple acres."

"That's most of the houses around there," Hadley said.

"Keep your results open, and you'll need to do a couple of different searches. One, you can look up the sales and rent listings on any real estate site. They all feed off the same MLS database. That will show you what's available, but that doesn't mean it's vacant. But it's a start."

"Got it. What else?"

Vince lowered his voice. "You need to check recent utility records. See if someone's electricity or water usage dropped from its normal rate to almost nothing. That's a good sign the property is vacant."

"We're talking about hacking here," Hadley said.

"Affirmative."

"You can't talk about this because the sheriff is in the car with you."

"Affirmative."

"No problem. I can hack."

The real estate listings were easy enough to obtain. There were only four properties for sale within the area they were looking for. One of them was close to the highway, so Hadley eliminated it. The other three were similar to the locations where Victoria and Shelly had been held.

It took additional effort to get into the utility records. The county had a stronger firewall than she had anticipated, but she found an entrance and worked her way to the search she needed. She started by looking at the three houses from her for sale list. One of them showed a significant drop in water usage from the previous six-month average. Two of them had private wells, which complicated things. She bookmarked the listing that looked vacant and widened her search parameters to all properties in the area.

She realized it would take her more time than she had to look up each property's utility records individually. She poked around and found a report she could run. It looked like it was intended for the county manager's use, but since she had gotten behind their firewall, she had full control. She ran a report for electricity billing from six months earlier and saved the results in a separate window. She re-ran the report but asked for the results from the last billing cycle.

With the two reports side by side, she scanned each property looking for a precipitous drop. She found two more properties that looked like decent candidates. Back on the property records search she recorded the owner information for each of the three properties. One showed the county as the owner; probably a foreclosure, she thought. It took a few minutes with an additional search tool to produce phone numbers for the owners of the other two.

The first owner, Wendy Slauson, did not answer, and the call never went to voicemail. Hadley assumed it was a landline without an answering service. She moved to the next owner, Chad Olson. He picked up on the first ring.

"Hi, Mr. Olson. My name is Hadley Collins, and my team is researching property ownership in Burgess County. Can you tell me if you still reside at the house on Wildcat Road?"

"Not interested," he said. The call ended.

Hadley dialed again, and the call went straight to voicemail. She bit her lip and tried once more. He picked up on the first ring, "I said I'm not interested."

"Wait," Hadley said. "One question. Yes or no. Do you still live on Wildcat Road?"

He didn't answer. She checked her phone. He had hung up while she was talking. Satisfied that she had more than nothing to show for the morning's work, she gathered her laptop and notes and took Vince's car to the police station.

•   •   •

The tips had stopped coming in. Brad was ready to end his volunteer police work and drive out to the motel to see if Corey Holgate had stayed there. Before he could voice his idea, the sheriff and Vince bounded into the room.

"What've we got?" Yellington asked.

Eddie nodded at Brad, who led the sheriff to the map and showed him where the calls had come in from. "Aside from the race volunteers, our potential sightings are south of Broadwood at the bottom edge of the county. We think he's operating out of there somewhere."

"Makes sense," the sheriff said. "Except, if he's seen the news, he knows that we know about the other two. My guess is he's probably packed up and headed someplace else by now. We'll search that area, but based on what we've seen of this guy, he covers his tracks well."

Brad suppressed an eye roll. Maybe he wanted to manage expectations, but Sheriff Yellington had to be the most pessimistic investigator he'd ever come across. At least he'd committed to searching the area. Brad kept quiet about the motel. He'd do that on his own, outside the sheriff's official purview.

"Any luck with the mother?" Eddie asked.

"We got a phone number," the sheriff said. "Deputy Cooper is working the warrant for it, so we can review the data and see if Holgate has even been in the state."

"He has," Hadley said from the doorway. Her cheeks were flushed and her eyes danced with excitement.

The sheriff scowled and crossed his arms. "How would you know that?" he asked. "How would you even have the phone number?" He cast a suspicious look at Vince.

"It's better that you don't know my sources," Hadley said. "Keep working the warrant angle in case you need something admissible, but I can tell you for a fact that Corey Holgate made phone calls from Idaho and Montana. He hasn't been in Texas."

"Or at least his phone hasn't," the sheriff said. Deputy Cooper crowded into the shrinking room.

"What, your theory is that someone who looks like Holgate stole his phone in Texas, called his mother up here, committed these crimes, and posed as a volunteer at the race?" Eddie asked. "Nonsense. If someone's trying to set Holgate up, why not identify himself as Holgate on the volunteer form?"

The sheriff looked exasperated, and Brad didn't feel one bit sorry for him. He had an actual homicide detective in the room, but he insisted on following his own plodding course.

"I have three candidate properties, too," Hadley said. She popped open her laptop. "I found three places that have indicators of being vacant, and they would fit the abductor's M.O."

"What indicators?" Yellington asked. "Know what...never mind. I don't want to know. Let's see the properties."

Hadley mapped each of the three locations. The sheriff watched the screen before pinning each of the places on the wall map. He plopped into a chair in front of the computer. "You got a satellite view?"

Hadley switched the map layers to bring up satellite imagery of the area. She zoomed in on the first property. It covered several acres. Looking over the sheriff's shoulder, Brad saw a main house and several outbuildings, along with plenty of tree cover.

Hadley moved to the next property, which was not as large, and only had one building. The building was hidden in trees, though. Brad squinted at the screen. The road into the property approached from the south. To the north, just beyond a band of forest, a larger road skirted the area. The abductor would have to hike in and out, but it was possible to stage a car near the big road for a cleaner getaway.

Hadley pulled up the final candidate. Like the first property, it sprawled with a large building and several outbuildings. It featured plenty of open space, with sparse greenery.

"I like the ones with the trees better," the sheriff said. Brad hated to agree with Yellington, but he liked the others better, too. "Got any ownership information?"

"Yes," Hadley said. "One is for sale. The other two have owners, but I haven't been able to make contact." She explained her earlier calls.

"How far away are we?" Brad asked. "We should just go check them out."

"I think I've explained about my limited resources," the sheriff said. "Me and Coop will talk this over and decide what to do."

Brad wanted to announce that the detectives' partnership with the police had outlived its usefulness. He felt confident he could take down Corey Holgate himself, particularly if Holgate didn't know he was coming. Before he could say anything, the conference phone rang. Aaron put the call on speaker and reached for an information form.

"This is Phil Jeffries," a voice high-pitched with panic said. "My family and I saw that guy on the television. He went in the back, and someone screamed."

"Slow down," Yellington said. "Are you in any danger right now?"

"No," Phil said, panting. "I don't think so."

"Are you driving?"

"Yes."

"I need you to pull over safely, put the car in park, and let's have a calm conversation," the sheriff said.

The call took Brad back to his EMT days; he heard numerous 911 calls where the dispatcher had to settle people down to get enough information to help them.

"I'm parked," Phil said.

"Where are you?"

"In Stanton." Brad and Eddie made eye contact, exchanging a silent "knew it" moment.

"Who did you see?" Yellington asked.

"We were in the 287 Diner, south of town," Phil said. "It was dead in there. Sorry, that's a bad choice of words."

"Go on," the sheriff said. He seemed on the verge of losing his patience.

"There was another guy at a back booth. He went to the register to pay, and we saw a notice on the news that the police were looking for him. It was the same guy. I'm sure of it. Same hat and sunglasses and all that."

"Then what happened?"

"The waitress went back to the kitchen, and he ran around the counter. The waitress screamed, and it sounded like there was a fight going on back there."

"What did you do?"

"I got my family packed up and we left. We drove into town, and I called it in."

"Sheriff, we got another call," Officer O'Brien said from the doorway. "Someone just went in the 287 Diner down south and didn't find any workers. He called out to see if anyone was there, and when no one answered, he went in the back and found two dead workers. Blood everywhere."

Phil's breaths grew quicker over the speakerphone. "Coop, finish this up," the sheriff said. "I'm taking the other call."

Brad paced around the conference room as Cooper got Phil's contact information and confirmed he didn't have anything else to share. Behind a lectern at one end of the room, Brad found a stack of topographical maps of the county. He shoved one in his pocket.

The sheriff returned with a red face and beads of sweat dotting his brow. He ran his hand through his ponytail. "Coop, I'm going to call the state troopers and see if we can get roadblocks north and south of the county on 287. We want to check everyone coming and going. You start assembling our squad. We're going to the three properties these guys identified, and if we don't find anything, we'll keep searching every house within twenty-five miles of Stanton. Got it?"

Cooper nodded, and both men bustled out of the room. "I'm going, too," Brad declared.

"If you're in, I'm in," Aaron said.

"Boys, this is a police matter now," Vince said.

"I'd agree with you, except my expectations for the sheriff's office are extremely low," Eddie said. "They need our help, whether they want it or not. Let's head out now. We can stop at the lodge on the way and pick up some supplies and then meet them on the way."

"What kind of supplies?" Vince asked.

Eddie grinned. "Trent, my cousin who owns the lodge? He's kind of a doomsday prepper. His basement is basically a bomb shelter. Non-perishable food and water and...well, he has plenty of fire power down there, too."

"No," Vince said. "We leave the shooting to the professionals."

Eddie grinned again, and Brad knew it didn't matter what Vince said. They were bringing guns with them.

They gathered their belongings and made it to the lobby before the sheriff stopped them. "Bugging out?"

"Kind of," Brad said. "We need to make a stop, but we plan on searching these properties."

The sheriff looked skyward and chewed his lip. "I'm breaking every protocol, but we wouldn't be this far without you. You can come with us. It would actually help if you could identify Holgate as the volunteer from the race. Assuming we find him, that is. And, assuming it's Holgate."

"Glad to help," Brad said.

"You go where we say to go, and you do what we say to do," the sheriff said. "Understood?"

"Got it."

Vince declared that they didn't need all five of them hanging onto the police's search, so he would stay at the lodge and continue researching alternate properties. Brad agreed that having some back up places to search made sense, but he also knew the guns were a big reason Vince wouldn't go. Too much history from Vince's military days. He would help them more back at the lodge.

Eddie, Vince, and Hadley departed for the lodge in Vince's car. Brad and Aaron would follow the police in Brad's truck and let Eddie know when and where to join them. Brad stared at his tattooed fingers again as his uncle's lesson echoed back to him through the years.

CHAPTER 33

Six Years Earlier.
March 24, 2019. Monument, Colorado.
A delivery truck blocked the driveway that ran behind the building where Brad always parked. Brad pulled behind it and honked. He waited a few seconds and laid into the horn, staying on it for a five count. Brad cracked his knuckles and ground his teeth. Finally, the driver emerged from the pet store next to the lab. A middle-aged guy with a mullet, his thick arms peeked out of his uniform shirt, which puckered around his doughy middle. He offered an apologetic wave and climbed into the truck. Brad pulled forward until his front bumper almost touched the truck.

The driver got out and approached Brad's truck. He motioned for Brad to roll down the window. Instead, Brad leaped out of the vehicle. He stood in front of the guy with his arms crossed over his chest.

"Hey, could you move your truck?" the driver asked. "I need some space to back up, and then I can turn around and be out of your way."

"So, you can see that you're blocking my way?" Brad asked. He took a step forward.

The driver blew out a frustrated sigh. "Look, I'm on a schedule, and I need to get on the road."

"Yeah, I've got someplace to be, too," Brad said. He dropped his arms and cracked his knuckles. He could drop the driver with two punches, and he could tell the driver knew it.

"Just move your truck, and I'll get out of here," the driver said.

Brad stepped forward again, and the driver moved back toward the delivery truck. "Everybody should just move out of your way and let you go where you want because your schedule is so important. Is that it?" Brad's voice raised as he spoke, and he continued in a near shout, "Don't want to get blocked? Don't block me. You're lucky I didn't move your truck myself. You block the driveway again, and I'll put it in a ditch and see what that does to your precious schedule. Don't park here again."

Brad stormed back to his truck and backed up a few feet. The truck driver moved the delivery truck back but needed more room. Brad gave him a few inches at a time, until the truck was turned around. The driver flipped Brad off as he drove past. Brad responded in kind.

With the truck out of the way, Brad caught sight of his uncle standing in the door to the lab. Brad looked away, parked behind the lab in the employee spot next to his uncle's, and went in the back door.

"You okay, Brad?"

"I'm fine, Uncle Doug."

His uncle shook his head, disapproval etched across his face. "You don't seem fine. You've been on edge with everyone lately. You're lucky that driver didn't escalate things with you."

Brad looked up. "Trust me, that wouldn't have been a problem."

"No? What if he had a weapon? Knife in the ribs makes you the loser. That's the way I keep score."

"I can handle myself," Brad said, moving from shame to annoyance.

"I don't doubt that," Doug continued. "What if he took a swing at you, you punched him, and he hit his head and never got up? Prison is full of guys who can handle themselves."

Brad didn't respond. His uncle sat at a table and motioned for Brad to take the seat across from him. Doug took off his hat, revealing his close-shaved head. He ran a hand over the stubble. "What's really bothering you, Brad?"

Brad looked at the Formica tabletop. He checked his watch. "I need to check the sample shipments for this morning."

"They're fine, Brad. I checked them already. Something's bothering you. What I've found is that we all want peace in our lives, but there's a price to get it. Know what that price is?" He waited a beat, and when Brad didn't answer, he continued, "It's truth, Brad. Peace and truth. They go together. If you can't be honest about what's going on inside, it'll just keep eating you up."

Doug stopped talking, and Brad continued staring at the table. He cracked his knuckles, one at a time on his left hand, then one at a time on the right. Finally, he spoke. "I don't want to lose you, Uncle Doug," he said. Tears stung his eyes, and he blinked them away. "After what happened to Dad, it's not fair to lose you, too."

Doug put a hand on top of Brad's. Brad looked up and made eye contact with him. Doug had kind eyes. The green had dulled over the past six months, but the compassion remained. "Two things, Brad," he said. "One, Mullet Man out there has nothing to do with that, so you shouldn't have taken it out on him. The next time he comes by with a delivery, you better apologize to him."

"Fine," Brad muttered. "What else?"

Doug tightened his grip. "We play the hand we're dealt. Nothing any of us can do about what the cards are, but we can control how we react to them."

"It's just not fair," Brad said, aware that he sounded like a child.

Doug shrugged. "It is what it is. If you don't like the cards, maybe you should talk to the dealer." He looked skyward and pointed up.

Brad thought about his uncle's words for the rest of the day. He didn't know what he believed about God, spirituality, or the afterlife, but he knew that Doug was right: the longer he ignored what he was feeling, the more it would eat at him.

That night, he sat at his dining room table, a hand-me-down from Uncle Doug. An uneven leg made the table wobble when he touched it. He wrote a letter detailing everything he felt. He spilled out how angry his father's death had made him and how seeing Uncle Doug dying, too, brought up all the old wounds. He wrote out how scared he was to take over the business by himself and how he worried he'd make bad decisions that would cause the lab to fail. He concluded by writing about how much he missed Chicago and his friends there and how far from being an MMA fighter his life had fallen.

When he finished writing, his cheeks were damp with tears and sweat beaded along his brow. He had three pages, written in terrible penmanship. He folded the pages and put them in a box on his dresser, where he also had a picture of his father and a flyer advertising a Chicago MMA tournament.

He closed the box and realized he felt lighter. After months of pretending everything was okay, he'd finally told the truth. He slept better that night than he had since he moved to Colorado.

CHAPTER 34

July 25, 2025. Burgess County, Montana.
Brad spied Eddie's Jeep as they rolled past the entrance to the Double T Ranch. He waved for them to fall in line, and the Jeep joined the convoy. The sheriff led the line of vehicles in his truck, one of his officers riding shotgun. Next came Deputy Cooper and Officer O'Brien in a standard sheriff's department cruiser. Brad and Aaron took the third spot, with Eddie and Hadley bringing up the rear.

The officers kept their lights off and sirens quiet but increased their speed as they got further away from town. Brad kept his foot on the accelerator and his eyes on the cruiser in front of them.

"Talk to Shelly again?" Brad asked.

"Yeah," Aaron said. "Just before we left the sheriff's. The doctors think they'll release her today. She and her sister will start the drive back to Chicago tomorrow."

Brad didn't know what to say to that. He felt an obligation to express some kind of well-wishing sentiment to Aaron, but he couldn't come up with anything. Despite Aaron staying to help with the investigation and seeming genuinely concerned for Shelly's wellbeing, Brad thought Shelly was better off without Aaron in her life.

"You guys will figure things out," he said, thinking that a clean break was a way of figuring their relationship out.

Aaron kept his eyes on the hills and trees passing by, a constant blur of brown and green out the windows. He didn't speak until several minutes had passed. "I'm not the same guy I was when you knew me," he said. "That was a long time ago, and I was a jerk back then. I'm different now."

Brad let the comment hang between them. Ahead of them, Cooper tapped his brakes as they approached the town of Stanton. There wasn't much to the town, at least not that Brad could see from the highway. A few houses on large lots occupied either side of the road that intersected with 287. Beyond the houses, a few buildings that looked like businesses stood. Brad couldn't tell what they were; maybe a bank or a post office and a bar.

They left town as quickly as they entered it. A couple miles south, they slowed again, and Sheriff Yellington pulled off the road next to the 287 Diner. Cooper followed. Both law men exited their vehicles, but Cooper motioned for the civilians to stay put.

A sheriff's department car and a state trooper cruiser parked angled toward one another in front of the restaurant's tiny parking lot, blocking entry. Yellow police tape hung around the building. Brad peered past the window advertising a weekday brunch special and watched Yellington talk to the officers inside. They waved their hands a lot and pointed toward the kitchen.

Yellington and Cooper emerged from the building, returned to their cars, and started the convoy again. A moment later, they passed the motel Brad believed Corey Holgate had been staying at. He noted the location and decided to stop by if the property searches did not yield results.

The sheriff turned onto a side road, and the rest followed. They slowed considerably and turned onto a gravel road. Driveways peeked out of trees here and there, getting further apart the longer they stayed on the road.

The sheriff took one of the driveways. Around a corner, a house emerged, with a detached garage and several other buildings scattered behind it. Cooper put on his brakes and stopped a hundred yards from the house. The sheriff continued on.

Brad exited the truck, and Aaron followed on the other side. Behind them, Eddie and Hadley piled out, as well. Officer O'Brien stood next to the passenger door of Cooper's car, a hand on his pistol, eyes focused on the property as the sheriff pulled to a stop in front of the house.

"You all stay here," Cooper said. "O'Brien is going to hang back, too. Keep your eyes on the driveway behind us and the other buildings. Any sign of movement, O'Brien will radio us."

"The search will go faster with more people," Brad suggested, but Cooper shook his head.

"It's a risk having you out here to begin with. Do as you're told."

He spoke to O'Brien in a hushed tone before jogging down the driveway to join the sheriff. Brad sat on the hood of the truck, watching the buildings in front of them. The sheriff knocked on the door several times before using a tool that looked like a skinny crowbar to pry the door open.

O'Brien tensed as his colleagues entered the house. He stepped forward. With O'Brien's attention on the search, Brad looked back at Eddie and Hadley. Hadley watched the driveway, looking out for anyone approaching from the rear. Brad figured they would hear a vehicle long before they'd see one.

Eddie motioned Brad over. Brad looked in the backseat of the Jeep, where Eddie had stored four semi-automatic rifles. Eddie cast a wary glance toward O'Brien before whispering, "Take one for each of you. A box of ammo each, too."

Brad obediently hauled the weaponry to his truck and slid it into the backseat. Aaron raised his eyebrows but didn't say anything. Brad took his seat on the truck's hood once more. The sheriff and his men exited the house. Yellington pointed toward the garage.

O'Brien watched the building through a pair of binoculars. Brad slid off the hood and stood near the driver's door, feeling vulnerable in the wide open. He relaxed when the men emerged from the garage. Yellington pointed to the next building, and O'Brien pivoted in that direction.

It took them forty-five minutes to complete the search. When they finished the last building, O'Brien and Cooper rode in the back of the sheriff's pickup to the deputy's car.

"No signs of anyone here," Yellington said. "We're moving on to the next one. Go back to the main road and pull off until we catch up with you. You can follow us in again."

Brad and Aaron returned to his truck, while Eddie and Hadley climbed back in the Jeep. Brad kept his eyes straight ahead, not daring to look at the truck's backseat for fear the sheriff would see the weapons and throw them off the case.

They pulled off the road as instructed and formed the convoy again when Yellington and Cooper passed by. A couple minutes into the drive, Aaron's phone rang. His face lit up, and Brad assumed Shelly was on the other end.

"Hey," Aaron said. "I've been thinking about you. How are you?" He listened for a moment, and Brad snuck glances his way, alternating between keeping his eyes on the road and watching Aaron for clues about Shelly's condition. "He's right here," Aaron said, his voice flat. "We're searching some properties, looking for the guy who took you."

Aaron listened for a moment longer. "That's great," he said. "I wish you'd called sooner, and I could have met you at the hospital or the hotel. I can't really head back to town right now, but I'll be there as soon as I can."

Brad looked at him, keeping his eyes off the road for longer than he should have. Aaron mouthed, "They're releasing her."

Then, he turned toward the window and lowered his voice, though Brad could still hear every word.

"I still have the hotel room," he said. "You might as well stay there. We can probably get you a ticket for my flight if you don't want to drive all that way." Silence stretched out, and Brad wished he could be somewhere other than the awkwardness of the truck. At the same time, he was fascinated by Aaron's side of the conversation and wondered how well he was filling in the gaps.

"Yeah, I'm sure the manager will let you in the room to get your stuff," Aaron said. "Let me know what room you're in, and I'll stop by to check on you. Maybe we can get dinner." He paused. "Yes, all of us. You, me, your mom, your sister. Even Brad."

He clicked off the call and jammed the phone into the cup holder between the seats. He kept his body turned away from Brad. Brad focused on the road. He hoped they'd reach the next house before long.

• • •

He parked just off the road on the rise above the house. He didn't dare take the highway, and he knew if he parked at the house, he'd be too easy to capture. The image of his face on the television screen at the diner kept flashing through his mind. His hands shook with rage as he wondered how they'd managed to identify him and get those photos out in the public.

He paced a few feet up and down the road, breathing in the mountain air. The scent of pines and the cleanness of the day tickled his nostrils and brought him to a calmer state. He needed to take care of business. First, the girl. That was easy enough. Then, he'd torch the house and get out of the state. He had a credit card he never used. He wondered if the police knew about it. He'd rather use cash for everything and be untraceable, but he might need the option to pay at the pump, at least until he got a couple of states away. He'd figure that out. The important thing was to keep moving.

He took his binoculars from the truck, along with a shoulder holster and a pistol. He looked wistfully at the kerosene in the truck bed. He wanted to use all three cans, but he'd have to settle for one. He hauled the closest can from the bed and let it flop against his leg as he walked. He worked his way through the trees until he came to the place where he could see into the valley below and watch the house.

He focused on the house first. He didn't see any sign that his guest had found her way out. The familiar tingle ran through his body, shocking him with its electricity. He imagined his hand on her throat and the fear in her eyes as he squeezed her life away.

He scanned the rest of the property before focusing on the road. Everything looked clear. He kept the optics out, wearing them around his neck, and found his way to the game trail that would lead most of the way down the hill. Even in the thick of the trees, the heat and humidity of the day got to him. He slapped at mosquitoes as he walked, his hands leaving clammy prints in the sweat where he swatted his skin.

The trail bent to the east when he needed to go west. He ducked under branches and crawled around trees, making his own way. He'd climbed the hill a couple of times when he scouted the location and always varied his path. He wanted anyone who followed him to move east with the game trail and leave his hideaway alone.

He took a break to catch his breath and peek out of the trees. He could see the roof of the house just below his elevation. He'd almost made it all the way down. Once inside, he'd move quickly and be back on the hill in less than an hour.

He heard a sound and immediately thought it was a car engine. Perhaps more than one. He used his binoculars to watch the road leading to the house. He didn't see anything. They'd surprised him by figuring out his ID, but there was no connection between him and this house. No paper trail, nothing to follow. Whoever was driving around in the woods was on their way to somewhere else.

He dropped the binoculars, letting them thud against his chest, and covered the rest of the distance to the bottom of the hill. Before he left the cover of the trees, he listened again, but he did not hear anything. The way the roads twisted and wound, and the way sound echoed in the valley, the car he'd heard before could have been miles away or on its way out of the woods. He breathed easy. Everything would be fine.

He dropped the kerosene by the back door and unlocked the deadbolt he'd installed. Instinctively, he reached for his ski mask before realizing he left it at the truck. He shrugged. It no longer mattered if the woman saw his face.

He kept his gun on but left the binoculars on the kitchen counter as he moved toward the bedroom.

"Honey, I'm home," he called out. He laughed when he heard her whimper in response.

He entered the room where she lay face down on the bed. He remembered a time when his mother had put out a glue trap to deal with mice, supposedly the more humane option. In the morning, they found a mouse caught in the glue, a leg ripped out of socket from trying to escape and its feces covering the adhesive pad. His mother had sent it outside with him, where he put it out of its misery with a hammer.

Ronda reminded him of that mouse. The sheets and blankets swirled around her body in a sweaty tangle. Red skin showed on her wrists where she'd rubbed them raw trying to break free of the cuffs. He'd seen it before with the other women.

"It's almost over, little mouse," he said, his voice a mere trace of a whisper. Still, she shuddered at the sound of him so close to her.

He pulled the bedding away, leaving her uncovered and vulnerable. She kicked as soon as he grabbed her legs, so he punched the small of her back. She cried out but stopped moving until he had the ropes and tape free. Then, she kicked again, her legs a frenzy of movement.

He punched her again in the same spot. A muffled howl tried to escape through the tape on her mouth, and her legs slowed down. He punched her once more.

"Listen," he said, leaning close to her. "We're taking a trip to the basement. If you fight me or make any trouble at all, it will be 100 times more painful for you. I promise you that."

He fumbled with his keys and unlocked the handcuffs. She tried to draw away from him, but he twisted an arm behind her back, bending it between her shoulder blades until her resistance stopped.

He kept the duct tape on her mouth. With rough hands on her arms, he guided her to the kitchen. He unlocked a door next to the pantry, flipped on a light, and told her to go down.

"Nice and slow," he said, keeping his grip on her arms. They made it to the bottom of the stairs. He opened another door, threw on another light, and pushed her into the room. The room was empty except for a freezer in one corner and a chair chained to a support column in the middle of the concrete floor. The place smelled musty, the air stagnant from lack of circulation.

He twisted her arm behind her back once more and led her to the freezer, a horizontal box about six feet long and four feet high. She dug her heels into the ground as he reached for the lid, but dehydration, hunger, and sleep deprivation had left her weak, and he easily pushed her forward, bending her chest down, so she could see into the appliance.

She shrieked when she saw the other body, a woman who looked much like her but lifeless and frozen. He was glad he left the tape on her mouth. She screamed again, and he backhanded her across the jaw. She fell to the ground. In the intervening silence just before her next scream, he heard a noise from outside.

He dragged her to the chair and fastened a handcuff to it before rushing up the stairs. The sound was unmistakable. Tires on gravel. Car doors opened and footsteps pounded the earth.

He beelined for the kitchen and the back door, his gun in hand. As he reached it, wood splintered at the front of the house, and the door swung inward. He could see the front door from his position. The long-haired sheriff stood in the doorway, gun drawn, and his deputy stood next to him with a crowbar.

"Don't move," the sheriff shouted, swinging his gun into a shooting stance.

The man raised his gun as the sheriff spoke and squeezed off two rounds. The sheriff jerked backward as a bullet ripped into his shoulder. The man fired at the deputy, too, but didn't check to see if he hit him. Instead, he sprinted out the back door to the trees.

He thought about the woman escaping from the previous place. The tables had turned. If she could escape his grip, he could slip away from the police.

Shouts emanated from the house. He was several feet into the woods before he heard someone yell, "He's not here."

"Check the trees," came the answer. He continued into the woods, staying as silent as possible. His objective was to reach the game trail and get to his truck. If he saw a clean shot at any of his pursuers, he'd take it, but it had to be the perfect opportunity. He didn't want to miss and give away his position in the process.

His blood boiled as he considered the woman in the basement. Another one that he would not get the pleasure of killing. He gathered himself and focused on navigating the woods without leaving a trail for the cops to follow.

CHAPTER 35

They parked closer to the second house, but Cooper still insisted the civilians stay behind his car and well back of the action. The deputy accompanied Yellington and the other officer to the house, leaving O'Brien to watch their backs. Brad stood in the bed of his truck to watch the action unfold, elbows propped on top of the cab. Hadley and Eddie sat on the tailgate, watching the road behind them. Aaron stayed inside the truck, probably brooding over his phone call with Shelly, Brad thought.

"If this isn't the right place, we'll need a new plan," Brad said.

"There's one more house on our list," Hadley said.

"I'm with Brad," Eddie said. "I don't like option three. If it were up to me, I'd be sending every police officer I could spare door to door to see if they can uncover anything."

"Any word from Vince?" Brad asked.

"Just that he doesn't have anything new," Hadley said. "No known connections between Holgate and any of the victims. No known connections among the victims. He's trying to track down employment information on Holgate, but it turns out there are more than a couple oil companies in Texas."

"Go figure," Eddie said.

Brad leaned further over the top of the truck as the sheriff and his men approached the house with deliberate steps. Using his binoculars to watch the windows in the house, he looked for any sign of movement inside. Unfortunately, the blinds were closed, blocking out his view.

Yellington stood by the front door. Cooper took a wide path along the left side of the house, with the other officer mirroring his movements on the right. They retraced their steps and conferred with the sheriff.

Yellington stepped forward and beat on the front door. The echo of his fist on the wood reverberated through the valley. The police officers tensed. When no one answered, the sheriff pounded the door again. When there was still no response, he stepped aside and Cooper stepped to the door with the tool that looked like a thin crowbar.

He inserted the device between the door and the jamb, just above the doorknob. He slid it up. He pointed at a spot on the door about head height and said something to Yellington. Brad wished he could hear their conversations.

The deputy removed the tool and reinserted it at the spot where he had pointed. He moved it from side to side, gaining momentum with each push. After a few seconds, he put his back into his work, forcing the tool further into the door frame and jerking to his right.

Wood splintered with a crackle as loud as a gunshot. Eddie and Hadley both jumped from their spots behind Brad and came around the front of the truck to watch. Even Aaron left his seat to see the source of the commotion.

Yellington and Cooper drew their guns. The third officer kicked the door inward, and the sheriff and deputy rushed inside. "Don't move," Yellington shouted.

Brad's heart raced as adrenaline surged through his body. He stood straighter and kept his binoculars trained on the now-empty doorway.

A gunshot rang through the valley, followed by several more. The sheriff surged backward through the door and collapsed on his back on the dirt in front of the house.

Cooper shouted, "Go after him," from inside the house. Officer O'Brien forgot about his post at the back of their formation and rushed forward.

Brad jumped from the truck bed, grabbed a gun from inside the cab and sprinted to the house. Footsteps pounded behind him, and he knew it had to be Aaron. Neither Hadley nor Eddie could keep pace with him.

He reached the door as Deputy Cooper stumbled out. "Back to the truck," he commanded, kneeling next to the sheriff. "O'Brien, Kitts went out the back door. Go around and see if you get a bead on the shooter."

O'Brien took off. "Back. To. The. Truck." Cooper repeated, his face flushed and his voice hoarse.

"I'm an EMT," Brad said. He took a knee on Yellington's other side and quickly assessed the sheriff. The lawman breathed quick, shallow breaths. He had one gunshot wound to his right shoulder. Brad didn't see any other signs of injury.

Brad yanked off his own shirt, wadded it into a ball, and placed it against the sheriff's wound. Blood seeped from underneath Yellington. "This is gonna hurt," Brad said, and he lifted the injured man's shoulder to see the back of it. He looked at Cooper, "You got a first aid kit in the car? I want to patch him up before he loses more blood."

Cooper regained his feet and ran back toward the police vehicles. Eddie met him on the way and thrust the first aid kit at him. "Go back and watch the road," Cooper instructed. He brought Brad the medical supplies.

"Good news, Sheriff," Brad said, as he unzipped the black backpack with a white cross emblazoned across it. "Looks like the bullet went all the way through, so it's not rattling around inside you where it might do something nasty. It's gonna hurt for a while, and the doctors will have to check for nerve or muscle damage, but there's nothing vital where he hit you."

The sheriff grunted an unintelligible response, but at least he was conscious.

Brad used scissors to cut away the sheriff's uniform shirt all the way from the front to the back, exposing his shoulder. He rolled the sheriff to his side and bandaged the entry and exit wounds. Then, Brad rolled gauze over the entire area, binding it as tightly as he could.

Cooper returned from his car as Brad finished. "Sheriff, do you think you can get up?" Brad asked.

Yellington muttered under his breath, and Brad still couldn't understand him. He looked at Cooper, who just shrugged, and Brad motioned for him to help.

With Cooper under the sheriff's good shoulder, and Brad lifting the other side, careful to avoid the wounded area, they got the sheriff to his feet. "We'll get him to his truck," Brad said, "and let him sit up for a while. Help's on the way?"

"Ambulance and more police," Cooper answered.

O'Brien and the other officer, Kitts, came back around the house. "No sign of him," Kitts said.

"He's in the trees," O'Brien added. "Has to be."

"He left a fuel can by the back door," Kitts said. "He may have been planning to blow the place up."

The officers helped the sheriff back to the truck before reconvening at the front of the house. Brad told Cooper about his theory that someone could stash a vehicle on the road above the hill.

"That's a decent climb," Cooper said. "I don't care what kind of shape you're in. I'm going to have one of the responding cars check out that road. O'Brien, you and Kitts keep watch at the back of the house, in case he tries to come back this way."

"Did you get a good look at him?" Brad asked.

Cooper shook his head. "Everything happened too fast."

"Would have been nice to confirm he's our guy," Brad said.

"If he's not, he's got something to hide," Cooper said. "He didn't want us coming in the house." The deputy surveyed the situation. "You two, stay with the sheriff," he said to Brad and Aaron. "O'Brien and Kitts, come inside with me."

"I'm going in, too," Brad said.

Cooper looked like he wanted to protest, but Yellington cut him off. "You know how to use that thing?" he asked, nodding toward the gun.

"Yeah," Brad said. He'd shot before; the sheriff didn't need to know it had been a few years earlier and with a different type of rifle.

"Let him go in," the sheriff said. "Extra manpower won't hurt."

Aaron stayed at Yellington's side, as Brad and the three officers formed up outside the door. Kitts went in first, with O'Brien a half step behind him. Kitts turned to the left as O'Brien went right, both keeping their guns pointed up and at chest height. Cooper went between them, and Brad brought up the rear.

With the deputy and Brad pointing their guns at the living room, Kitts and O'Brien checked the kitchen. When they declared it clear, the four moved down the hall. There were three doors, two on the left and one on the right. Cooper motioned for Brad to stay on one side of the door on the right; he took the other side.

Kitts and O'Brien moved into the first room. Through the open door, Brad could see it was a bedroom. The door next to it was open a crack, and Brad thought it looked like a bathroom. A moment later, his suspicions were confirmed when O'Brien kicked the door open and quickly searched it.

Finding no one, they burst through the door on the right; Brad kept watch on the hallway as they searched it.

"The place is a mess," Cooper whispered as he exited the room. "Bedding strewn about. Stinks like body odor. Back to the kitchen; I saw two more doors there."

The group crept through the house and found two doors side-by-side at the back of the kitchen, near the back door to the house. Cooper slung one open, revealing an empty pantry. The deputy pushed against each of the walls, but they all held firm.

Next, Kitts opened the second door, revealing a dark cavern. Cooper shined his flashlight and revealed a set of stairs. O'Brien found a wall switch and flipped the lights on. He led the way down the stairs, followed by Kitts and Brad. Cooper came last, keeping his body turned and his back pressed against Brad's, so he could watch for movement above them.

In the distance, a siren wailed, and Brad hoped that meant the ambulance was getting closer. A moment later, all thoughts of the siren exited his mind as he saw a woman chained to a chair in the middle of the basement.

She looked terrible, as though she hadn't eaten or bathed in days. Tear streaks lined the dirt on her cheeks, and fresh tears joined them when she saw the officers. She had blond hair and blue eyes and bore a striking resemblance to Shelly and Victoria Owens. A strip of duct tape ran over her mouth and into her hair.

As Brad peered closer, he saw that the woman had been handcuffed to the chair. A chain secured the chair to a support column.

Cooper moved in, his eyes darting around the basement. "Ronda?"

The woman nodded, and Cooper continued. "I'm going to take that tape off your mout. It might hurt. Is that okay?"

Ronda nodded again, and Cooper worked the tape free from her lips and pulled delicately to the outsides. A shiver ran down Brad's arms as the tape pulled her hair from her head. If the woman felt any discomfort, she didn't show it.

"Did you get him?" she asked. Cooper shook his head, and more tears gushed down her face. Her shoulders shook.

Cooper examined the handcuffs. He produced a key ring from his pocket and flipped to a small brass key.

"Most of the commercially available cuffs use a pretty simple locking mechanism," he explained. "This key should do the trick." Within seconds he had freed Ronda. She stood and wrapped him in an embrace before slumping back into the chair and rubbing her wrists. She eyed a horizontal freezer in the corner.

"There's someone else," she rasped. "In there." She pointed at the appliance.

Brad gripped his gun tighter until he realized what she meant. Cooper flipped the freezer lid open, and the other three men gathered next to him. Another blond-haired, blue-eyed woman lay dead.

Cooper slammed the lid, fire and fury in his eyes. "Let's get her upstairs," he said. "I think I heard the ambulance." He turned to Ronda. "We'll have questions for you, but let's get you checked out first."

Kitts let her take his arm. O'Brien led the way up the stairs, gun ready. Cooper and Brad followed.

Outside, a medic tended to Sheriff Yellington. A second ambulance and two more police cars squeezed past the other vehicles and parked near the house. Brad gestured to the hill behind the house.

"How long do you think it would take to climb that hill?" he asked Cooper.

The deputy wrinkled his chin. "If you knew the area and had a trail mapped out, not long. If that's where the guy went, I'd say he's reaching the top about now."

"I'm going after him," Brad said, stepping toward his truck.

"Don't bother," Cooper said. "I sent a car to check it out. If he comes out of the woods up there, he's ours."

"I'm going," Brad repeated. The time had come to end this thing, and he wasn't leaving it to chance. Aaron stood by the sheriff's truck. Brad put on a fresh shirt from his backpack. "Reynolds, you coming?"

CHAPTER 36

They flew across the dirt road, kicking up dust behind them. Keeping his foot on the gas, Brad hoped Eddie kept enough distance between them to maintain visibility. Having now seen four of the guy's victims—Shelly, Victoria, Ronda, and the unknown woman in the freezer—Brad wanted to catch him and bring him to justice.

Brad glanced at the map on the dashboard and peered ahead. They approached the road he was expecting, and he whipped a left turn onto it. The tires hit the pavement, and Brad mashed the accelerator down further. In the rearview mirror, he spied Eddie emerge from the dust cloud and join them on the pavement.

Brad didn't slow until he saw a sheriff's car. He screeched to a stop and pulled off the road behind it. As he rushed toward the car, an officer stepped into his path, arms held up.

"Slow down," he said. "I need to see some ID."

Brad held his hands up. "I just came from the house down below," he said, pointing toward the valley. "Yellington got shot, and Cooper is there with him."

"ID," the officer repeated. Brad opened his wallet and held up his driver's license. The officer stepped closer and squinted at it before looking at Brad's face. "Who are they?"

Brad realized Aaron, Eddie, and Hadley had joined. "We're private detectives," Brad said. "We've been helping with the investigation. It started with my friend, Shelly Cantwell, and it's expanded from there. You can call Cooper."

"Coop said you'd be coming," a second officer said, approaching from behind a tree. He held a shotgun.

"Find anything?" Brad asked. He took a tentative step forward, and when no one stopped him, he continued until he stood next to the second officer. A set of fresh tire tracks marked where another vehicle had been. Based on the width of the tread, it was probably a truck.

The officer shook his head. "We must have just missed him. We'll find him, though. He shot the sheriff, and he can't stay out here forever."

Brad walked back to the road looking up and down. He pictured the map in his mind. The road ran northeast to southwest. "My guess is he went that way," Brad said, pointing to the northeast. "Lots of areas to hide out in up there, and he can work his way out to a larger road and eventually catch the interstate."

The officer didn't look impressed. "You could say the same about the other way."

Brad went back to the truck, Aaron, Eddie, and Hadley in tow. He made his decision. "The cops don't have enough manpower to hunt this guy down, and I'm not letting him get away. I'm going after him."

"You don't know where he went," Hadley said.

"I'm taking a chance on a gut instinct," Brad said. "There's no other play at this point."

"Want to split up?" Eddie asked. "We can each take a different direction."

Brad had no doubts about Eddie's or Hadley's bravery, but he couldn't live with himself if either of them got shot because they agreed to his reckless plan to hunt down an armed madman in the woods. He shook his head.

"Nah, I've got it. You should go back to the scene and see if they've found anything else. Maybe you can listen in on an interview with the woman, see if she knows anything helpful. You can call me with whatever intel you get."

"I'm going with you," Aaron said.

"Reynolds, this isn't about Shelly anymore," Brad said. "You should get a ride back with the others, maybe go see her at the hospital."

"I want to do this," Aaron said. "I can't have you getting all the credit."

Brad could see that Aaron wasn't changing his mind. "Fine," he said. "You can drive, and I'll navigate with the map. Just know there's a good chance we're both getting shot."

"That's a good reason to come back with us, Brad," Hadley said.

Brad shrugged. "We all have our strengths. You and Vince dig up information and produce clues out of thin air. I rush into danger without thinking."

"You're just going to leave me out of the skills discussion?" Eddie said.

"You're an excellent fisherman, and I hear you make a great cup of coffee," Brad said. Hadley rolled her eyes before stepping up to hug Brad.

"Be careful," she whispered. "Seriously. If you get into trouble out there, get away and call in the real cops."

•　　•　　•

How could he have been so stupid? After all the precautions he'd taken, he let the police see his face in the house where the girl was. He should have had his mask. He should have dragged her to the woods and strangled her there. He could have made a clean getaway and left the body for the animals to dispose of.

He pounded his fist against the padding of the steering wheel. He let out a scream that rattled the windows and slammed his open palm against the dashboard. Dust motes floated into the sunlight. Pain seared through his hand, which blazed red, as though he had touched a hot stove.

Think, he told himself. Regretting the past would do him no good. He had to make quick decisions and keep moving forward.

The road cut up a hill. At the crest, he pulled to the side and peered through his binoculars at where he had been. A police car had arrived, right where he had been parked, and two civilian vehicles joined it. He had slipped away just in time. He studied the two vehicles, a green Jeep Wrangler and an ancient white F-150 that made his own truck look brand new. Three men and a woman gathered around the vehicles and gestured at the road. He wondered who they were. Consultants, perhaps. Maybe the local police knew they were in over their heads and called in expert help.

He tossed the optics into the passenger seat. In another mile, the spur he was on would connect with Highway 287, which would continue north, bend back to the west, and connect with Interstate 15. He didn't know what direction he would go then, but he needed to clear the current area fast.

He threw the truck into gear and continued his journey northeast. He approached Highway 287 and groaned when the police roadblock came into view. Without hesitating, he whipped the truck into a U-turn and got back on the spur, the truck fishtailing like a stunt car in a movie.

He mashed the accelerator before taking his foot off and letting the vehicle coast. He did not want to cross back over the road he had come from, where the police were. He needed to find a turn before that spot, and if he went too fast, he'd miss it.

With a gulp of air to cleanse his lungs, he steadied his hands on the wheel at 10 and 2, just like in driver's ed, and maintained

45 miles an hour. He scanned both sides of the road, looking for any turn that looked promising.

The road curved to the left, and he took it slowly, pushing on the accelerator as he came out of the turn to give the engine more power. The road straightened, and he gritted his teeth.

Coming toward him was the ancient truck he had seen through his binoculars. He felt certain it was the same one. He assured himself that they wouldn't know what he was driving, and if he looked the other way as they passed, they wouldn't recognize him from the photos.

He eased the accelerator down further, picking up speed. His stomach dropped. The truck wasn't going to pass him. Instead, it turned crosswise on the spur, creating a roadblock.

CHAPTER 37

Brad checked the map again. He traced their route with his finger. They were gaining elevation. Once they passed the top of the hill, they wouldn't have far to go before they caught up with Highway 287. Hadley had texted that the sheriff's office was setting up roadblocks on the highway to keep Holgate within the county.

"If we don't find him before we get to the highway, we'll need to come back and look for a side road he might have taken," Brad said.

"This is pointless," Aaron said. "There's too much ground for us to cover alone."

Brad was about to point out that Aaron chose to tag along, but a truck coming toward them caught his attention. He grabbed his binoculars and focused on the driver.

"Turn the truck," Brad said. "Quick. Make a roadblock."

Aaron slowed the truck and pivoted it at a ninety-degree angle to the road. Before he had completely stopped it, Brad slid out and grabbed a rifle from the backseat.

"Stay there," he commanded.

The other truck slowed, almost stopping. It was still 300 feet away, and Brad beckoned the driver to come forward. He prepared a story about helping the police with a manhunt and needing to check everyone's license and registration.

Ahead, the other truck revved its engine and jerked forward as if propelled from a slingshot. Brad swung the gun into a shooting position, but by the time he had sighted the truck, it was too late. The driver pulled onto the shoulder and blurred past them, kicking up gravel. A loose rock thunked into the bed of Brad's truck.

Brad scrambled into the passenger seat, still grasping the rifle.

"Follow him," he said.

It took Aaron a couple of seconds to straighten the truck and accelerate. Brad wished he had done the driving. They went back over the hill. Ahead, a cloud of dust served as a landmark to where their fugitive had fled.

"Right there," Brad said.

"Got it," Aaron answered.

They hit the dirt road, and Brad relaxed his grip on the gun and made sure the barrel pointed out the window at an angle. He didn't think modern weapons fired just because they got bumped, but he didn't want to lose a piece of himself finding out he was wrong.

Aaron steered through several twists and turns. The air whooshed by the open windows, and the dust cloud grew thicker.

"We're gaining on him," Brad said.

"Can you get a shot off?" Aaron asked.

Brad weighed the options. With a handgun, he might be able to lean out the window and squeeze off an accurate round or two, but the length of the rifle gave him little room to maneuver. He wouldn't admit it to Aaron, but he wasn't a good shot to begin with, and firing at a moving vehicle from a moving vehicle through of cloud of dust on an open road had almost zero chance of success.

"Just keep driving," Brad said. "We'll catch up to him or corner him eventually."

Aaron kept his foot on the accelerator, and Brad opened the map app on his phone. He sent their location to Hadley with a note, "On Holgate's tail. Close."

A moment later, Hadley's reply lit up the screen. "Sending police. BE CAREFUL."

He looked up to see a T intersection approaching. Aaron slowed almost to a stop. They had to let the dust settle before looking down each direction to see where a new cloud had formed.

"To the right," they said at the same time.

Aaron took the turn, speeding up to make up for the time they had lost. Brad looked at the topographical map again.

"This is going to loop around," he said. "We're going to end up where we started."

"Should I turn around and try to catch him from the other direction?" Aaron asked.

"No. Let's stay on his tail. We can't be far off."

Brad planned out an approach when they caught up with Holgate. He assumed the fugitive was armed and had no qualms about taking another life. He would know Brad was armed because Brad pointed a gun at him already. Brad moved his seat back as far as it would go and reclined it, giving himself as much room as possible. He didn't want to shoot from inside the truck, but he might not have a choice. If nothing else, the gunshots might panic Holgate into making an error.

Ahead, the other truck came into view. It wasn't moving. Aaron slowed to a stop behind it. Brad didn't see movement from inside. A fallen tree lay across the road in front of it, along with several medium-sized boulders. Brad looked at the rocky hillside near the road. Piles of dirt lined the bottom, where the earth had been washed away, perhaps in the thunderstorm a few days earlier.

"I don't see him," Aaron said.

Before Brad could answer, gunshots filled the air, and the windshield exploded into shards of glass.

•   •   •

Eddie drove too fast on the way to the lodge, muttering most of the time about the sheriff needing all the help he could get and still not letting them sit in on the interview with Ronda.

"They have to get her to the hospital first, anyway," Hadley said. "There wasn't room for us in the ambulance. We're better off helping from the lodge."

While Hadley would have loved to interview Ronda and compare her statement to Shelly's to see what patterns emerged, she also knew time was of the essence. Brad had sent her a location with a Holgate sighting, and the sheriff's office said they were trying to get a helicopter in the area.

They rushed into the lodge, and Hadley hurriedly set up her laptop. Vince joined them in the kitchen, and she caught him up on what was happening as she sent Brad a text asking for a status.

"What about you?" Hadley asked. "Any luck with any of the background work?"

Vince shook his head. "As far as I can tell, Corey Holgate did not know any of the victims ahead of time, and none of them were connected. It appears to be a random series of crimes. He had a type of woman he preyed on, but everything else was up to chance."

Hadley shuddered. The thought of becoming a victim based on your looks and being in the wrong place at the wrong time made her nauseous. She looked back at Vince. His expression grew grimmer.

"I did some more digging on Holgate, since I had some time. I cross-referenced everything we knew about his background, where he's been, his phone numbers, and the IP addresses you traced. I had to use KryptoSearch to review unindexed sites. I found a couple of hits on a message board using the same IP address around the same time he was registering as a volunteer for the race."

"What kind of message board?" Hadley asked.

"Not good," Vince said. He opened his laptop and thrust it at her.

The discussion thread was dedicated to the art of murder. A lot of the posts were graphic musings about ways to end someone's life. A new wave of nausea swept through Hadley.

"These are the worst kinds of people," Eddie said, reading over her shoulder. "Which one do you think is our boy?"

Vince commandeered the laptop and scrolled before turning it back to them. "This one at the top. Uses the screen name Abbasid871."

Hadley read the post. "Everyone on this site knows none of us would ever actually hurt anyone," it began. Many of the messages Hadley had read began with that type of disclaimer. "This is all hypothetical and philosophical. That said, I think the coolest way to kill someone would be up close. Not with a gun or a knife but with your bare hands. I think I'd get a rush out of feeling someone's life leak out of them as I squeezed."

Hadley closed the laptop and pushed it back to Vince. "That screen name?" he said. "I looked it up. It's believed that one of the oldest serial killers lived in the Abbasid Caliphate, what's Baghdad today, in the ninth century. He strangled women and buried them in his house. The guy was never caught."

Hadley grabbed her phone. Brad still hadn't responded. She dialed him, but he didn't pick up. She thumbed out a quick message: "Get out of there and wait for the cops. I'm serious."

"I hope he listens," she said.

"When has Brad ever listened to us?" Vince asked.

Hadley wondered if they should go find him. As if reading her mind, Eddie started for the door, keys in hand. "Let's go get him," he said.

CHAPTER 38

Brad bailed out of the truck, keeping the passenger door open, and rushed to the back end. He squatted behind a rear tire. A moment later, Aaron joined him on the driver's side. Gunshots peppered Brad's truck, but none came close to the two men.

The acrid smoke from gunfire filled Brad's nose. One thought occupied his head: survive. That meant changing the equation. Holgate's shots missed because he didn't see them or he had terrible aim. They couldn't count on that holding out forever.

A new volley of shots crackled, and the truck listed to the left as Holgate shot the driver's front tire.

"He's at eleven o'clock," Brad said. "I'm going to roll out to my right and shoot at his position. That should buy you some time to grab a gun and get off the road. Go to the trees over there." He gestured to their left.

Aaron looked scared. His skin had paled, and his eyes looked hollow. Brad didn't have time to give him a pep talk, so he just said, "Got it?" Aaron nodded.

Brad stood in a crouch and readied the rifle. He sprinted to his right, squeezing off rounds in Holgate's direction as he ran. Holgate returned fire, missing badly, before his gun fell silent. Brad fired a few more shots before flattening himself against the rocky hill. He hoped the soil would hold firm.

The truck door slammed shut, and Brad watched Aaron run toward the trees. More shots issued from Holgate's area, and the dirt between the truck and the trees exploded in tufts of dust and gravel. Aaron took cover behind a tree and gave Brad a thumbs up.

In his rush to get them free of the truck and the line of fire, Brad hadn't come up with more of a plan. They had no way to communicate. In a perfect world, Aaron would engage Holgate and keep him pinned down, while Brad flanked him and overpowered him. Instead, Aaron stood behind the tree, as motionless as if he had become part of the trunk himself.

"Corey Holgate," Brad bellowed. "We know it's you. The police talked to your mother, and she gave up information about you. The police can place you at the scene of each kidnapping. This doesn't end with you getting away. Turn yourself in to us, and maybe they'll go easy on you." Brad didn't think there was any chance of that happening, especially since Holgate had shot the sheriff.

He waited for gunshots. Nothing happened. He sprang from his position and fired at where Holgate's shots had come from before flattening himself against the rocks again. Corey didn't return fire.

Brad sprinted back to the truck, ducking around the back of it and using the bed for cover. "If he shoots, return fire," Brad yelled.

"Got it," Aaron said, but Brad didn't like how shaky his voice sounded.

Moving as quickly as he could, Brad retrieved his backpack from the backseat. He shoved the boxes of ammunition inside. Then, he stretched into the front seat to grab the map. The sun glittered off the glass bits that filled the cab, and the air rushed through the gaping hole where a windshield used to be. If Holgate chose that moment to take a shot at him, he'd be a dead man.

Brad snatched the map and got away from the truck, joining Aaron in the trees.

"Did you see any movement?" Brad asked. "Any sign of him?"

"No," Aaron said.

Holgate had been shooting from a small hill. He could be lying in wait on the back side of it, or he could have taken off. Brad secured the backpack on his shoulders and shoved the map in his pocket. He grabbed Aaron's arm and pointed to two different locations in the trees.

"We're going to move around in here," he said, "and make sure we have cover. You'll break off and go to the edge of the trees right up there. I'm going to go further to the left to get behind his hill."

Aaron nodded. "Then what?"

"I'll shout 'now.' When I do, start shooting toward the hill. I'm going to swing out and try to pin him down from the other side."

"What if I shoot you?"

"Don't," Brad said. "Shoot at the top of the hill. And don't shoot continuously. Take a breath between each trigger pull, so you can see if he's shooting back. Stop shooting if he doesn't return fire. There's a chance he took off."

With that, Brad pointed Aaron in the direction he wanted him to take before heading further into the woods. He picked his way around and under branches, trying to keep as quiet as possible and maintain an element of surprise.

When he passed the hill, he moved to the edge of the trees. He double-checked the rifle. His heart hammered. Fighting MMA and taking trauma calls in Chicago had hardened his nerves, but those activities were a far cry from engaging a known killer in a gun battle. He knew what Hadley would tell him if she were there. He remembered her text about a helicopter and wondered where the police were.

He breathed in and out and counted to ten. Mustering all his nerve, he yelled, "Now." Gunshots popped from Aaron's direction, and divots blew out of the top of the hill. No one moved or returned fire from that position.

Brad ran from the trees, angling himself to get a good look at the back of the hill. He prepared to flatten himself and start shooting if he took any fire, but no gunshots came. He reached the bottom of the hill and saw no sign of Holgate.

Brad ran back to the trees and yelled for Aaron to come to his position. He kept the gun level and ready to provide cover fire should Holgate emerge.

Aaron reached Brad's spot in the trees, his face flush with excitement. The timidness Brad had observed earlier had vanished. Aaron checked his phone and held up the screen for Brad to see that he had no service.

"I think we should go back the way we came," Aaron said. "We could find the cops at the roadblock or call for help as soon as we get service."

"No," Brad said. "We're too close. I'm not letting him get away." Aaron opened his mouth, and Brad cut him off. "Go back if you want, but I'm staying. And we're way better off together than walking into an ambush alone."

Aaron scowled but did not argue. Brad took out his map and found their location. He saw where the road that had been cut off by the rockslide looped around to their starting point. It did not show smaller roads or driveways, but Brad imagined there were cabins nearby. He could picture Holgate forcing his way into one and hunkering down or taking someone's vehicle and finding a back road out of the area.

"This is our best bet," he said. "We'll follow the road. See how the trees border it along the way, with the rocky hill on the other side? Let's stay on the tree side, so we can take cover if we need to. If he fires on us, take cover behind a tree and shoot back in the direction the shots came from."

Aaron agreed, and they made their way back to the road. While Brad kept watch, Aaron climbed over the fallen tree. Then Aaron watched until Brad joined him. They made their way to the trees, walking in the clear but ready to dart inside the forest if necessary.

The map showed that they would start down an incline. When they reached it, Brad told Aaron to wait, so they could survey the area from the high ground. He shielded his eyes from the sun and scanned the land in front of them. He saw no sign of Holgate, which bothered him. Holgate knew he had to move quickly, and following the road would be much faster than fighting through the trees. It would be quieter, too. He either had a huge lead on them or he had set up somewhere, ready to attack.

"Stay alert," Brad whispered.

"Yes, sir," Aaron said, an edge to his voice.

Brad gritted his teeth but didn't reply. He pointed down the incline, and they started down, Brad first with Aaron a few yards behind him. Halfway down the hill, the gunfire began anew.

The shots came from inside the trees ahead of them, where the road curved slightly. Brad fired two shots and sprinted into the woods. Aaron took a position behind a tree and shot. The bullet took out a chunk of wood from the trunk Brad hid behind. He glared at Aaron and waved his hand in front of his throat in a cut-it-out gesture. Brad moved further to the left, making sure he was clear of Aaron's firing line.

When no more shots came, Brad retreated to Aaron's spot. "He's probably waiting for us to come forward again, and he'll try to take us out. I'm going to climb the rock hill and see if I can spot him from above. You stay here and be ready to return fire."

Aaron nodded. His skin had gone pale again. The rush of playing soldier had subsided, and the frightened Aaron had replaced the brash one. Brad preferred the frightened one at that point. He was creating plans on the fly, and he needed Aaron to go along with him without arguing.

Brad raced to the base of the rock hill. He slung the rifle over his shoulder, letting it slap against his back. He grabbed a sapling and tested it for sturdiness. It held, and he pulled himself onto the hill. Loose gravel slid under his feet, and he tightened his grip on the tree until he was sure he had his feet under him.

He started upward, turning his feet sideways for maximum traction. Just like running an adventure race, he told himself. It was a combination of navigation, which he excelled at, and overcoming unknown obstacles. The big difference was he'd never run a race where one of the obstacles wouldn't hesitate to blow his head off.

With that reminder to stay focused, he continued his trek up the hill, grabbing trees for support as he went. He heard movement above him. He looked in its direction. A rifle slid past him, clattering on the gravel. It bounced off a tree trunk and continued its descent down the hill.

Brad ran harder. The prospect of catching Holgate unarmed renewed his energy. He reached the top of the hill and took the rifle off his back. The summit came to a narrow peak, just wide enough for a person to stand, with crevasses and sheer drop offs lining the sides. In the places where the hilltop was wider, trees and boulders dotted the peak. He peered over the edge of the hill, but Holgate was not descending. He scanned the summit, trying to find his quarry behind a boulder or tree.

Brad turned to his left and baby-stepped toward the edge of the hill, checking for Holgate as he went. Footsteps crunched on the gravel behind him. He spun. A rock smashed into his chin, and he crumpled to the ground.

CHAPTER 39

Shooting had never been his thing. Despite growing up in the West, where some boys learned to shoot before they learned to ride a bike, he had never taken to hunting, and target practice seemed like a waste of time, bullets, and cans. He longed to find the boys he had grown up with and brag about the hunts he had been on and how much more exquisite his prey was than a moose, bear, or elk. He'd love to see the looks on their faces when he told him he did his killing with his bare hands.

That didn't help him with the two guys on his trail. He obliterated their windshield but didn't wound either of them. When the leader yelled his name at the hill and said the police had spoken to his mother, he knew he had to get out of there. While they expended perfectly good ammunition on an empty hill, he got back to the road and found the perfect spot to set up a blind.

He climbed a tree where the path curved. He had good cover from the branches while maintaining a perfect sightline on the road he had traveled down. He couldn't ask for a better set up. None of that helped him if he didn't shoot any better. He needed to take them out, find a new vehicle, and get out of Montana.

He would head south, out of the country and into Mexico. Maybe he'd keep going south, assume a new identity in Panama or Costa Rica.

The men came into view. He aimed, held his breath, and pulled back on the trigger—squeezing, not jerking, like he'd always heard.

He missed. He fired more shots, raking bullets across his field of vision, but the shots came up short, and within seconds, the men fired back at him. When their volley ceased, he shimmied down the tree and started up the rocky hill that bordered the other side of the road. The men would seek his position, and he'd have a new blind and be ready to execute them. He just needed to land one shot on each of them.

He clambered up the hill. His side was steep, and the loose rocks made it difficult to keep his footing. By the time he reached the top, his chest heaved, and the heat of the day left his palms and brow sweaty. A noise from below caught his attention.

He crept to the edge of the hill and looked down. The leader climbed the hill, having a much easier go at it.

The man stepped back, out of view. Luck had finally smiled on him. He'd get the cleanest shot he'd had at either of them, and he would not miss. He found it hard to steady the gun with his sweaty hands. He put the butt of the gun on the ground and leaned the barrel against his body. He wiped his brow with one arm. As he dried both hands on his shirt, he upset the balance of the gun, and it tipped over. He lunged for it, but he was too late. The gun slid off the edge of the hill, past the guy, and continued its descent.

He jerked back from the top of the hill, cursing himself for his clumsiness. He guessed where the guy would come up the top of the hill and hid behind a boulder a few feet away. At his feet, he found a flat stone about the size of his palm. He picked it up and hefted the weight in his hand. It would do.

The leader emerged on the precipice, looking each way. He rushed to one side of the hill, keeping his back to the man. The man took the stone and crept out of hiding. When the other guy turned around, the man bludgeoned his face with the stone.

The guy howled in pain and fell to his back. He dropped his gun, and it clattered off the side of the hill, sliding down to join the man's weapon. The man didn't care. He'd killed by hand before, and he'd do it again.

He straddled the guy, putting a knee on each of his shoulders, put his hands around his throat, and squeezed.

•   •   •

Brad remained conscious, but he had no idea how. Blood flowed from his mouth, and the air rushed from his lungs as he thudded to the ground. Holgate straddled him and started choking him.

Brad jerked his head to the side, keeping Holgate's hands from his carotid arteries. Holgate leaned forward, repositioning his hands. Brad couldn't gain much leverage with his shoulders pinned down, but he punched his assailant's kidneys. If the blow hurt, Holgate didn't show it.

Brad had been in similar positions in the ring. There was no ref to stop the fight, so he had to escape on his own. He thrust all of his weight to one side, freeing his right arm. While Holgate was still off balance, Brad chopped down on his hands, knocking them away from his neck. He reached for Holgate's face, planning to put a thumb in his eye, when bullets pinged off the rocks around them.

Dirt clods and pebbles flew into the air, pelting both men as the gunfire continued. Holgate slid off Brad and took off toward a nearby boulder. Brad flipped onto his belly and looked off the hill to see Aaron shooting at them.

"Hold your fire," Brad shouted, but the bullets continued. They landed further from Brad, so Aaron had at least differentiated between the two men. Brad rolled sideways until he was just below the top of the hill, using the rise for protection.

The shooting stopped. Brad hopped back up and looked for Aaron, who stood below them, examining the gun. He must have run out of bullets. Brad turned his attention back to the hill and rushed for the spot where Holgate had hidden. No one was there. He pushed his back against a boulder to prevent a sneak attack and scanned the area, searching for the killer who had once again slipped out of his grasp.

Brad ran his tongue around the inside of his mouth and discovered most of his bleeding came from the space where a tooth used to be. As the adrenaline wore off, his chin screamed in pain. He cracked open the first aid kit from his backpack and found a roll of gauze. He tore off a piece, wadded it up, and shoved it into the gap where Holgate had knocked out a bottom incisor. He used a handful of the remaining gauze to mop up his chin. He had a cut just below his bottom lip. He stuck an adhesive bandage over it, slung his backpack over his shoulders, and prepared to start the hunt again.

"Did I get him?" Aaron asked as he climbed to the top of the hill.

Brad glared at him. "No. I had him, but you started shooting, and he ran off."

"It didn't look like you had him," Aaron countered. "It looked like he was in control." He gestured at Brad's bloody face and clothing. When Brad didn't respond, he added, "You're welcome."

Brad wheeled on him, arm drawn back for a punch. He stopped himself. Reynolds was as annoying as ever, but he was not the enemy.

"He needs transportation," Brad said. "Even if he could get his truck turned around with mine blocking the way, the police have all the information on it now. He's going to go back to the road and find a car he can steal."

In the distance, the rotors of a helicopter cut through the air. It was about time, Brad thought. He didn't know where they could land. The hilltop didn't present a wide enough surface for the skids, and there were too many trees and rocks in the wider spots. They'd have to stay airborne, and they wouldn't be able to spot Holgate through the trees. They needed boots on the ground, and he wasn't waiting around for them to figure that out.

"Let's go," he said.

They descended the hill at the least steep part. When they reached the road, they took off at a jog, running shoulder to shoulder. Each step jarred Brad's chin and mouth, and the coppery taste of fresh blood flitted across his tongue.

They reached a driveway on their right. It wound around a curve with numerous oaks and pine trees limiting the visibility. They stopped behind a tree, and Brad reloaded the gun Aaron carried. He kept hold of it as they started again, and Aaron didn't protest.

The driveway led to a cabin. There were no cars outside and no fresh tracks. Brad peeked into a window. The lights were out. He tried the doorknob to no avail. A detached garage stood behind the cabin. Like the cabin, it remained dark inside and locked tight.

"He's not here," Brad said. They returned to the road. After another hundred yards, they reached a driveway on their left. This one had a clear view from the road to a larger cabin with a carport, where an SUV and a station wagon stood motionless.

They started down the driveway. The cabin's front door swung open. Brad grabbed Aaron, and both men hid in the trees. Brad crept forward along the tree line, staying out of sight but watching the scene in front of him.

A man who looked to be in his seventies stumbled out of the house, his hands raised above his head. A key ring dangled from his right thumb. Corey Holgate exited right behind him, a butcher knife in his hand, pointed at the man.

Overhead, the rotors of the helicopter grew louder, and the aircraft came into view. Holgate stepped closer to the man, and they lurched forward toward the carport. The police must have caught a glimpse of what was happening before Holgate and his hostage made it under the shelter because the chopper circled back.

"What's the play?" Aaron whispered.

"We stay here and wait," Brad said. "I don't want to put the old guy in danger. They'll have to come back this way in one of the vehicles. We'll follow them on foot, and as long as they stay on the road, the police can track them from the air."

The helicopter circled again. A voice issued a command from its speaker, but static and the noise of the rotors obscured the words. Brad tensed, expecting to see one of the vehicles pull out from under the carport. He craned his neck to see what was going on. He could see inside the windshield of each vehicle, and he didn't see the men in either of them.

"This doesn't make any sense," Brad muttered.

An engine sputtered to life, cutting his thought short. Exhaust appeared between the two vehicles in a puff. An engine revved.

"They're not taking the cars," Brad said. "It's an ATV."

He exited the woods and ran full throttle for the carport. He squeezed between the two vehicles and saw the ATV disappear into the woods behind the cabin. Holgate would have cover from the police, the trees rendering his escape invisible to the watchers overhead.

The old man was not behind the cabin; Holgate must have taken him. A second ATV sat empty along the back wall, out of view from the driveway. Brad checked it but did not see the keys. He rushed into the house, Aaron behind him.

"We need keys to that ATV," Brad barked. He went straight to the kitchen, opening drawers and cabinets. Aaron searched by the front door and in the living room. Finding nothing, Brad took off down the hall. He spotted a bedroom with an unmade bed, a television still playing. Brad looked on the dresser and found what he needed.

Outside, the police helicopter continued past the cabin and over the woods. Brad jumped into the driver's seat of the side-by-side buggy. Aaron took the passenger seat, and Brad floored the accelerator. The little vehicle jerked to life, and Aaron flopped sideways, righting himself before he fell out. He hastily fastened his seatbelt.

"We left the gun in the cabin," Aaron said as they entered the woods.

"No time to go back," Brad said. "Keep your eyes open and let me know if you see any signs of him."

Brad found the tracks from the first ATV and followed them, keeping the accelerator mashed down. Branches whacked the sides of the vehicle, splintering off the trees with loud cracks. The helicopter noise diminished, and Brad guessed it had repositioned near a road, trying to spot Holgate as he exited the woods.

Aaron's phone pinged with a text message. Brad cast him a sideways look. "You have service?"

"Must have just come back," Aaron said, digging in his pocket. Brad hoped that meant they were nearing civilization and Holgate would run out of forest to hide in.

"Shelly got settled into a new hotel room with her sister," Aaron said. "They'll leave in the morning."

Brad didn't have the relationship with Aaron to delve into personal details and the time wasn't right, but he blurted his question, anyway. "What's going on with you two?"

"No idea," Aaron said. "Things have been tense for a while. I don't know what happened to her when she was held prisoner. She doesn't want to talk about it with me, and it seems like she wants some space. Indefinitely."

"I guess that's normal after something like this," Brad said. Aaron didn't answer.

The tracks ahead swerved off their course and into thicker tree growth. Brad let up on the accelerator and made the turn. He slammed on the brake when he saw the old man lying next to a tree.

Brad was out of the ATV while Aaron fumbled with his seat belt. The man was conscious and seemed to have his wits about him.

"Are you okay?" Brad asked. The man nodded. Brad looked for blood but saw none. "He didn't cut you?"

"No," the man said. "He put the knife down, and when he slowed for this turn, I bailed."

"How far ahead is he?"

"Two minutes," the man said.

"Can he get out to a road from here? Something secluded; not the highway?"

"Not the way he's going," the man answered. "He was headed due west when I jumped. He'd need to head back to the northeast. There's a dirt road up there that eventually catches up with a farm road."

"Aaron, call for help," Brad said. "You can stay with our friend here. Sorry, what's your name?"

"I'm Walt. I can walk back to my house."

"Aaron will go with you," Brad said, keeping his voice firm. "Aaron, call for help. Walt should get checked out."

With that, Brad climbed back in the ATV and resumed his hunt. He flew through trees and bushes, eyes glued to the tracks in front of him. He turned to the left before going back to the right. After several minutes, the trees thinned into a clearing, a rocky hill in front of him. It looked much like the one he and Holgate had fought on earlier.

Brad shielded his eyes from the sun and saw the first ATV making its way up the hill, spitting gravel and dust in its wake. Probably trying to scout a path out of the maze of trees he'd gotten himself caught in.

Brad hit the gas to climb the hill. There'd be no taking Holgate by surprise. He didn't care. He'd just make sure Holgate didn't get a shot at his chin with a rock again.

CHAPTER 40

The second ATV growled behind him. Those guys were relentless. He wished he still had his hostage, but he'd have to confront them without a bargaining chip.

He reached the top of the hill and slowed to a crawl, surveying the space in front of him. The road he had chosen had led him into the woods, away from civilization. That worked great for keeping the cops off his back, but he needed to get out of the state. He could only hole up in the forest for so long, especially without any supplies.

He turned the wheel and made a slow, looping turn. The other ATV approached. Beyond it, he could see a dirt road that looked like it went for miles. The police helicopter hovered further to the south, guarding the exit that would take him to the highway. It would be the dirt road, then.

He revved the engine and cranked the wheel hard as he approached the second ATV. He peeled out, showering the area with loose rocks. His front bumper mashed into the side of the other man's ATV, and they both spun.

He righted the vehicle, but before he could make his getaway, the other guy rammed him, pushing both vehicles to the edge of the hill where it transformed into a cliff, with a sheer face running almost vertical.

He grabbed the butcher knife, switched off the engine, and jumped from the vehicle, hoping momentum would carry the other guy over the edge and save him the trouble of what he needed to do.

No such luck. The guy followed his movements, exiting his ATV and squaring up against him. The man waved the knife.

"Just get out of here," he said. "I'll let you walk away if you forget you ever saw me here."

The guy sneered and shook his head. "I'm sorry, Corey. That's not gonna happen."

•   •   •

Eddie pulled to a stop behind the wreckage of Brad's truck. Shards of the windshield littered the area, and bullet holes riddled the sides. Two flat tires caused it to list to the left.

"What happened here?" Eddie asked.

"Looks like Afghanistan," Vince said, as he climbed out of the Jeep. His stomach tightened, and he took a deep breath as he tried to ward off the memories.

"You gonna be okay?" Hadley asked.

"I'm fine," Vince said.

The tree and boulders made the road impassable, so they set out on foot toward Walt Carmine's house, following the offline map Hadley had downloaded. Hadley led the way in a near jog. Vince struggled to keep up but managed to stay within a few paces. Eddie straggled behind.

They reached Walt's driveway and waited for Eddie. He wheezed as he walked and patted his stomach. "You'd think all the fish I've been eating would have slimmed me down."

"When you fry it and eat it with onion rings and beer, it really doesn't matter how healthy it started," Hadley said.

"I could go for a beer about now," Eddie mused. Hadley rolled her eyes, and the three headed for Walt's place.

Aaron and the older man met them at the door. The man was in good condition, especially for someone who had been kidnapped at knifepoint less than an hour before.

"You made good time," Walt said. "Police haven't even made it yet."

"We were already on our way," Vince said.

"I was just telling your friend here that I have an idea of where they could be. Come with me." Walt led them around his house, past the carport, and into a patch of wild grass that stretched between them and the tree line. "See how it's all woods in here? Well, if you look that way, toward the west, there's that big hill. We call it Lookout Point because you can see everything from there. The guy was headed west already; if I saw that hill, I'd go up it and try to find a way out of here. Otherwise, you can wander around lost in these woods for days."

"How do we get there?" Eddie asked.

"Need an ATV," Walt said. "Unless you want to go on foot."

"How far is it?" Hadley asked.

"Two, three miles. It would be slow going on foot."

"I don't suppose you have another ATV lying around?" Vince asked.

Walt offered him a sad smile and shook his head. "Wait," he said. His eyes flickered with recognition. "Jumbo, my neighbor has one. He'd let you use it."

Vince scanned the area. All he saw were trees and Walt's place. "Neighbor?"

"You have to go back out to the main road and then take the next driveway. I can take you to the spot where the road's blocked."

Walt went inside. Several minutes later, he emerged, keys in hand, and a smile on his face. "Jumbo says it's fine. Let's go."

He climbed into the SUV, and the others piled in, Eddie up front and Vince, Hadley, and Aaron in the back. They arrived at the roadblock at the same time a state trooper showed up, an ambulance right behind him.

"I don't need an ambulance," Walt said. He turned to the others and gave them directions to Jumbo's.

The trooper cleared his throat and looked unsure of what to do with a crowd of people trying to leave a crime scene. Walt strode over to him and started telling him his story. As Walt talked and the paramedics buzzed around him, Vince, Eddie, Hadley, and Aaron got in the Jeep and took off.

Vince expected Jumbo to be a human mountain, something out of the lore of the Wild West. Instead, they reached the house of a man standing five foot three and who needed a couple of meals with Eddie before he'd reach 115 pounds.

"Walt okay?" Jumbo asked in his squeak of a voice.

"Seems fine," Vince said. "Paramedics are checking him out."

Jumbo nodded and led them to his garage. Right out front, his ATV gleamed in the sunlight. "Who's driving?" he asked.

Eddie, Vince, and Aaron all said, "I am," in unison.

"I'm going," Aaron said. He cocked his head to the left. "No offense, but I'm in the best shape to take this guy down."

"I'm going, too," Vince said.

"This is more of a job for a former police officer," Eddie said.

"I've been shot at in combat," Vince answered.

"And I've actually been shot."

"Boys," Hadley said, shaking her head. "It needs to be Vince. Eddie, you had a hard enough time catching your breath on the walk to Walt's. Let Vince do this."

Aaron took the keys from Jumbo and settled into the driver's seat. Vince climbed into the passenger seat next to him and buckled in. Jumbo went into the garage and came back with an M4 machine gun.

"Know how to use this?"

Vince inhaled sharply and blew a breath out over the count of ten. He swore he'd never touch a gun like that again. He could do it for Brad. "Yeah," he said. "It's been a while, but I can shoot it."

"Safety's on now, and it's fully loaded. Good luck out there and bring my ATV back."

Jumbo gave them directions to the hill, and Aaron took off, going faster as he grew more comfortable with the ride. A thousand thoughts passed through Vince's mind: Afghanistan, Lisa Dillon, Nick Batson, and Hassan Abdallah foremost among them. He focused on Brad. The mission was to save Brad and apprehend Holgate. He could wallow in his memories later.

"Cummings still do any fighting?" Aaron asked.

"No," Vince said. "At least not that he's told us about. He works out like a maniac, though."

The hill came into focus, and Aaron jammed the gas down further. At the crest of Lookout Point, two men grappled. Vince couldn't tell which one was Brad and which one was Holgate. One of them appeared to have an advantage over the other. Vince hoped it was Brad.

CHAPTER 41

During his time in the ring, Brad had learned to watch his opponent's core. A fighter could feint in any direction with a hand or a foot, but his body always moved with his bellybutton. Watch the core, and he knew where the attack was coming from.

He'd never stepped in the ring with a guy holding a weapon. Despite the years of training trying to kick in, Brad could not tear his eyes away from Holgate's knife.

The two men circled. Brad bent forward at the waist, keeping his shoulders over his toes and his arms bent. Holgate twisted his wrist from side to side, bouncing the sun's rays off the gleaming steel.

Holgate had a thick build, and his T-shirt clung to the muscles of his chest and biceps. His eyes held a calculated cruelty, as though he could slit Brad from navel to chin and drive off without a second thought.

The helicopter grew louder. Brad didn't take his eyes off Holgate, but he could imagine the chopper moving closer. Perhaps they'd gotten a call from Aaron or the old man, or maybe they'd seen the ATVs climb the hill. Either way, Brad didn't see how the police could help much. Like the previous hill, the crest was uneven, and there were too many boulders and trees to offer much in the way of a helipad.

Holgate lunged forward, taking a deep step with his right leg as he thrust his right arm forward in the style of a practiced fencer. Brad sidestepped the stab and grasped at Holgate's wrist, but the attacker pulled his arm back as quickly as it had shot forward. Brad stumbled, off balance, and Holgate moved in again. He stayed low on the second attack, slashing the knife at Brad's knee. Brad regained his feet enough to leapfrog the swipe. By the time he landed, Holgate had retreated.

Brad squared up to his opponent, and they circled again. Brad wanted to be the aggressor, but he worried about the knife. If he couldn't immobilize Holgate's arm, he'd be giving his opponent a clean shot at him. Holgate could take his pick: throat, back, kidneys. Instead, Brad continued to circle.

Holgate lurched forward again, his body a blur of speed and precision. Brad dodged the blade and grabbed Holgate's wrist. He twisted, but Holgate didn't let go of the knife. With Brad's attention on the weapon, he didn't see the kick coming. Holgate landed a roundhouse to Brad's lower back. Brad kept his grip on Holgate's wrist, and Holgate followed the roundhouse with a knee into Brad's groin.

Brad doubled over, and Holgate twisted free. He grasped the knife handle in both hands and swung the blade down as though swinging a sledgehammer. Brad dropped to the ground and rolled, taking Holgate's legs out. Scrambling to his feet, Brad kicked Holgate's wrists. The knife clattered away along the rocks.

Brad dropped to his knees, intending to put an elbow in the back of Holgate's head, but the other man slid away a half second before the blow. Brad slammed his elbow into the hard ground and pain resonated through his humerus and into his shoulder. Holgate kicked Brad in the chin, and blood immediately flowed from his earlier wound.

Brad fell and Holgate was on top of him, raining blows on his back and head. Brad absorbed the pain, but the hits continued, and his grasp on consciousness grew more tenuous by the second. While he looked for an escape move, two sounds filled the air. A vehicle engine hummed nearby. It sounded like a riding lawnmower on steroids.

Additionally, the helicopter rotors grew louder as the bird approached. It cast a shadow over the hill and dropped in altitude. Holgate continued his assault.

"Get on the ground and surrender immediately," a voice from the helicopter thundered. "This is an order from the Burgess County sheriff."

Brad turned enough to see a smile slither across Holgate's face, disappearing an instant after it appeared. The police wouldn't fire on them for multiple reasons: neither man had a gun, they wouldn't risk shooting Brad instead of Holgate, and the rocking of the helicopter would make it unlikely to get a good shot. Holgate knew that, and he wasn't about to surrender.

Holgate's eyes glanced upward at the helicopter for just a second, though, and it was the instant that Brad needed. He put his hands under his chest and exploded upward in a push up, continuing until he could get his feet under him, sending Holgate to the dirt below.

Brad wheeled, but Holgate was already on his feet and moving away. The guy was quick, Brad would give him that. He saw Holgate's target. The knife lit up like a spotlight in the sun.

Ignoring the pain that racked his body, Brad lurched forward, catching Holgate and shoving him a step away from the knife. Holgate kept moving, though, and Brad knew he wouldn't be able to pick up the knife without giving Holgate the time to attack again. Instead, he kicked it, sending it over the edge of the hill.

He turned as Holgate's next punch came. Brad ducked, and the blow connected with the top of his head, which was much better than taking another shot on his chin. Brad stepped forward, throwing a punch of his own. Within seconds, the two men engaged in a freestyle, bare-knuckled brawl, moving to the edge of the hill as they threw punch after punch.

Brad stepped into a right hook, driving all his energy through his hips and into his knuckles. Somehow, Holgate dodged the punch. Brad's momentum continued beyond his target, and he stumbled, dropping to one knee. Holgate shoved him, two hands on his chest, and Brad slid backward and over the side of the hill.

His body thudded against the rocky side of the rise, white hot pain searing through his chin and jaw as he dropped like a stone. He shot out an arm and caught a rock embedded in the hill. He looked down, and his spirits sank.

The fight had carried the two men to a crevasse that dropped straight down. Whether Holgate had intentionally brought them there or just got lucky didn't matter; all that kept Brad from a death drop was his white-knuckled hold on the rock.

Brad stared up, beyond his extended right arm, wondering when he'd see Holgate's victorious face. He felt alongside the rock with his left hand, trying to find another handhold.

Sure enough, Holgate appeared. Brad had fallen about two feet below the lip of the hill. The smile filled Holgate's face again, and it didn't disappear. The guy still had problems; he'd have to deal with the police and whoever was in the other ATV, but Brad would be one less thing on his list.

"You should've stayed out of this," he hissed, his voice cutting through the helicopter noise. He stepped down with his right leg, about to stomp Brad's hand. Brad closed his eyes and waited. Before he felt the foot on his fingers, a gunshot ripped through the sky.

Brad opened his eyes. Holgate stood in suspended motion, his leg hanging over the side of the hill, his head turned to the side. A second later, Aaron Reynolds wrapped Holgate in a bear hug, and they disappeared from Brad's view.

Vince Marcotte's face appeared over the side of the hill. "Hang on, Brad," he said. He moved away, and Brad called out, "Hurry."

Vince reappeared, assessing the situation. He lay on his belly and shoved both arms down to Brad.

"Are you strong enough to do this?" Brad asked. Vince nodded. Brad had his doubts, but the rock under his fingers had grown slippery with sweat and Brad had seconds, not minutes, to get in a better position.

He reached up with his left arm, and Vince grabbed it with two hands. Brad gripped Vince's arm and braced his feet against the side of the hill. With a deep breath, he let go with his right hand and quickly grabbed Vince's other arm. He pushed his body up a foot with one step, then covered the rest of the distance with the next. He flopped onto the hillside, his legs hanging out into the air, and gasped for air.

Vince helped him over the edge of the hill and onto his feet. Brad caught sight of a rifle lying nearby, which Vince picked up. Aaron had Holgate facedown on the ground, hands behind his back, with Aaron's knees pinning them down.

A rope ladder extended from the helicopter, and a police officer climbed down. Vince ran over and started talking a mile a minute, but the officer raised his hands to quiet him.

"We saw enough from the air," the officer said. "We know exactly what's going on."

With Aaron's help, the officer cuffed Holgate and hauled him to his feet. Above, the ladder retracted into the helicopter, but the chopper continued to hover in the area.

"They're going to keep an eye on us until help arrives," the officer said. "We have officers coming in ATVs. We'll be taking everybody back to the station and getting statements." He looked over his shoulder at Vince. "You can put the safety on and set that thing down, if you don't mind."

"Gladly," Vince said, complying with the instructions.

"Did you shoot at him?" Brad asked, motioning at Holgate.

Vince grinned. "Just a warning shot. Got his attention long enough for your buddy to move in and take charge."

Brad bit back a retort about Aaron not being his buddy. After all they'd been through over the past week, he wasn't sure what they were at that moment, but archenemies no longer seemed to fit the bill.

CHAPTER 42

July 26, 2025. Burgess County, Montana.
Shelly gazed at her reflection in the hotel mirror. She looked better than she had in the hospital. Some color had returned to her face, but she still looked too tired, too thin. She lay awake the entire night, unable to sleep, despite her body's longing for rest, despite the presence of Kristin, her sister, in the bed next to her and her mother on a cot next to the wall. Recovery would take time. She already had appointments booked with a therapist in Chicago, and she planned to stay at Kristin's for a while.

She put her hairbrush in the suitcase and zipped it closed. She wheeled it to the door, where Kristin waited in the hallway. Her sister snatched the luggage handle.

"Kristin, I can roll a suitcase through the parking lot," she said. She resisted adding, "I killed a mountain lion with my bare hands." Kristin was having none of it. She took the luggage, and Shelly followed dutifully to the car.

A crowd waited in the parking lot: Aaron and Brad, of course, and Brad's detective friends, along with Deputy Cooper. Aaron stepped forward, and Shelly motioned with her head for him to follow her closer to the building where they could talk out of earshot, despite being under so many watchful eyes.

Aaron gave her an awkward, sideways hug, like one might offer a stranger he thought he was related to but not completely sure how. Shelly turned into the hug and wrapped her arms around him. She pressed her head against his strong chest.

"You okay?" Aaron asked.

She stepped back and looked up at him, taking his hands in hers. She shook her head. "Not really. Not yet."

Aaron nodded, though Shelly could see in his eyes that he didn't understand. "I'm happy to ride back with you all," he said. "I can do some of the driving. It's a long trip."

Shelly let go of his hands and shook her head. "That's okay. I need some time alone."

He looked hurt, and she knew he was wondering how she could be alone when she was with Kristin and her mom. What she really meant was she needed some time without him; she suspected he understood that but not why, and that probably deepened the hurt for him.

There was so much she wanted to say. He needed to hear that the reason she'd been so cool to him was that when she was with him, she could only be with him. He dominated the relationship and made everything about him; she rarely had space for her own thoughts and feelings. After everything that happened to her, she needed to think and feel, to process the past week. The more she thought about it, the more she realized that when that madman had her locked up, she thought about Brad coming to rescue her because their friendship was about the two of them equally. It was a much healthier relationship than she'd ever had with Aaron.

She couldn't say any of that to Aaron. Not right then. She felt fragile, as though she would break into a million pieces if she expressed any of the thoughts raging through her.

"I'm..." Shelly started, but didn't complete the thought. She wouldn't tell him she was sorry; she'd been through an ordeal and deserved time to heal in her own way. "I'll call you when I'm ready," she said.

Kristin appeared over Aaron's shoulder. "Come on, Shel," she said. "Still some more people who want to say hello, and then we have to hit the road."

Shelly smiled at her older sister, always her protector. They returned to the crowd, and Brad introduced Shelly to his partners. Brad looked terrible with his bruised and swollen face and missing tooth. He didn't look like he'd slept anymore than she had the past few days.

"Old Yeller wishes you the best," Deputy Cooper announced. "He's recovering from that gunshot from yesterday, but he'll be on his feet again soon."

The crowd backed away from the car, all except Brad, who hugged her goodbye. "Call me if you need anything," he said. "Or just to talk. I'll be there."

A lump formed in Shelly's throat and tears filled her eyes. She wiped them away and said, "I'm not done racing. I'm going to find another course for us, so you better keep training."

Brad smiled at her. "We'll make sure the obstacles are the most dangerous part of the next one."

"Deal," she said. She climbed into the car, and her mom put it in gear. Shelly looked over her shoulder and watched the group grow smaller as they drove away from a place she'd never forget. She faced forward, closed her eyes, and focused on the return home.

•   •   •

"Holgate's not talking," Cooper said after Shelly had departed. "We have him on shooting the sheriff. That's a slam dunk. We have him on Ronda's kidnapping, too. She saw him without the mask. We have witnesses that place him at the diner, so that one will be easy enough. Your friend's case is a little trickier, since he always had his face covered, but the hypodermic needle you all found will help. The dead girls are tricky, too. We're bringing in forensics specialists from the state and FBI, and we'll put a strong case together on those crimes. It'll just take a little longer. I personally won't rest until we have enough evidence to convict him on every crime he committed."

"Any idea how many other victims he might have had?" Hadley asked.

Cooper's eyebrows shot up. "That's the big question, isn't it? We hope it's just the four we know of, but you can bet the state and FBI will search every house in these woods over the next week."

"Wouldn't hurt to search the surrounding states, too," Brad said. "We know one of his victims was from Idaho."

"They'll be running searches to match missing women against Holgate's profile," Cooper said. "Right now, it looks like he started with meticulous planning. The first two kidnappings, the ones that ended in murder, appear much better thought out than the rest. Old Yeller says his pride may have gotten the best of him. He thought he could outsmart the cops forever. I think he needed a bigger rush, and the spur-of-the-moment crimes offered him that."

"Maybe a combination of both theories," Vince said.

"Let's just hope the charges stick," Eddie said. "Anything the police need to move this forward, let me know, and I'll help however I can."

Cooper shook their hands, wished them well, and double checked he had good phone numbers for everyone, particularly Brad and Aaron. The group watched him drive off.

"We're packed, too," Hadley said. "Back to Denver for us." Vince and Hadley thanked Eddie for his hospitality, and Hadley gave him a warm hug. Vince jingled his keys and started toward the Subaru, Hadley on his heels.

"I'll be right there," Brad said. "Just need to take care of a couple of things here."

"I'm still up for giving you a ride to Bozeman tomorrow," Eddie said to Aaron.

"I appreciate it. Thanks for all you did this past week."

"Yeah," Brad added. "We couldn't have done all this without you. You sure you don't want back in the game?"

"Positive," Eddie said. "Now, promise me you'll come back to visit, and I'll teach you how to fly fish, and we won't get involved in a kidnapping or murder investigation."

"You got it," Brad said as they shook hands.

Eddie drove off, pointed toward the fishing resort. Brad and Aaron stood without speaking for several minutes.

"You were right not to trust me," Aaron said, breaking the silence. "Back in Chicago. I was a jerk then, but I've changed. I never laid a finger on Shelly."

"I believe you," Brad said. "Sorry I acted like I did when Shelly disappeared."

Aaron shrugged. "You were doing what you had to do to find her. Thank you, by the way."

"That's like the thousandth thanks," Brad said. "Seriously; you don't have to say it again."

"I wouldn't have found her on my own," Aaron said. "The cops wouldn't have found her, either. You and your friends made all the difference."

"Well, you stepped in at the right time up on the hill," Brad said. "Truce?" He stuck out his hand. Aaron shook it.

"What's next?" Brad asked.

"Don't know. Back to Chicago tomorrow. Back to work Monday. Maybe someday Shelly and I will get back together, but it feels like we're moving in different directions."

"Best of luck to you," Brad said. They shook again, and Aaron headed back into the motel. Brad walked toward Vince's car. He held his hands up just before he ducked inside and looked at the tattoos. Truth and peace.

He remembered his uncle's words. "If you want peace, get to the truth." Brad thought about his uncle as he joined his partners for the ride back home. Doug had no way of knowing it, but working for him was the best preparation for being a detective that Brad could have asked for.

AUTHOR'S NOTES

January 2025. Denver, Colorado.
If you've read the previous Vince and Hadley books, you'll realize this is a departure from my normal settings. I decided it was time to give them a view of the world outside Colorado, and visiting Eddie in the wilds of Montana seemed like a good way to do it. I'm not nearly as familiar with the geography of Montana as I am Colorado, so I set this story in fictional towns. Any resemblance to actual locations in Montana is coincidental, but as a lover of small, mountain towns built around outdoor activities, I would enjoy visiting a place like Broadwood (provided they have their serial killer problem under control).

As you're reading this, it's been more than four years since I first started writing *Foxholes*. I'd used Vince in previous, unpublished work, but Hadley, Eddie, and Brad have all been new arrivals into my literary universe. Bringing them to life has been more rewarding than I could have imagined, and I hope they've brought you some measure of entertainment over the course of the four books. With no immediate plans to write another in the series, I miss them already. I'll never say never for writing another Vince and Hadley mystery because they are characters worth revisiting, so I'll just say that this is a farewell for now.

I hope it's not a farewell to all of you. Visit my website, https://travistougaw.com, to stay updated on future books and activities. You can also subscribe to my newsletter there. Finally, I'm always open to hearing from readers at travis@travistougaw.com.

This feels like a good place to offer my heartfelt thanks to you for reading this book (and, I hope, *Foxholes, Captives,* and *Last Call*). Writing can be a lonely business, but it's worth it when I find out a story has resonated with readers. Thank you for being a part of what I do and making the journey so meaningful.

While writing itself is solitary, at least for me, putting out a book is not. You hold this in your hands because of the work of Reagan Rothe and his team at Black Rose Writing and Cindy Bullard, my agent at Birch Literary. I've received encouragement, critiques, pointers, and fellowship from a group of writers along the way. I'm grateful for the Rocky Mountain Fiction Writers, as well as the International Thriller Writers. In particular, I'm thankful for the support of Cam Torrens, Gary Gerlacher, Jeff Circle, C.S. Abbott, Ivanka Fear, Carla Seyler, Bret Hurst, Kay Smith-Blum, Lena Gibson, Mark Stevens, Andre Gonzalez, T.O. Paine, and many others. They are all great writers, and you should definitely check out their work!

My parents, siblings, in-laws, and extended family have been a great source of encouragement as these books have published. Thank you for buying books and telling your friends about them.

Carvin and Miles, you are my inspiration, and these books are my legacy for you.

Jennifer, these stories would not exist without you. Words are not sufficient to thank you for the brainstorming, the critiques, and the encouragement and for not letting me give up.

Finally, *Death Grip* is a story of hope, of finding a spark in the deepest darkness. I'm thankful to my Hope Giver for illuminating my life.

ABOUT THE AUTHOR

Travis Tougaw grew up in a military family. As a perpetual "new kid," he quickly learned the value of sharing stories to connect with others. Having settled down after his own stint in the Air Force, Travis stopped relocating, but he's never stopped telling stories. He's always on the lookout for characters and storylines that will grab readers' attention and keep them turning pages. Travis lives in Colorado with his wife, children, and an enormous dog. When he's not writing, he enjoys reading, outdoor activities, playing musical instruments, and trivia competitions.

NOTE FROM TRAVIS TOUGAW

Word-of-mouth is crucial for any author to succeed. If you enjoyed *Death Grip*, please leave a review online—anywhere you are able. Even if it's just a sentence or two. It would make all the difference and would be very much appreciated.

Thanks!
Travis Tougaw

We hope you enjoyed reading this title from:

www.blackrosewriting.com

Subscribe to our mailing list – *The Rosevine* – and receive **FREE** books, daily
deals, and stay current with news about upcoming
releases and our hottest authors.
Scan the QR code below to sign up.

Already a subscriber? Please accept a sincere thank you for being a fan of
Black Rose Writing authors.

View other Black Rose Writing titles at
www.blackrosewriting.com/books and use promo code
PRINT to receive a **20% discount** when purchasing.

9 781685 136482